The
Cottonwoods

The Cottonwoods

LYN FARRELL

CAVEL
PRESS

Kenmore, WA

A Camel Press book published by Epicenter Press

Epicenter Press
6524 NE 181st St.
Suite 2
Kenmore, WA 98028

For more information go to:
www.Camelpress.com
www.Coffeetownpress.com
www.Epicenterpress.com
www.lynfarrellcom

This is a work of fiction. Names, characters, places, brands, media, and incidents are either the product of the author's imagination or are used fictitiously.

Cover design by Scott Book
Design by Melissa Vail Coffman

ISBN: 978-1-94207-826-5 (Trade Paper)
ISBN: 978-1-94207-827-2 (eBook)

Printed in the United States of America

*This story is a tribute to my grandmother,
Lillian Remund, who gave me a decade of
halcyon summers at the farm
&*

*To Aunt Irene who loved secrets,
wrens and four-leaf clovers*

*Cottonwoods is dedicated to my
seven cousins who still remember the farm:
Phyllis Moffat, Evone Petersen, Fred Remund,
David Sakumura, Eric Sakumura,
Marty Sakumura Iriarte, Marybeth Sakumura,
and to my sister Kelly Tompkins*

ACKNOWLEDGMENTS

The process of writing *The Cottonwoods* was a decade-long endeavor in which many people were involved. Despite multiple submissions and rejections, Jennifer McCord never gave up on helping me elicit and write the story. I will always be indebted to her.

Given that my memory is fallible, if I have forgotten to include you, please forgive me. The MSU Writing Group was invariably helpful, but three from the group (Cele, Karen and Linda) took the time to read and comment on longer sections of the manuscript. Family friends Christy and Roberta read the story in its entirety and gave me very helpful feedback. I also hired three professional reviewers, Sandra Judd, Scott Driscoll and Tara Gavin who were immensely helpful. Thank you all!

ONE

Amber Morand Bradshaw sat in the parking lot of the Apple River Falls Nursing Home listening to the click of her car's cooling engine, mentally preparing herself for the task that lay before her. She had driven nine hours to meet with her mother's Great Aunt Irene, get the keys to the family's century-old farmhouse in Wisconsin, and assess what renovations would prove necessary to put the place on the market.

It had been fifteen years since Amber's mother told her there was treasure hidden at the farm. "Listen to what I am telling you, Girl, there are gold coins in that farmhouse. My great grandparents brought it with them from Romania during World War I." Grace's hoarse whisper resonated in her hospital room. She died two days later, having made Amber promise to care for her sister and their father. And someday, when she was ready, to find the family treasure.

It's silly to the point of ludicrousness to think that piles of golden coins have been lying undiscovered in a derelict farmhouse for a hundred years, Amber told herself, shaking her head. And yet, she had come. It was time to begin. She cracked a window for her dog, sleeping soundly in the back seat, and got out of the car. As the wind lifted her dark curls, Amber took a deep breath and strode the long stone sidewalk to the entrance to the facility.

The receptionist at the front desk asked her who she was visiting. Her name tag read Mrs. Worth.

"Miss Irene Morand," Amber said.

"Room 109," the woman said pointing down the hall.

"Thank you," she said, heading in the direction the receptionist indicated and knocking on the door.

"Come in," a high-pitched querulous voice responded.

When the door swung open, Amber saw her mother's ninety nine year-old Great Aunt Irene. She was sitting in a chair by the window and the late afternoon light slanted across her features. Ancient and tiny, Irene Morand was no bigger than a gnome. The old lady had a pointed chin, wispy white hair and wore silver-framed glasses. Her face was so wrinkled it might have been carved from half a walnut shell. She wore a faded housedress, colorless from a hundred washings. Her legs looked swollen and pink slippers were tight on her tiny feet.

"Hello, Aunt Irene," Amber said tentatively.

The old lady peered intently at her with piercing black eyes. "Well technically, I am your Great Great Aunt, but Aunt Irene will do. You're Amber Bradshaw, I assume. Your father left word you were coming. I haven't seen you since you were a girl. I remember your mother, Grace. She used to bring you and your little sister to the farm when you were young. She's been gone a decade or more now. Breast cancer wasn't it? Sit down," Aunt Irene said peremptorily.

"Yes, she has been gone fifteen years," Amber replied and took a shaky breath, feeling a recurring melancholy for her mother who died when she was twelve.

When her father opened the door to her mother's hospital room, Amber had bolted. Running down the hall, she came upon a cluster of tropical plants and a bench. She sat there a moment, breathing hard. A young nurse found her and joined her on the bench. No words were exchanged until at last Amber stood up. The nurse took her hand and walked with her into the room where her mother was to meet her maker two days later.

Aunt Irene reached for her purse on the window sill. "Your father said you are going to sell the Morand House." She rummaged in her purse and pulled out two keys.

"That's right," Amber said. She was surprised by the irritable note in Aunt Irene's voice and felt a bit irked. It really wasn't any of her business. Aunt Irene only owned the farmland, not the house. The house belonged to her.

"Here is the key to the front door and this one is for the summer kitchen. You probably have no idea what a summer kitchen is, do you? Well, what do you have to say for yourself, Girl?"

Amber took a breath and said, "I've taken a leave of absence from my job to renovate and sell the farmhouse. I plan to get it done this summer."

"The Morand House you are planning to sell has been in our family for over a hundred years. You were lucky enough to have inherited it from your mother and here you are ready to shunt it off to strangers. No sense of continuity, the young. No respect for history," Aunt Irene said. Her lips were pursed and her mouth twisted in a tight grimace.

"My father said you would give me directions," Amber said, struggling to regain her composure in the face of the old lady's fretful remarks.

"To get to the farm, you take W 21 east past the reservoir. It will be dark soon, but you will see lights around the water. Four miles past the lake, turn right on Morand Road. Stupid County officials renamed the road Main's Crossing a few years ago, but everyone hereabouts knows it as Morand Road. The first farm you drive past belonged to my brother, Charles. Nobody lives there now. Dead, dead, dead, they are all dead." Aunt Irene coughed and her voice trailed off as she gazed out the darkening windows, lost for a time in her cobwebbed memories.

Moments later, Aunt Irene took a deep breath and resumed her narration. "About a mile past the first farm, you'll see a big red barn on your left. The Morand farmhouse is at the end of the driveway that runs past the barn. There's a carriage house beyond the cottonwood trees with an apartment on the second floor. After my brother married, I moved out of the main house and made the carriage house my home. Don't go up there or touch anything," Aunt Irene said, looking at her sternly.

"I won't," Amber said, quailed by the fierceness of the old lady.

"I own the whole 500 acres now," Aunt Irene said, smiling grimly. "My father willed the farm to my brothers, Paul and Charles. Property always goes to the men, you know. Women are expected to *marry*." Her lower lip quirked in irritation.

OMG, the curmudgeon is a feminist, Amber thought, suppressing a grin.

"Obviously the house will be filthy. It's been empty for fifteen years. However, I assume even someone as feckless as you seem to be should be capable of cleaning." She gave Amber an oblique glance from eyes as dark as ink.

"Guess I'll be going then," Amber said and stood up. She could hardly wait to leave the old grouch.

"One more thing. It's about my mother, Ina. She kept a journal. My brother translated about half the entries. It tells about the early days before our parents left the old country." Aunt Irene reached into her nightstand drawer and pulled out a handful of winkled, tissue-thin papers. "The Journal itself is somewhere in the farmhouse. If you find it, bring it to me," Aunt Irene said with a severe glare.

Amber took the pages, thanked her and said good-bye. Just as the door swished shut behind her, she heard Aunt Irene's voice. She was talking to herself in her empty room. "Girl's a nincompoop. High-heeled leather boots on a farm? Little Twit won't last a week." She gave a chirpy little laugh.

TWO

WALKING OUT OF THE NURSING HOME in the gathering darkness, Amber realized it was too late to go out to the farm. She drove down Orchard Street with its one red light to the town's only motel, parked and went inside. She asked about having her dog, Camelot, sleep in the room. After agreeing to a pet fee, Amber walked along the sidewalk of the single story building until she reached her room. Standing outside with the dog for a moment, she listened to the sound of spring rain that pattered softly as raindrops hit the unfolding leaves of the trees. Aunt Irene's critical observations and the likelihood that there really wasn't a treasure descended heavily on her. It was going to be a long summer in the tiny town of Apple River Falls, a world away from the busy life she had in Chicago. Shaking off her reservations as best she could, she inserted the key in the lock.

Once inside the motel room, Amber set her suitcase on the bed, took a shower and got into her pajamas. Toweling her dark hair dry, she opened the suitcase and removed an ancient photograph album she had brought along. The first page showed a family tree with names in black-bordered squares.

"This is your mother's family," her father had told her. "These two men here, Frank Morand and his brother came to the States with their wives in 1917. Frank and Ina were your mother's Great Grandparents. They had two sons, Paul and Charles and one daughter, your Aunt Irene. She's the person who owns the farmland now."

The album was filled with wedding pictures of men in military uniforms with mutton-chop beards and women wearing long dresses and high-buttoned shoes. One dark-haired young woman held a baby dressed in a simple linen dress and embroidered cap. The child had a mutinous expression on her face. Although ninety-nine years had elapsed since the picture was taken, Amber had no difficulty recognizing that cranky face—it was Aunt Irene.

Hoping to learn more about the old family history from the woman who had emigrated here a hundred years earlier, Amber picked up the first thin pages of Ina's Journal.

Ina Nicolescu Journal Entry
Timisoara Commune, Romania, 1915

Summer has started and the cottonwoods are releasing their white fluffy seeds. My father complains that they will take root in his fields, but I think they are beautiful. There are so many in the air now, it's like snow in summer. I am writing this entry in my journal, something I have wanted to own for so long. My mother doesn't understand why I want to record things—she didn't even approve of me learning to read and write, but because I am marrying into a wealthy family, she relented. My fiancé, Frank Morand, is an Officer in the Romanian Army.

My wedding dress is almost finished. Mother took hers apart to make into mine. It's light brown and beaded, but the waist is dropped and the neckline high. I wanted a sleeveless white gown with an open back. I have seen pictures of dresses like the one I wanted, but my mother said I would look like a "curva." I was offended. How could my mother say such a thing—that I would look like a woman who would sleep with a man for money? I have never known a man in that way. I am only eighteen, and according to my grim-faced father, not ready to be a wife. When he left the house, I asked mother what he meant.

"You have lived on the farm all your life, you know about breeding," she said. The blue eyes in her face were hard. I felt myself coloring. "Some women learn to enjoy it. I never did. Remember, you wanted a life away from the farm." Her words were clipped.

It was true. I detested the dusty farm where my parents grew rutabagas, turnips and raised pigs. Grubbing in the earth, getting coated with dust, never feeling clean. The constant grind of farm life wore on me. If we had had a cow, I might have felt differently. Our neighbors had one. Their ridiculously long eyelashes and gentle faces always made me smile.

Ina Morand's distinctive voice was so vivid, Amber thought. She already had a strong sense of her character. Setting aside the thin papers, she laid back, pulled the bed covers up to her chin and closed her eyes.

Her dog, Camelot, had been dozing on the floor. When Amber's breathing slowed, he surged up on the bed and settled down beside her with a ridiculously self-satisfied expression. He was well aware that sleeping on the bed had been frequently and expressly prohibited.

AMBER ARRIVED AT THE MORAND FARM early the next morning. She parked near the two ancient cottonwood trees in front of the carriage house with its upstairs that had been Aunt Irene's dwelling before she entered the nursing home. The trees were enormous with wrinkled gray bark and a cumulous of triangular toothed leaves. The metallic-colored leaves clattered lightly in the morning wind.

Those trees must have been planted a century ago, Amber thought and wondered if Irene's mother, Ina, could have carried the saplings with her all the way from Romania. The trees seemed to guard the place like sentinels. A morning mist rose off the dark plowed fields and the early bird calls carried clearly. Amber took a deep breath, feeling calmer than she had last night.

Calling her dog who had wandered off, she walked up to the house and unlocked the back door to the summer kitchen. The dog followed her inside. The room had only one window and inside the light was dim. Feeling around for a light switch, Amber spotted a single bulb hanging from frayed wires in the ceiling. She had to stand on her tiptoes to pull on the string that turned on the fixture. A faint yellow light illuminated the dusty space. Curling strips of yellowed flypaper hung down from the ceiling, looking like waxy crepe-paper streamers. The floor was made of rough reddish boards coated in peeling paint. Along the far wall, Amber saw an ancient wringer washer and a cupboard with missing doors hanging above a rusty sink. Beside the washing machine was a small ice box with its door open. Camelot headed determinedly toward the far corner of the room, barking loudly.

"What is it, Cam?" Amber asked. She directed her cell-phone light toward a pile of dried leaves in a corner and grabbed the dog's collar. "It's only a pile of leaves, you silly nut," she said, but just then the brush pile began to walk. Two glittering black eyes peered out at her from under its leafy coat. The opossum bared its yellowed teeth and hissed.

Quickly grabbing an old broom from the corner, while still holding tight to the struggling dog, Amber gently nudged the animal toward the back door. With one furious backward glance, the critter lumbered out to the stoop and vanished around the rear corner of the house. Camelot growled low in his chest.

THREE

AMBER SLID THE HEAVY WOODEN DOOR between the summer kitchen and the main house to the left. The rollers squeaked as the door opened and she stopped for a moment, feeling as if she had walked into a child's favorite storybook, one she had read a thousand times. Entering the house brought back her childhood visits in a rush of memory. There was an enchanted feeling to the place that came from the beauty of old wood and a faint scent of lavender. This house and her ancestor's lives—dominated by the turning of the seasons—had emerged seemingly intact from a century ago. She had walked back in time.

Camelot wriggled out of her grasp and loped into the room. With a keen sense of anticipation, knowing that the long-delayed treasure hunt actually beginning, Amber followed. There was no furniture in the dining room except for an antique light fixture hanging above the area where the table should have been. Natural light flooded the space from a large window facing the front yard. A china cabinet had been built into the wall between the kitchen and the dining room. She opened the cabinet door, surprised to see a set of hand-painted dishes, frilled with dust. She turned a plate over carefully and read the word Czechoslovakia. Ina's dishes were so old, they came from a country that hadn't existed for decades. Pale pink geraniums with silvery leaves had been hand-painted on the dishware. How lovely they are, Amber thought.

Beyond the dining room, a staircase rose to the second floor. There was a small nook at the base of the stairs furnished with a faded loveseat upholstered in decaying chintz. It faced a wooden bookcase. A wide casement arch beyond the staircase led into the living room. She walked into the room, still feeling the timelessness of the place. There was a baby-grand piano in one corner covered in a white dust sheet and a brick fireplace on the opposite wall. She walked over to the piano, lifted the sheet and touched the keys. A note of music hung like a single hair in the silent air. Raising the panel above the keyboard, Amber saw the yellowed rolls of a player piano. Seeing a lever marked "play," she lifted it and stood entranced as the keys rose up and down playing an evocative melody. It filled the space like a moving river of sound. She could practically see her mother's grandmother, Lillian Morand, dressed in a white gown, sitting at the instrument and swaying to the beautiful melody.

As the music played, Amber noticed a main-floor bedroom beyond the living room visible through interior windowed doors. She wondered if those were original to the house. Opening the French doors, bordered with thick damask drapes, she walked into the room. The bed was covered with an Amish quilt in bright velvet squares. Amber reached down to touch the soft fabric thinking of the generations of her family who had slept here.

Walking back to the bottom of the staircase, she noticed there was a globe-shaped light fixture installed on the newel post. The stairs were open to the dining room on her left, but the right hand wall had been papered in a floral botanical, much faded now. The wallpaper had a black background that was nearly covered in overlapping green leaves and an occasional peach-colored flower. The wallpaper looked like it came from the Art Nouveau period.

Climbing the stairs with her dog behind her, Amber opened the door to the first bedroom off the landing. Camelot bounded inside, swishing his tail. The room was furnished with an antique spool bed, a dresser and a painted dressing table. A thick layer of dust lay over everything.

Amber leaned across the bed and raised the window sash. An early morning wind billowed the tattered lace curtains and dispersed dust from the quilted bedspread. Below her in the yard she saw a ragged hammock hanging between the two cottonwood trees. It moved slowly in the breeze, as if pushed by an invisible child. The second bedroom was furnished with only a mattress on the floor and an antique cradle. Amber wondered if her little sister, Claire, had slept in that cradle when they came to visit the farm many years ago.

Looking around the old place, Amber felt a warmth, as if a sunbeam had hit her in the breastbone. She recalled the picture of Irene's mother,

Ina, from the photo album. She and her husband Frank had come to America as war refugees to claim this tract of land in the wilderness. Aunt Irene, that cantankerous old lady in the nursing home, had once been a child who played with her little brothers in these rooms. The significance of the place struck Amber with a powerful thump. Her heartbeat caught.

AROUND MID-MORNING HER CELL PHONE RANG. The name on the screen read Andrew Bradshaw. It was her father. He was a different person now from the man he had been in the first years after her mother died, a person she had learned to love and respect again. Their memories of Amber's mom and their love for Claire had drawn them back together. It had been her father who encouraged Amber to take the summer off, fix up the old place and search for the treasure. He said the time had come. If she didn't go now, both the farmland and the farmhouse would be sold and the treasure, if it ever existed, might never be found.

"Hi Dad. How are you?"

"I'm having some tests done that my orthopedist ordered. He thinks I need a knee replacement," he said gruffly. "What do you think of the house?"

"It's gorgeous. I'd forgotten how large it is. How could they possibly have built such a big place that long ago? They couldn't even have had power tools."

"It wasn't built all at once. Originally, there was a log cabin on the property with a cellar underneath for storing food. Frank Morand tore it down and built what we call the summer kitchen. He and Ina, with baby Irene, lived in that single room until he added the rest of the main floor. Irene's brother, Paul added the second floor and the upstairs attic after he married. What has to be done to sell it?"

"The whole place needs a deep cleaning. The kitchen is a total gut, and there is only one bathroom in the house. I want to put in a second bath, a Jack-and-Jill, between the upstairs bedrooms and a powder room in the summer kitchen. Nobody will buy a house these days with only one bathroom."

"No problems getting it done then?"

Amber hesitated for a moment before saying, "Well, it's a lovely morning, Dad, and I keep telling myself it's only going to take the summer. And who knows maybe there really is a treasure? In any case, I promised Mom I would come."

"That's my girl. Did you see Aunt Irene last night?"

"I sure did. The woman is a Grinch!" Her father's laugh hooted across the distance. "I heard her call me a nincompoop as I was leaving."

"I warned you," he chuckled. "It's just the way she is. Kind of a burnt marshmallow, crusty on the outside and melty on the inside. She was always my favorite person at the farm," his voice trailed off.

Amber smiled at the marshmellow description. "I haven't seen the melting part yet, Dad, but will keep my hopes up. Why is she your favorite person here?" She found it intriguing that her father would respond so positively to the sharp-tongued old lady.

"Miss Irene doesn't suffer fools gladly and I find her tart commentary on life amusing. She's one of a bygone breed of farm women who respected their menfolk and gave their lives to keep those old family farms going."

"She didn't seem to have much appreciation for what I've taken on here," Amber said, feeling a prick of resentment.

"Give her some time, she'll grow you," Dad said.

"We'll see. Anyway, I'm obviously going to need a contractor to get this job done. I already called the Chamber of Commerce. They recommended a local man named Ryan Amherst. He lives just down the road and is apparently an expert in restoring old homes."

"Sounds like you are making progress."

"Sorry, I have to run. Cam got outside again. I just spotted him dashing down the road. Oh my God, he's chasing a runaway cow. Bye." Amber clicked off the phone.

After retrieving the dog and shooing the cow through a gate into a nearby field, as a herd of Holstein's looked up in open-eyed blinking surprise, Amber called the contractor's phone number. Ryan Amherst agreed to come out the next day to discuss what she wanted done with the house. Concluding the call, Amber grabbed her suitcase from the car and took it into the house. Climbing the staircase to the bedroom with the white spool bed, she decided she wouldn't go back to the motel for a second night. She stood at the bedside for a while, listening to the breeze blow through the towering cottonwood trees, feeling connected to something ancient and powerful she couldn't even name.

Amber loaded Camelot in the car the next morning and drove back to the village of Apple River Falls for groceries and cleaning products. On her return, Morand Road already felt familiar. It was bordered by slender trees that made a green arch over the dusty gravel road. Farm fields beyond the rows of trees rolled away into the distance. Pale lime-green shoots, planted in perfect geometric symmetry, were just emerging from the dark brown soil.

She was driving slowly past the farm Aunt Irene said had belonged to her brother, Charles, when she spotted a slender man walking down the hill toward the barn. Remembering Irene say the place was deserted, Amber bumped her car down the dirt driveway.

She rolled down the window and called, "Hello?"

"Hi," he said. The young man was lean and attractive with copper-colored skin. His dark hair was wavy and touched his shoulders. He looked to her as if he might be part Native American. She was startled to feel a frisson of attraction to him. A farmer wasn't her usual type.

"My name's Amber Bradshaw. I'm here to fix up and sell the old Morand farmhouse. I didn't think anybody lived at this farm. Who are you?"

"Name's Hunter Freedman. I live across the road. I'm feeding the calves."

"The calves?" Amber couldn't fathom why anyone would keep calves on an unoccupied farm.

"Yes. I'm coming by your place later to feed yours."

"I have calves?" Amber frowned, perplexed by the calf mystery.

Hunter nodded looking down, prodding the dirt with his foot. "Just a few, in the barnyard." He acted like it was an ordinary thing—like everyone kept calves in the barnyards of derelict farms. She shook her head in confusion but let it go. She would probably learn more when he came by later.

"I noticed the crops on both sides of the road. What do you grow in those fields?"

"Winter wheat," he said. "We plant it in autumn and it grows under the snow all winter. It comes up early in the spring. We harvest in August."

"Guess I'll see you this afternoon then," Amber said and turned her car around. Continuing down the road, she envisioned winter wheat with its pale green seedlings that were strong enough to grow under snow. Perhaps this task and lovely old place will make me strong enough to grow through the loss of my mother . . . and my failure to keep the promise I made, she thought.

The bleak anguish she felt in the years after her mother died had been worsened by her father's despair (which he tried to drown in alcohol) and her sister being so young and needy. And your own stupidity, she thought. Remembering the day she forgot to pick Claire up after school was like pushing on a bruise. In her mind she always thought of it as the Day of Disgrace. With an effort, she pushed the memory away.

Pulling in next to the big red barn, Amber spotted a half dozen black-and-white calves milling about in a small fenced area. She hadn't noticed them before. Those must be my calves, she thought and felt a little quirk of pleased surprise.

SHE WAS CARRYING A PLASTIC BAG full of junk looking for a trash bin late that afternoon, when she saw Hunter again. He was in the back yard playing with Camelot.

"Hi," she called out. "Do you know what I am supposed to do with the trash?"

"There's a burn barrel," he said. "It's behind Miss Irene's carriage house. What's your dog's name?"

"It's Camelot. I call him Cam."

"Want to help me feed the calves?" Hunter asked.

"I would love to," she said. The day was warm and throwing out all the old broken stuff made Amber feel lighter, as if she had cleaned herself of unwanted emotional garbage. They walked to the burn barrel and Amber deposited the trash.

"Isn't there curbside trash pick-up and re-cycling here?" she asked as she followed him toward the barn.

Hunter gave a surprised laugh. "No. We're too far out in the country. That service is only for people in town. I guess you could haul stuff to the dump if you wanted to," he said. "Or you could just light the barrel like we do." His mouth curved up in one corner when he smiled and his eyes sparkled when he looked at her.

It was strange, she thought. She was clearly attracted to him, but normally she was drawn to driven men—stockbrokers, bankers or lawyers—men whose ambition virtually crackled. Hunter seemed pretty laid-back. He did have an awfully cute smile though, she thought.

They reached the barnyard with a half-dozen milling black-and-white Holstein calves with pink noses and fat tongues. Hunter went into an adjacent cement block building and came out with two enormous baby bottles topped with red nipples and filled with white foamy milk.

"Want to feed one?" he asked. He vaulted over the fence and Amber noticed his muscular physique. Farm work was hard enough to keep a person in good shape without resorting to a gym, she realized. She normally went to the gym to work-out every few days, but hadn't seen any signs for gyms in the little village of Apple River Falls.

"I'd like to try," Amber said, glancing down at her high-heeled footware. "But I don't want to ruin my boots."

"There's an old pair of rubber galoshes in the milk shed. I'll get them for you."

Putting the rubber boots on, Amber opened the barnyard gate and stepped gingerly into the paddock. She instantly sank down in muck half a foot deep. Hunter handed her a bottle and she held it low enough that the calf could drink. One of the calves came blundering over and knocked against her. The bottle fell and the nipple came loose, spilling most of the milk.

"Hey there, stop," she told the calf, laughing.

"Put your back against the fence so he can't knock you around. Little buggers are getting strong. Here, I'll get him started." Hunter rapidly replaced the dirty red nipple with a clean one and guided the calf's mouth toward the bottle. "You just don't have the knack yet," he said. Amber flushed and Hunter grinned at her naiveté.

No re-cycling, having to burn trash in an incinerator made out of a barrel and feeding calves with huge baby bottles. Clearly, there's plenty to learn here, Amber thought. Although it's probably not worth the effort since I'm leaving by the end of the summer. The calf emptied the bottle in short order, giving her a sense of pleasure that pervaded her chest. When the little guy looked up at her, she saw a spiral of hair between his eyes. She started to laugh. "This little calf has a cow-lick," she said.

"Lots of them do." Hunter smiled and took the bottle from her hand, grazing her fingers. His eyes lingered on hers for a moment and he smiled. "I'll fill 'er up again," he said.

Leaning against the fence with the afternoon sun on her shoulders as the calves made a bumping circle around her, Amber felt herself start to relax. One of the calves took her fingers into his mouth, startling her with his gritty tongue and strong suck. "This little fellow needs a cow mom," she said. Looking around the barn she noticed several birds darting in and out of the haymow. They had dark blue wings, long forked tails and amber breasts. Their sharp crescent shapes and little chittering noises made her smile. "What kinds of birds are those, Hunter?" she asked.

"Barn swallows. They leave in the fall and come back in the spring. Swallows eat mosquitoes and lots of other bugs so they are always welcome."

"You seem to know everything about this place. Have you lived here all your life?"

"Yes, I was born here. I went away to art school in Santa Fe when I was seventeen, but I didn't finish the program." His tone was suddenly clipped.

"I went to art school too, and I work in an art gallery in Chicago. I'd love to see your work sometime." When he frowned, Amber realized she had hit upon a touchy matter.

"I used to be a pretty fair painter. Can't seem to get started again," Hunter's voice trailed off.

Hillside Gallery where Amber worked was always on the look-out for new talent. In the last five years, she had spotted several promising young artists and helped get them going in the field. Hunter's inability to paint on this tranquil farm intrigued her. Maybe later she could unravel that little mystery. "Why do you keep calves here when there aren't any mom cows to feed them?" she asked

"The farm down at the other end of Morand Road belongs to Mr. and Mrs. Lundgren. They keep about a hundred milk cows. Miss Irene gave them permission to keep their calves here for the summer—until they go to other farms or to slaughter," Hunter said.

What would happen to these little adorable little guys at the end of the summer, she wondered and felt a spike of apprehension.

IN THE MIDDLE OF THE NIGHT, a clap of thunder woke Amber. She sat up in bed and quickly pulled the bedroom window down, shutting out the rain. Thinking of all she had to do to get the house ready to sell, she was unable to fall back to sleep. Perhaps reading more of Ina's story would help, she thought and picked up another of the translated pages with their thin spidery writing.

Ina Nicoleu Journal
Fall 1915

I sleep in a loft above the kitchen in my parent's farmhouse. The cook stove provides our only heat and my father cut an opening in the floor of my room, when I complained about how cold it was. The heat rises now and I will be warmer this winter. I can hear my parents talking through the hole in the floor. I wrap my red shawl around my shoulders and tiptoe from my mattress to kneel down close to the vent.

"I think you're rushing her, Husband. You said yourself she isn't ready to be a wife."

"The German Army has already conquered Belgium and northeast France. Our rulers are sympathetic to the Nazi cause. If the Germans get this far, I fear for our beautiful country."

"Will she be safe, though? You know her fiancé, Frank, is estranged from his father. Apparently, he isn't even going to attend the wedding."

"When a grandson comes, the father will come around. He is Boier, of the hereditary nobility. I don't know what issues the father has with his sons, but he will want to have an heir to his titles and lands. If the rift is so deep he doesn't will the property to his sons, a grandson would be welcome."

"I only wish Frank's mother were still alive. A mother would want to see her son's wedding. But it's late. Let's go to bed, Husband."

I breathed out shakily and a small cloud of mist from my breath shone white in the moonlit room. Creeping back into my bed, I looked out my tiny window. It was snowing hard. I had learned about war in school and seen a map that showed the countries of Europe. Austria and Hungary stood between Romania and Germany. Surely no Army could come that far. But I shiver, wondering what my future holds.

Setting the pages down, Amber clicked off her lamp. Her knowledge about WWI was sketchy but she remembered the Austro-Hungarian Empire declared war against the Serbs over an assassination of an Arch Duke, although the Germans didn't reach Romania until several years later. Despite the war, Frank and Ina managed to survive and make it all the way to the U.S. It would be fascinating to learn the whole story, but she was going to run out of translated pages in a few days. If only she could get Aunt Irene to tell her the location of the journal itself.

Secretive old sourpuss, Amber thought, exasperated. I'm pretty sure she knows where it is. She just wants to see if I can find it.

FIVE

A VAN PULLED INTO THE DRIVEWAY around four o-clock that afternoon. The truck's logo read "Amherst Construction." A Victorian house with multi-colored gingerbread trim had been stenciled on the side panel.

"Ryan Amherst," the young man said, extending his hand as Amber walked outside to meet him. He was tall and slim with a nice voice. "I'm the contractor. We spoke on the phone yesterday."

"Right, sorry. Lost track of time. I've been cleaning, as you can see," she said, rubbing a grubby hand across her forehead. Her long hair was hot on her neck and she gathered it up, twisting it into a knot. "Thought I could do it in a day. What was I thinking? The house is enormous. Come on in."

She held open the door and followed him inside. He wore blue jeans and a white T-shirt printed with a faded emblem of his company. When Ryan's shirt sleeves rode up, she could see evidence of his farmer's tan. A baseball cap with its brim turned backward covered his light hair. He had the loose-limbed walk of a man who did a lot of physical work, a man comfortable with his body.

"Before we start, are you the legal owner of the house?" Ryan asked. "I know it's the old Morand property, and you said you are Irene Morand's grandniece, but I can't work on the place without permission of the owners."

"Yes, the house was willed to me by my mother, Grace Morand Bradshaw. She inherited it from her grandmother, Lillian Morand. I brought the paperwork."

"I'm excited about the possibilities here. I've always been curious to see the inside of this place. I specialize in historic renovation and the Morand house is the oldest house in the county."

After checking the deed, Ryan began assessing the kitchen. The room was empty except for an antique stove and an old pine table topped with tin and placed below the front window. A second window to the west framed a view of the big red barn.

"I want the kitchen completely gutted," Amber said. Noticing a frown on Ryan's face, she paused. "Unless, that is . . . is there something here worth saving?"

"Did you not see the cook stove?" Ryan raised his eyebrows questioningly.

Amber looked in dismay at the antique stove. It was a metal appliance that looked like a clothing dresser with decorative curvy legs. She had no idea how one would even turn it on.

"This is a beauty, I'd say turn of the century," Ryan said. "Those wrought iron discs on the surface are the burners. You put kindling under them and start a fire. The fire warms the burners and does the stovetop cooking. The two bulging doors above the burner surface are the oven and the broiler. The stove has been converted to use bottled gas for the ovens, but stovetop cooking is done over a wood fire. This baby is solid cast-iron with an enamel finish. Just look at her," Ryan said, his voice was admiring.

"Can't you sell these things?" Amber asked, frowning. The antique stove didn't look that wonderful to her. She had been thinking stainless steel for the appliances.

"You can, but I wouldn't. There's a guy in town who restores them, but this one is fine as she is."

"I don't think a woman would want to have to build a fire just to heat soup, would she?" Amber asked, doubtfully.

"My wife, Megan, does," Ryan said, cheerfully.

And I bet she hates it, Amber thought. "I had actually been thinking stainless steel for the appliances."

Ryan looked positively crestfallen at the thought of stainless steel appliances and shook his head gloomily. Seeing his reaction, she said, "Or maybe we could keep the stove as a decorative item?"

"You are paying the bills so you have the final word, of course, but how about a compromise? Would you agree to use the antique stove if I electrify the burners?"

She hesitated a moment before saying, "Ryan, I know you're an historic renovator and can see how much this means to you, so I will agree to keep the stove, but *only* if you can get the electricity working. It would be a pain in the bum if I had to build a fire every time I wanted to cook something."

"It's a deal. Beyond the stove, the only thing worth keeping in the kitchen is that table by the window. It's probably been here for close to a century. Has some real history, I'd bet."

"Thanks, I'd like to refinish it," Amber said, recalling a story her mother told her of sitting at this very table, waiting for her grandfather to bring milk up from the dairy for her breakfast cereal. "Could you get a new sheet of tin to use on the top? This one is all scratched up."

"I could, but I'd rather just repaint the legs. I prefer to keep the things that are left in an old house pretty much as they are. I assume you would like an historic renovation done on the place?"

"What would that involve?" Amber asked. She was beginning to be concerned that Ryan's passion for the history of the place was going to be a problem.

"Peeling back the layers of paneling, wallpaper and linoleum that were added over the years and restoring this old beauty to her original style," Ryan said.

"Wouldn't that cost more?" Amber asked.

"Not a lot," Ryan said. "And it's the right thing to do for this gracious old lady."

"Okay, but please keep in mind I'm planning to sell the house when the renovation is complete and the finished house needs to appeal to today's buyers."

Ryan nodded, although Amber wondered if she had really gotten through to him. They continued to discuss his ideas for period-appropriate kitchen cabinets, soapstone countertops and tearing out the old peeling linoleum on the kitchen floor. He lifted up a corner and said there was heart-pine under the cruddy linoleum.

"I could sand the floor down. I think I can bring it back," Ryan said cheerfully. "I'll do final calculations later and call you with my estimate for the labor. The way I usually work is for the property owner to purchase the materials for a project locally. I have an account at Latimer's Lumber Yard. If you get your cabinets there, you can tell them we're working together and they will give you a contractor's discount. I'll get my guys in here to demo the kitchen tomorrow, all but the stove and the table. Sound good?"

"Fine," she said, startled at the speed of his calculation and smiling at his incisive grasp of the situation. They shook hands on the deal. A moment later, Ryan looked at her and Amber realized she was still holding his hand. It was the first time she had touched a man since she had broken up with her boyfriend, Brock.

She left the Gallery to grab lunch one day when she spotted her boyfriend across the street walking beside a blond girl. She wasn't even positive it was him until he bent his head to the girl's laughing face. His hand rested on her back in an oddly possessive gesture. When she phoned him that night, saying she had seen him with another woman, Brock said he had something to tell her. He was sorry but their relationship was over, he had fallen in love with the blond girl. Amber adored him so completely she hadn't realized he hadn't felt the same—until he broke her heart. Afterwards, she could see there had been clues, times when he was simply unavailable, his stalling over meeting her father and his avoidance of the subject whenever she'd hinted that they might move in together.

"Sorry," she said, dropping Ryan's hand, "Just deep in thought. I'd like to have the house ready to go on the market by the end of the summer. Is that possible?"

"Don't see a problem," he said, his mouth rising in a grin. "All the ladies love me because I clean up a construction site at the end of the day. Not all of them want to hold my hand that long, though," he raised his eyebrows and chuckled. Amber felt herself redden.

WATCHING RYAN'S PICK-UP DEPART, Amber realized her dog was missing again. She walked down the driveway toward the barn and whistled for him. Camelot bounded up and out of the muddy calf pen, raced up the driveway, and practically flew through the air toward the house. When he skidded to a stop, Amber looked down at her beautiful white Afghan hound. He could have passed for a mud-coated chocolate retriever.

The first time she fed the calves, she worried that Cam would scare them, but Hunter said Aunt Irene owned a border collie to bring the cows from the pasture to the barn. When she entered the Nursing Home she gave the dog to the Lundgren family. The calves were used to dogs and Cam just seemed to love being around them. They would lower their necks to sniff his head and he would lick their mouths. Predictably trying to scrounge a few drops of milk, Amber thought. Chow hound.

Pulling her cell phone from her pocket, Amber took Cam's picture and sent it to her best friend in Chicago, Cassidy Dillon. Cassidy had gray green eyes, sun-streaked hair and eyebrows that were arched as perfectly as seagull's wings in flight. Of the two of them, Cassidy was the one who took life calmly—as it came. Amber was far more emotional, keenly feeling life's ups and downs. She could see those beautiful eyebrows rising when she saw the picture of Cam.

"Pix of my immaculate dog," Amber texted.

Cassidy texted back immediately saying, "Ready to come back to the city? Ha, Ha."

"I wish! Lots to do here yet," Amber replied.

LISTENING TO THE WIND BLOW through the cottonwood trees as she got in bed for the night, Amber decided to read another page of Paul Morand's translation of Ina's journal. She was restricting herself to one page a night. It was difficult. She was already caught up in Ina's story.

Ina's Journal
November, 1915

I will put all my hidden thoughts in this journal. My fiancé can never read it. Frank Morand, the man I am soon to marry, is short, thin and intense. He is not handsome, but he wanted me and no one else did. He courted me for two years before I finally gave my reluctant consent. His eyes went dark and glittered when I said yes. His gaze made me feel like a goose stupidly waddling toward a man holding an ax behind his back. I wanted to escape the farm, but blood pounded in my ears when I thought of what being married to Frank would mean.

As is traditional in our culture, our betrothal ceremony took place almost a year ago on a cold autumn day. The priest recited blessings and pressed his thumb into my forehead three times. We held lighted candles in our hands. The flames symbolized our willingness to receive the blessings of God. The village women have fashioned garland wreaths into crowns made of dried mock-orange blossoms and myrtle for my wedding. My mother still has her crown, dried and crispy with age. She pulled it from a round-topped trunk, telling me she wanted to be buried with it on her head. Soon, we will have my crowning, the part of the wedding ceremony most filled with meaning.

My father says I am lucky to be marrying into such an important family but I feel uneasy. As far as I can tell, Frank doesn't talk with his mysterious well-to-do father who will not be attending the wedding. His mother died years ago. Even sadder, to my woman's heart, Frank has never said he loved me. My mother says love is not important in a marriage, but I ache to feel a profound love like my friend Sarah did. She went laughing to her wedding.

But Sarah died in childbirth a year later and her baby is cared for by her mother. Sarah's adored husband drinks in the taverns, frequenting the injuratura women of our town and stumbling through the streets. The older women have nothing but contempt for him.

Tonight as I kneel by my bed to say my prayers, I beg for the blessings of God and for my heart to open to my husband-to-be. A pulse in my throat beats with trepidation thinking of my wedding—and what lies beyond the ceremony on my first night as a married woman.

SIX

RYAN'S CREW BEGAN DEMOLITION on the kitchen the next morning. Although Amber knew it had to be done, she found it hard to watch. She was surprised by her strong sense of connection to the old place. By noon, the kitchen table had been moved out to the front porch for painting and Ryan was running a power sander over the floors. The machine made a high whine and sawdust hung like a reddened curtain in the air. The house was emerging from ill-considered renovations done over the decades and becoming the beauty it deserved to be, although Amber knew she would have to keep a sharp eye on her contractor and his plans if the house were to sell.

Wanting to escape the construction mess, she decided to go back to the nursing home and visit Aunt Irene again. Perhaps she could pry something out of the old lady about Ina's journal. She left Cam in the summer kitchen, closing the door tightly and telling Ryan not to let him escape, but a mile down the road she spotted a whirling cloud of dust in her rear-view mirror. Amber stopped the car beside the silly mophead who kept trying to express his doggy gratitude with wild licking. She got out of the car, opened the rear door and the dog climbed into the back seat.

"Twit," she said, grinning at Aunt Irene's word. To his voluble dismay, Amber left the dog in the car with windows cracked when she walked into the Apple River Nursing Home. He barked once loudly and she called, "Tough, Cam. Just deal with it."

"You're back. It's nice to see you," Mrs. Worth said as she entered the facility.

"Is Aunt Irene in her room?" Amber asked.

"Actually, she's not. She had a doctor's appointment for congestive heart failure this morning. It was to deal with the edema in her legs. I hope it went okay." She chewed on a fingernail, looking toward the sliding front door. A handicapper van was pulling up. A white-coated driver and his assistant got out, walked around to the side of the car, lifted Aunt Irene out and placed her in a wheelchair. Even through the glass doors, Amber could hear the stentorian tones of Aunt Irene's voice instructing the attendants.

"Slow down, you idiots," she stormed. "You're going to drop me. You're supposed to wait until I'm *dead* before you kill me!"

"General Irene Morand still issuing orders to the troops, I see," Mrs. Worth murmured with an amused twitch to her lips. Amber followed the shrieking wheelchair occupant down the shining hall. Her nurse opened the door to Aunt Irene's room, gesturing for Amber to wait.

"You can go in now," the nurse said after a few minutes and Amber opened the door to see the old lady in bed, propped up against her pillows.

"Hello, Aunt Irene," Amber said. Her great aunt was coughing. It was a wheezy cough, similar to an asthmatic's. Her chest sounded like a washing machine agitating in the wash cycle.

"Stupid quack says congestive heart failure is going to kill me in six months," Aunt Irene said. Her nostrils flared. She seemed more furious than depressed by the horrible prognosis.

"Oh dear, I'm so awfully sorry," Amber offered, feeling the ordinary words too paltry. "Maybe the doctor's wrong. You could get another opinion."

"No. Damned charlatan is right. Dead and buried by fall. Won't make a hundred now." Her face stiffened and Amber could see the bones beneath her near-transparent skin. Aunt Irene had struggled to say the last few words. She started coughing again before catching her breath and saying, "There's a bird-feeder outside the carriage house. My wrens need feeding and I've been cultivating a patch of four-leaf clovers under the feeder. Don't let Hunter cut them down when he mows the yard." Aunt Irene was still having trouble breathing but added, "I found a couple more translated pages from Ina's journal." She took them from her side table and handed them to Amber.

"Thank you. I've been reading a page at a time. Going to run out soon. Do you know where your mother's original journal is?"

Aunt Irene frowned and said, "Wasn't going to tell you. Thought you should have the challenge, but given my useless doctor's diagnosis, I will. It's in the cellar." She laid back breathless, her face white as her starched pillowcase. "Leave, Girl," she said.

Clutching the additional pages, Amber departed. As she reached the front desk, Irene's nurse called out. "Wait a minute, Miss Bradshaw. I wanted to talk to you. I'm Emma Clarkson, Miss Irene's nurse."

"I'm Amber Bradshaw. Thank you for helping her."

"You know Miss Irene has congestive heart failure, right?" Emma asked.

Amber nodded. The phrase, *congestive heart failure*, gave her an awful sinking feeling. She felt a sudden stab of pride in the strong-willed woman who faced her fate with rage instead of despair and realized she was, as her father had predicted, already becoming fond of the old curmudgeon.

"When you have congestive heart failure, the heart is not as powerful as it once was. As less blood is pumped out of the heart, the blood returning to the heart backs up. The back-up is what causes her shortness of breath. The medicine Miss Irene is on gives her some relief, but she has already had CHF for five years," Emma shook her head, touching a finger to her mouth, adding, "I'm afraid she's running out of time."

"The doctor told her she only has about six months left," Amber said.

Emma reached out and patted Amber's shoulder gently. "Since you're her only family, could you stop by to visit every couple of days?"

"I'm remodeling a big house, so it's going to be tough," Amber said, hesitating. She really didn't want to promise more than she could deliver. She remembered all too well her young years devoted to her little sister after her mother died. Mixed with the sadness about the loss of her mother, Amber still felt the weight of the heavy burden her mother had laid upon her young shoulders.

She recalled one day when she visited the cemetery. Kneeling at her mother's gravestone, Amber hadn't heard her father climbing the hill behind her.

"Didn't know you came here," he said gruffly.

"It's been a year today," she said, setting a small collection of acorns and bright autumn leaves on the flat granite marker which read, "Grace Morand Bradshaw, Beloved Wife and Mother." The wind was cold and she shivered.

Later, as they walked down the hill toward her father's car, he stumbled. Cursing, he pulled himself up and opened the car door. She could smell alcohol on his breath. "We are out of food," she told him coldly. "You promised you would go to the grocery store. We had to eat at O'Brien's again last night. Claire is starting to think she lives there."

Pulling her mind back to the present she said, "I'm sorry, Emma, what were you saying?"

"Just that you are her last relative. She needs you," Emma's expression was determined. "Plus, she told me she has a secret she's kept for a long time. I've gathered it's some mystery connected to the farm and her mother's journal."

"I don't suppose you know what this secret is, do you?" Amber asked, wondering if there really could be a treasure. And if there was, whether Ina's journal would reveal its location.

"I don't," Emma shook her heard ruefully. "She'll tell you when she's darn good and ready, I suppose. Could you pick up one of those lined paper notebooks for her? Miss Irene's had such a long and interesting life, it might help her to write things down. And who knows, she might forget herself and write something about this long-held secret."

Like that canny old woman would forget to keep a secret. Not likely, Amber thought.

Driving down Morand Road on her way back to the farm, she remembered her father saying the family home had been built on the site of an old cabin with a root cellar underneath, but she hadn't seen any entrance to a cellar either inside the house or out. If Ina's journal was down in the cellar it was going to be tough to find. Aunt Irene could have given me a bit more information, she thought. Exasperating old biddy.

WHEN PHONE RANG AROUND SEVEN that evening, Amber grabbed it. "Hi, Dad. How are things going there? Are you going to have surgery?"

"Yes. The doctor said it was *past* time to schedule the knee replacement. The surgery is pretty routine these days. I'm not worried about it," he said, but Amber caught a tiny note of concern in his voice.

"I'll come home for the procedure. I don't want you to go through that alone."

"Actually, Mrs. Miller said she'd take me to the hospital and stay during the surgery. You don't need to worry."

"Mrs. Miller? From next door you mean?"

"I should have told you before, Amber," he hesitated. "Ever since her husband died last year, Joanna and I have been . . . seeing each other."

"Goodness," Amber paused to digest the news. "Well that's just wonderful, Dad. I'm happy for you."

"Thanks, Honey. Anyway, how's Aunt Irene?"

"I don't know how much you know about her condition. I hate to tell you this, especially over the phone. I know she is one of your favorite people. Her doctor says she is in the last stages of congestive heart failure. She only has about six months left to live."

When he spoke her father's voice was constricted. "I know she's an old lady, and everyone's life must come to an end." He cleared his throat. "But that's an awful shame. How did she react to the news?"

"She wasn't sad at all, more like enraged. Told me she had planned to make a hundred. She gave me several more pages from Ina's journal that her brother translated. Apparently the journal itself is in the cellar, but I haven't found a way to get down there yet. Do you know where the entrance is?"

"I sure don't, Honey. As you know, your mom believed her great grandparents brought valuables with them from the old country. She said there was a stash of gold somewhere in that house—maybe it's in the cellar." He chuckled. "I never believed those old stories. Even if the Morands did bring gold with them, it's probably long gone by now. But if you can find Ina's journal, it would make for interesting reading."

In bed that night, Amber reached for one more of the translated pages from the journal. Ina had been expressing reservations about her marriage to Frank, Amber wanted to know what would happen next.

Ina Nicholescu Journal
December, 1915

From the window in my parents' house, I can see the women of my village, dressed in long dun-colored dresses, with their clumsy wooden shoes and head scarves. They are carrying flowers into the dark church. My wedding is tomorrow. After the service, I will no longer be Ina Nicolescu. I will become Ina Morand, always known by my husband's last name. My childhood self will be erased, as if all eighteen years of my life until that day, had never existed.

Frank has a younger brother, Charles, who is also an Army officer. Charles has a lower rank than Frank in the army, and is not paid as many golden lei for his service. He is married to a woman named Alene. She is a cheerful bustling woman with a hearty laugh. They are the only people from Frank's family who will attend our wedding. Frank says his father lives in a castle. I doubted him at first, but then I remembered the conversation I overheard between my parents. They said Frank's father was a Boier, a member of the aristocracy.

I try to raise my spirits, thinking of living in the city of Bucharest on the Dambovita River. Frank said we could have a house near the parade grounds where the soldiers under his command practice marching. They wear smart navy uniforms with red epaulets on their shoulders and hold shining silver swords at their sides. Frank's men have to do whatever he says. Like the soldiers, I also must obey him, he says. He takes this for granted, but I feel a scalding bitterness tighten in my chest. A burn of anger rises in me that my parents fostered this union, despite my misgivings.

Amber put the pages down, looking out the window at the moon-drenched cottonwood trees recognizing how much she and Ina shared. She hoped Ina had eventually learned to love Frank and forgave him for insisting on her obedience as part of the marriage ceremony.

Will I ever be able to forgive myself for the day I almost cost my little sister her life? Her remorse rose and she wondered if being at the farm, or just the simple passage of time, would someday permit her to forgive herself.

SEVEN

THE SOFT PURR OF A CAR COMING TO A STOP behind the farmhouse woke Amber's dog. He nudged her with his cold nose until she raised her sleepy head and looked at the clock. It was four o'clock in the morning. A gentle wind floated in through the tall open window. The air felt like silk against her skin and starlight glinted on the leaves of the cottonwood trees. She smiled sleepily, recalling an old nursery rhyme about a fisherman's net filled with "stars caught in a twinkling foam."

Then a car door slammed, startling Amber into full wakefulness. She sat up in bed, looking down on the driveway from her second floor window. The moon caught a young woman's silvery hair as she pulled a bag from the rear seat and headed directly toward the door to the summer kitchen.

Whoever this is knows exactly how to get into the house, Amber thought uneasily. Although she hadn't felt afraid living on the farm since Cam had rousted all the critters, a quiver of alarm crossed her shoulders wondering if the visitor were a messenger carrying news of life-changing importance. The dog stood up on the bed, white and ghostlike, making a low rumble in his chest.

"Shush, Cam," Amber whispered. "We better see what this is about." She pulled a robe on over her nightshirt and walked downstairs. When she switched on the light over the back stoop and looked out through the window, she saw her little sister.

She opened the screen door slowly.

"Claire, is it really you?"

"Good, you're up," it was her sister's matter-of-fact voice. "Aren't you going to let me in?"

Stunned, Amber stepped back and opened the door wider. The slender girl standing in the starlight seemed insubstantial, surreal. Claire had been away at college for two years following a huge fight with their father. Despite the many phone calls which were rarely answered, Amber hadn't seen her since she was eighteen. She would be twenty now.

"Wait a sec," Claire said, handing her bag to Amber. "I have to get something else from the car."

Amber walked slowly into the kitchen. She reached under the stove for the basket she had filled with paper and small chips of wood for kindling. Ryan was still stalling on hooking up the burners to electricity. She struck a match, irked to realize it was already starting to feel normal lighting a burner this way. No doubt part of Ryan's diabolical master plan. Drat the man and his blasted cheerful persistence. Filling the teakettle, she set it on the wrought-iron burner to heat.

"I'm in the kitchen," Amber called, hearing Claire come back into the house. She reached out to touch her only sibling, the child she had raised nearly single-handedly from the day their mother died. Their father had been so consumed by grief he drowned himself in alcohol, trying to blot out his depression, seemingly confident in Amber's twelve year-old inadequate parenting skills.

Claire was holding some blankets in her arms. The dog walked forward from the corner, eyes bright, watching.

"Look what I have," Claire said softly and pulled the blankets away from the tiny face of a sleeping infant. Camelot moved so quietly he almost seemed to tiptoe. A delicate pink foot stuck out of the blanket. The miniature toes were so interesting, the temptation so irresistible that the dog licked the tiny toes that curled up reflexively. The baby's face was rosy and perfectly curled eyelashes rested on her chubby pink cheeks.

"I call her Minna. Her full name is Cosmina Morand Bradshaw."

"Oh my God, Claire. You had a baby?"

"I did indeed," Claire said looking at the child and smiling fondly.

Amber reached out and touched her sister's cheek. "I can hardly believe you are here. Sit down at the table. We have some serious catching up to do."

The two sisters sat at the tin-topped kitchen table drinking cups of tea as the baby slept in Claire's lap. "Your little one is just darling, Claire, but what about her father? Where is he in this picture?"

"He's not," Claire said softly.

"Why?" Amber asked.

"He told me he's not ready," Claire said looking away and shrugging her shoulders.

Amber frowned—exasperated at Claire's lack of responsibility as well as the boy's—before feeling a pinch of guilt. Had she never even talked to Claire about birth control?

As the first light hit the kitchen windows, Claire handed Amber the baby saying, "Here, you take her. Sorry, Amber, but since I had the baby, I never get enough sleep."

Claire climbed the stairs and disappeared into the bedroom. Amber carried the sleeping baby to the chintz-covered loveseat at the bottom of the staircase and looked up the name Cosmina on her I-pad. The name meant order and beauty in Romanian. *The opposite of my sister's crazy life,* she thought. With Cam at her feet, Amber sat watching the baby sleep until her eyes fluttered open. They were gray green, the color of pebbles under water. The moment Amber looked into baby Minna's eyes, she felt a profound qualm. She really didn't want to be responsible for a little one again, but to her dismay realized she was already falling for baby Minna.

THAT AFTERNOON AMBER RETURNED to the Apple River Falls Nursing Home. She had been reluctant to leave her sister and the baby at the house, fearing Claire might vanish while she was gone, but her sister promised she wouldn't leave. They had agreed to spend some more time talking soon. Amber wanted to hear her sister's entire story.

Emma was sitting at the nurses' desk in the patient wing recording data in a chart. Her ash-blonde hair fell forward as she bent to her computer. Amber didn't disturb her. Opening the door to room 109, she saw Aunt Irene asleep. She stood near the bed for several minutes before noticing the notebook on Aunt Irene's lap. It was the one she had purchased at the drugstore. Idly, she picked it up and began to read.

I am Irene Morand, 99 years old and the last of the Morand family. Wanted to make 100, won't happen now. Just before my mother died, she showed me an ancient icon, a religious painting of Mary with baby Jesus in her lap. She told me my father brought it with them when they came to this country. Its beauty took my breath away . . .

Amber heard a sound and looked up. Aunt Irene had woken. Her furious eyes were fixed—like a barn owl ready to pounce on a foolishly irresponsible mouse.

"Hello," Amber said, feeling guilty. "I was reading your notebook. You said your mother showed you an icon? I studied them in art school. They have been around forever. Icons of Mary and baby Jesus were already being produced in the third century. Do you think her icon is still in the house? It could be very valuable." She realized she was practically babbling.

"Don't want you reading my notebook, it's private," Aunt Irene said, grabbing the notebook and yanking it from Amber's hands.

"I'm sorry. I won't do it again. Are you up to telling me more about your parents?"

"Yes," Aunt Irene's voice was slightly stronger. "You may ask." She waved her hand with the air of a queen bestowing a blessing on a lesser mortal.

"Did your parents have a happy marriage?" Amber asked, remembering Ina's feelings of trepidation before her wedding.

"They always seemed very much in love to me. They held hands all the time. My father laughed a lot."

The marriage must have turned out all right then, Amber thought, feeling relieved. "You said Ina's journal was in the cellar. I haven't found an entrance to it. Could you tell how to get down there?"

"Can't quite remember," Aunt Irene said, pursing her lips and giving Amber a sidelong glance, but from the expression on her face Amber knew she was teasing. Aunt Irene knew perfectly well how to get down into that cellar. She just wasn't ready to tell her. It was obviously a test.

"My turn to ask questions now. Are you married?" Aunt Irene asked.

"No. I was dating a man named Brock before I came here. I thought he was the one, but he found another girlfriend and left me for her."

"Useless tool," Aunt Irene said and Amber stifled a giggle.

"Aunt Irene, I'm shocked! What language." Amber grinned. "Where did you even hear such an expression?"

"I talk with the cleaning ladies at night," Aunt Irene said. "Interesting stuff."

"Do you think Ina's journal would tell us anything about the icon?"

"You are a vexation." Aunt Irene's mouth moved in a tiny reluctant tweak of a grin.

Amber was afraid she might laugh.

"Nuisance girl, leave," Aunt Irene said and waved her hand limply in the air, but she was smiling.

"Next time can we talk about the Morand Dairy?"

"Yes," Aunt Irene whispered and sudden tears trickled down her cheeks.

"I'll come back," Amber promised and patted her bony old shoulder gently.

CLAIRE WAS PUTTING BABY MINNA TO BED in the cradle upstairs when Amber returned to the farmhouse that evening. After leaving the Nursing home, she had spent the rest of the day with Ryan at the lumber yard. They had argued about every single decision—cabinets, countertops, fixtures and appliances. The problem was that she was slowly being converted to Ryan's vision.

"Do you want to talk?" Claire whispered when Amber came into the bedroom. She was sitting on the floor rocking Minna's cradle with one hand.

"For a bit," Amber whispered. "Come into my room so we don't wake the baby." Claire stood up and they walked into Amber's bedroom.

"I was wondering about Dad. What does he say about me?"

"He wishes you would come back home. He misses you, Claire." Amber saw a sudden wetness glisten in her sister's eyes. "I want to hear all about Minna's birth and how you have managed all this time. I just wish you had contacted me. I called you every week when you started college but after a few months it seemed to me that you were always running to class, or meeting friends, or on your way to get coffee. I felt you were avoiding me." Amber took a deep breath. "Now I know the reason. It must have been awful for you going through a pregnancy alone."

"It was pretty tough," Claire said in a shaky voice. "I'll tell you the whole story soon, but let's talk about the renovation now. What were you doing all day?"

"I want a modern farmhouse look, but my contractor, Ryan, wants 1920's accuracy so we shopped together, although I probably should say we *argued* together. What started it was that I had the temerity to purchase a microwave oven a week ago, which Ryan subsequently returned to the store," Amber rolled her eyes in exasperation. "You just can't have a kitchen these days without a microwave."

They could hear the baby fussing and Claire left, saying she had to settle the small one.

Amber sat down on her bed and reached for another translated page of Ina's journal. She wanted to read about Ina's wedding.

Ina's Journal
December 20, 1915

It is my wedding day. When we reach the church, my mother enters the sanctuary and takes her seat. I wait until the music starts and my father walks me inside. I clutch his arm, afraid I will stumble. Frank stands at the altar. He's smiling and looks proud. When we reach the front of the church, my father puts my hand on Frank's arm and I stand on tip-toe to kiss my father good-bye. My bridegroom's arm feels strong. I realize I've rarely touched him before.

We kneel before the priest. Holding our crowns in his hands, the priest crosses his arms three times in the air before placing them on our heads. We take three sips of wine from a shared common cup. It is the sign that we will share everything. The priest's assistant leads us around the altar where the Bible and the cross stand. Three hymns are sung as we circle. At the end of the ceremony, I kneel to Frank and although my voice quavers and I still have doubts, I vow to honor and obey him. The priest tells my husband to walk in righteousness.

To me he says I must multiply like Rachel in the Bible and fulfill the conditions of the law. The ancient phrase, "Na sisete," rings out over the congregation. It means, "May you live." I feel shivers across my shoulders remembering all the girls I've known who died in childbirth.

"Lord Jesus Christ, Son of God, have mercy on me, have mercy on me," I pray and the ceremony is over. Even now, Frank has never said he loves me. And I find myself married to a man I might never love either. Tomorrow I leave my parents' farm. After a long argument, my father finally agreed I could take my little dog with me to Bucharest. At least she loves me and I need someone who does . . .

Setting the pages aside, Amber laid back on her pillows, reaching down to pet Camelot sleeping on the floor. She was glad Ina had been able to take her dog with her to the city. During the time before her father went into treatment for his alcoholism, it was only the family dog who raised her spirits. He was a cocker spaniel named Sam who never left her side on long walks to the cemetery and through the fields. Sam had died years ago and her father bought Camelot as a bumbling puppy before her trip to the farm. He wanted her to have the company, he said.

EIGHT

"HAVE ANY OF YOU SEEN MY SISTER AND THE BABY?" Amber asked the workmen who were installing the plumbing for the half-bath the following afternoon. She had been at Latimer's Lumber yard checking on the estimated date for the kitchen cabinets to arrive. Some alterations had been made to the order, the clerk said, holding out the order form. She shook her head, seeing Ryan's initials authorizing the changes. The men working at the Lumber Yard clearly didn't seem to think she was in charge of the project. Neither did Ryan obviously.

"Sorry. I haven't seen your sister today," one of the workmen said and the others shook their heads.

After searching the entire house with no luck, Amber walked down to the barn with Cam walking at her side. He was getting so big, his head reached up to her hip. A wooden ladder rested at an angle leading up to the haymow. Amber remembered climbing up into the hawmow as a child. She would stand on the step behind Claire, encircling her little body so she wouldn't fall.

"Claire," she shouted. "Are you up there?"

Her sister came to the opening and gestured for Amber to come up. "Shhh. Minna's napping," she whispered, putting a finger to her lips.

Climbing the ladder, Amber looked down at her dog standing at its base. "You stay right there," she told him firmly, knowing he wouldn't. He would be in the calf pen the minute she was out of sight. Dratted scamp. How was she ever going to control Ryan if she couldn't even get her dog to mind? Aunt Irene was right. She really was a twit.

Reaching the opening, Amber looked around. The floor had been made a century earlier of ten inch-thick planks from the vast forest that once covered the whole state of Wisconsin. Stacked bales of yellow grain filled both ends of the haymow. Someone had piled them up step-wise, making what seemed a staircase for giants. The floor in the middle was dusty, empty except for baby Minna, sound asleep on a pink blanket.

"How the heck did you get the baby up here?" Amber whispered.

"I have this baby carrier that goes around my body. There was too much noise in the house. Minna is going to wake up soon and be hungry. I forgot to bring her bottle or diapers. I'm not very good at this mothering thing. Not like you," Claire said, her face a study in consternation.

Amber's voice softened. "Don't be silly. It's still new to you. You'll get the hang of it. I'll go get her bottle and diapers and find out how long the workers will be here today."

CLIMBING BACK UP THE LADDER with supplies later, Amber joined her sister who sat cross-legged by the baby. A stab of sunlight from an opening in the roof hit Claire's silvery blond hair; it shone lambent in the dusky barn.

"Being at the farm has been bringing back a lot of memories of Mom for me," Amber said. "Do you remember much about her, Claire? I know you were only five when she died."

"I remember her taking us to the farm for visits, picking blueberries and the sound the berries made when they plopped into the metal pail. I remember the cows turning their heads to look at us when we went into the barn. They were standing in a row waiting to be milked. But I try not to think about Mom too often."

"Don't you want to remember her?" Amber asked, feeing troubled and looking at her sister intently.

"Yes and no. I saw a counselor at school for a while. She said I was afraid to think about Mom too much because it would just bring back my feelings of abandonment."

"I won't ever abandon you, Claire," Amber said, softly. "I've told you that."

But you did, the voice in her head said. The shame of coming home stark naked, the ambulance lights and the police cars in the driveway returned—striking with a body blow.

"You didn't always want me tagging along after you and your friends when we were kids though," Claire said, smiling.

"There were some days when you were indeed a little pest." Amber said, struggling to sound cheerful despite the awful memory crowding in. "Tell me what else you remember about Mom."

"I remember the nurse coming to the house and checking the tubes that were connected to her arms. Once I took a little lotion and rubbed it on her hand. She made a small whimpering noise. I thought I hurt her." Claire winced.

Amber felt tears prick her eyes when she said, "The last thing I remember is going to the hospital to say good-bye. Dad must have known she didn't have much time left. Her face was as white as the sheets. She could hardly talk."

"I remember that day, too. Dad told me to kiss her good-bye, but I couldn't reach her skin because of all the tubes." Claire had tears running down her cheeks by then. "I'm never going to leave this little one like Mom left us," she said looking down at her baby.

"We weren't the only ones Mom left, you know. Dad was never the same after she died," Amber said.

"I just remember him being gone all the time. It seemed as if we had lost them both. Like we were orphans, living all alone in that big house." Claire took a deep breath.

"In those first years, Dad was seriously depressed. He started drinking heavily. He was driving back from the grocery story one night when he got pulled over. It was our neighbor, Officer O'Brien, who stopped him. He opened the trunk of the car. It was full of empty whiskey bottles. That's when we knew he was an alcoholic. "

"I remember Mrs. O'Brien," Claire said with a smile. "She was so nice. She took care of me before I was old enough to go to school all day. We never got hot food, except at their house."

"Mrs. O'Brien was an angel. She won't even have to stop at Heaven's Pearly Gates. Saint Peter will just wave her in. She basically added us to her family until social services stopped checking on us. If it hadn't been for her, we would have ended up in foster care."

Claire got a funny look on her face. "Did I get lost once? I remember crying for you to come for me, how dark it was and seeing a man with a flashlight. I remember my arm was hurting." She frowned.

Amber felt a burn of shame but kept her voice calm. "Yes, you broke your arm. The doctors put a cast on you and I drew little flowers on it," she said, trying to distract her sister from remembering more about that awful day.

"Did we live with the O'Briens for a while?" Claire asked. She frowned in confusion. "I seem to remember sleeping there. We slept in the same bed I think. Did I wet the bed?"

"Yes. Mrs. O'Brien expected it, she said it was a normal response to what you had gone through." Amber swallowed and took a deep breath realizing she was ready to apologize. "I'm so sorry I forgot to get you that day from school, Claire. I still feel just awful about it." She found herself in tears and wiped her eyes.

"That's okay, Amber. I'm sorry I wet the bed," Claire said and chuckled.

Amber tried to join her light-heartedness, but the memory of her failure returned with a hammer blow.

The school was close enough that Amber came home for lunch. She walked slowly into their house, dreading seeing how ugly it was now. There was a half-empty bottle of whiskey on the kitchen counter. Dirty dishes cluttered every surface. She remembered how the house looked when her mother was alive, every surface shining. Bright red tulips in a silver vase on the table, music playing and dinner baking in the oven.

"I should clean up the kitchen," she told herself, as she set her backpack on the couch cluttered with newspapers, toys and dirty glasses. But the dog cried to go outside for a walk and a spring wind was blowing. She decided she wouldn't go back to school. "The water in the lake would be warm enough for a swim," she thought. She couldn't stand being in the ugly house another second. Grabbing her father's half-empty liquor bottle, she took a swig. It burned all the way down her throat and she coughed. "Maybe enough of this will make me forget that I don't have a mother," she thought, and stuffed it in her backpack.

Outside, she climbed on her bike, whistled for the dog and left. It had started out as an adventure. If only I hadn't gone to the lake, drunk the liquor and gone skinny dipping. If only I had remembered I was supposed to get my little sister.

Baby Minna started to whimper, breaking Amber's train of thought. The baby was opening and closing her little fist and Claire picked her up. "Would you like to feed her, Amber? She's always hungry when she first wakes up. That little gesture means 'milk'. I've taught her a few signs from the language of the deaf."

"That is so cute! She's adorable, Claire." Amber picked up the bottle and took Minna into her arms. The baby gulped her bottle down hungrily. "I'm noticed a big improvement in Dad's spirits recently. I just learned he's started seeing Mrs. Miller."

"He's dating Joanna Miller?" Claire asked, raising her eyebrows. "Her son and I are . . . friends."

"All this happened since her husband died," Amber said. "Dad feels badly about being estranged from you, Claire. You two need to talk."

A frown crossed Claire's forehead. "I'm not ready for him to know about Minna."

"You can't exactly keep a baby a secret forever," she said, exasperated. "He's having knee replacement surgery and it's going to be tough on him. Go home for a visit, and bring the baby."

Claire stood up, walked over to the haymow opening and sat down. Her bare legs hung outside in the warm summer sunshine. Amber heard the sound of Ryan's pick-up truck pulling in. They could hear him chatting with some workers who were just leaving.

"That's my contractor, Ryan," Amber said

"He's headed this way," Claire told her.

Amber stood up and walked to stand behind her sister. "Ryan, I'd like to introduce you to my sister, Claire. She has a baby and it's a hot mess in the house. Are you about done for the day?"

"Nice to meet you, Claire. Yes, the crew is leaving. They've removed the ugly 1970's paneling and you'll never guess what they found! There's original *shiplap* on the walls," his voice rose with excitement. "I wanted to ask if you are okay with me keeping it. It's going to take a bit longer because all the nails have to be pulled out and the holes filled. It's worth it though. You know how I am about all this old historic stuff," he grinned.

Amber sighed. Damn man was clearly winning. "As long as the walls can still be painted white, or ivory that's fine. I'm sure it will look wonderful when you're done."

"We probably need to go to the paint store together," Ryan said, looking guilty, and Amber rolled her eyes. He obviously had another color in mind, in fact he'd probably already ordered it.

"Do you see Cam around?" she asked.

"In the pen with the calves," he said.

Of course he was. Dratted animal.

PREPARING DINNER THAT EVENING, Amber asked Claire to tell her about the day Minna was born. Her sister took a deep breath.

"Okay, here goes. My roommate at school was in the nursing program. When I went into labor, she brought one of her ob/gyn nurse friends over. She reminded me that women had babies at home for centuries and kept reassuring me that I would be fine. But it went on so long, I got scared and asked them to take me to the student health center on campus. Walking out to the car, it was raining and fall leaves were blowing all over the place. I almost slipped and fell. Once in the car, I kept screaming for them to drive faster."

"You poor kid, I still can't believe you did this all on your own," Amber said.

"The doctor at the Student Health Service wanted to send me to the local hospital, but I was too close to delivering. My labor lasted twelve hours and the whole thing hurt like hell. After she was born, the health center called an ambulance and I was admitted to the hospital for a couple of days. I had to meet with a social worker and sign some papers."

"Oh honey, I'm so sorry," Amber said, thinking Claire should never have had to go through all that alone and wondering where the hell the boy who got her pregnant was.

"You had just taken the job with Hillside Gallery when I started college. As you know, I had an awful argument with Dad the night before I moved into the dorm. But you probably don't know what it was about. He caught me in bed with my boyfriend," Claire looked embarrassed for a moment.

"Did I ever meet this boy?" Amber asked. "I don't remember him."

"You were in art school when we started dating. He joined a band in high school and was never around on week-ends when you came home."

"I take it he is Minna's father. Did you tell him you were pregnant?"

"I did. He said we could get married if I wanted, but sounded reluctant, said he wasn't ready for the responsibility of being a dad. Plus, he'd been taking drugs to fit in with the band, was stoned a lot of the time and didn't have any money. I got my back up and told him to forget it. But to tell you the truth, Amber, I felt the same way. I knew I wasn't ready for the responsibility either. I wasn't ready to be a mom."

Just like I wasn't ready, but that was no excuse, she told herself and winced.

"I never told Dad I was pregnant," Claire said. I called him once, toward the end. He sounded stiff. Asked me if I was behaving myself. It wasn't exactly the time to say I was about to have a baby."

"Oh, Claire, I wish you had at least told me. I called and left messages and texted over and over. I even drove to the college a couple of times, but nobody seemed to know where you were. Why didn't you call me?" Amber asked.

"I dialed your number so many times, Amber. A couple of times you answered and I hung up when I heard your voice." She took a shaky breath. "I knew you would be disappointed in me getting pregnant and if I gave the baby up for adoption, you would never have had to know. But when I saw her face, I just couldn't. I'm sorry, Sis. I should have told you."

"I'm sorry too, Claire. I certainly have no right to criticize. Brock dumped me for another girl a few months ago. I'm not any different from you, except for using the pill. Seems like we both picked losers."

"But look what I got," Claire said and the two women smiled at the sleeping baby. The baby stirred and smiled, a little bubbly smile. Looking down at her cuteness, Amber felt a rush of love for the little one.

But Claire saying she wasn't ready to be a mom made Amber's stomach churn. Her chest tightened. It was happening all over again. She just knew she was going to end up being responsible for both of them. At least I'm not twelve this time, she thought. If I end up with Claire and her baby now, I will never run out on them like I did on the day I forgot her.

THE FOLLOWING AFTERNOON, Amber went down to the barn to feed the calves with Hunter. When she got to the calf pen, Hunter was busy filling the bottles. He smiled warmly when he saw her. Standing beside the pen was an older man who wore his hair in a single long braid down his back. He was dressed in faded jeans and a denim shirt, his belt had an elaborate silver buckle. He looked more Native American than Hunter did.

"Amber, this is my dad, Ned Freedman.

"It's good to meet you, Mr. Freedman," Amber said, holding out her hand, "I'm Amber Bradshaw."

"Dad and I were talking before you got down here. What would you think about me cleaning out the barn and putting up the stanchions again?" Hunter asked.

Stanchions? More farm terminology she didn't know. "Sorry to be such an idiot, but what are stanchions?"

"Stanchions are sets of metal poles that lock around the cow's neck and hold them in place while they are milked. We still have the old stanchions from the Morand Dairy, but they would need to be put back in place, and we'd need some new milking machines. Plus, the barn isn't clean enough or insulated, Irene didn't feel she had the money to make the necessary improvements."

"It's nice of you to offer, Hunter, but I've put so much money into the house that the budget my father gave me for the project is fast disappearing."

"It would only take a few thousand dollars to get the barn and milking parlor clean and the milking machines working," Mr. Freedman said. "Irene Morand had fifty or sixty cows here originally, but over a period of years she cut the herd down to a half-dozen. That was all she could handle. Those six cows are over at the Lundgren's place. I'm assuming you know the Morands had a dairy here for almost a hundred years?"

"Aunt Irene told me."

"I've already sanitized the milking machines that still work," Hunter said, "And milk sells pretty well now. We figure we could pay you back for a small investment in less than a year."

"How much would it take to get the barn clean enough to produce good milk?" She felt herself reluctantly giving way in light of their enthusiasm.

"That depends on what grade of milk you want to sell. For lower grades we could get an operation going for less than five thousand," Mr. Freedman said.

"I hate to rain on your parade, but Aunt Irene has promised to sell the farm to a big agricorporation called Framingham."

"Would you at least talk with her about the idea?" Mr. Freedman asked. "Possibly she will change her mind." Amber nodded.

WALKING BACK TO THE HOUSE, she felt acutely frustrated at this latest turn of events. Originally, all she had to do was fix up the house and sell it. Then Ryan came into the picture wanting the house to look like it did a century ago. Now, the Freedman's wanted to re-start the dairy on farmland Aunt Irene had apparently committed to sell. And Claire had appeared with baby Minna.

"It will only take you the summer to get the house ready to sell," her Dad had said. "And it is so serene and restful at the farm."

Right, Amber thought, feeling exasperated. She knew what was happening. She was being drawn back into the role of the "big sister," the one who always took care of others. Except for the day I went to the lake, her conscience reminded her and the memory flared again like a forest fire.

When she reached the little lake near their house—just a pond really—the area was deserted. She stripped off her clothes, dove in the water and then popped to the surface, exhilarated and laughing. The water had been stingingly cold on her bare skin.

When she rose up out of the water, pushing her dripping hair off her face, she heard a boy's taunting laughter. She waited as long as she could, not wanting him to see her naked, but desperate to escape the cold, she scrambled up the bank. She waited there for several minutes, hunkered down in the brush, but hearing nothing more, dashed to the place she had left her clothes.

They weren't there.

NINE

AUNT IRENE WAS LOOKING OUT THE WINDOW when Amber arrived at the Nursing Home the following day. Someone had washed her hair and she'd been given a manicure. Her hands with their pink shiny fingernails rested in her lap, the swollen knuckles testament to the arthritis that afflicted so many hard-working older people.

"I have some more questions about the family, Aunt Irene. Is that okay?" Aunt Irene nodded.

"I read the pages of Ina's journal describing her wedding to Frank. It made me wonder why you never married. I can't believe you didn't have suitors, you were such a lovely young woman. I've seen your pictures in the old photo album."

A little more color came into Aunt Irene's face. Amber wondered if she was blushing.

"You are a . . . pest," Aunt Irene said. She pursed her lips but Amber could tell she was tickled by the question.

"Who was your favorite beau?"

Aunt Irene looked a bit embarrassed. "George Lundgren."

"Mr. Lundgren was your boyfriend?" Amber raised her eyebrows and frowned in confusion. "Hunter said the Lundgren family owns a nearby farm and have little kids. Aren't they my age?"

"It was the boy's great grandfather. He proposed to me in the spring. Knelt down under the cottonwood trees to ask me," she said, with a poignant smile.

For an instant, Amber saw the remnants of Aunt Irene's former beauty and the lovely young woman she had been. When the moment passed, Amber noticed how transparent her skin had become—so thin it looked like tissue paper.

"Why didn't you two get married?"

Aunt Irene closed her eyes and said, "He died in a silo. Crushed by wheat during threshing. I remembered him every time I looked down the road toward the Lundgren farm. Already had my wedding gown, you see." She looked down and started to cough.

"Oh, God. I'm sorry." Thinking of all the decades Aunt Irene had lived alone at the farm, running the dairy and grieving for a man she could never marry, Amber felt a groundswell of sorrow.

"I'm getting tired. Help me into bed, girl."

Amber did so and after Aunt Irene was settled, she asked, "Can we talk about the dairy?"

"The . . . dairy." Aunt Irene coughed. Then she smiled and Amber took her hand. She could feel pleasure warm Irene's small fingers.

"Mr. Freedman and Hunter want to clean out the barn and start milking again," Amber told her. "They want you to invest in the operation. Since the start-up money would come from you, and the profits would be yours, I want to know what you want to do."

"Tell them to use my money," she said. "How I *wish* they told me this before I had to come to live here." She gestured sadly at the small room.

"How much are you willing to invest?"

"All of it," Aunt Irene said. She started coughing. "Call Row . . . shay."

"Rowshay? Is he a banker or an attorney?"

"Banker." She lay back exhausted.

"I'll go to the bank and check how much you have in your account," Amber said. "However, I'm sure you would have to sign some forms. Would you like me to stay a bit longer today?"

"No. Vamoose, Wimp," Aunt Irene said, glaring at her but with a twinkle in her eyes.

Amber chuckled, she was finally catching on to her aunt's sense of humor. Aunt Irene's eyes closed and moments later her breathing deepened. Careful not to wake her, Amber bent down and kissed her forehead, feeling the blood flow beneath the fine skin at her temples. Aunt Irene was the last of the old people, the keeper of the family secrets.

DRIVING TOWARD THE BANK, Amber dialed her father's cell phone. "Hi Dad, it's me. What's happening?"

"I got some bad news yesterday. Turns out both knees have to be done."

"Oh, I'm so sorry. That's awful," Amber said.

"Well, they can only do one at a time, and once done I'm sure I'm going to feel like a new man, but two major surgeries are going to be tough."

"Are you sure you don't need me to come home?" Amber asked. "I'm happy to."

"I'll let you know. Don't think so, though. Mrs. Miller is here with me now. How's Aunt Irene? Has she told you anything more about the journal?"

"She said it was in the cellar. That's all she'll tell me so far and it wasn't very helpful because I can't find the entrance. You're sure you don't know how to get down there?"

"Not a clue," her father said. "Now I don't want you to get your hopes up about treasures at the house, Amber, but I always wondered how a young immigrant family could have purchased hundreds of acres of land, built two large houses, two barns and set up the Morand Dairy with no resources. There might have been a treasure once, but it was probably spent long ago."

As her father ended the call, Amber took a deep breath, trying to still her rising frustrations. She wanted to share everything with him, but he already had so much to handle with his upcoming surgery. Amber straightened her shoulders. Once Dad had his surgery, if Claire still hadn't told him about Minna, she decided she would tell him everything.

AMBER PARKED HER CAR IN THE BANK'S PARKING LOT, walked inside and asked a teller for a person named Row . . . shay.

"You must mean Mr. Rochet," the young receptionist said. "It's French. He's the president of this branch. I'll see if he has time to see you. Can I give him your name?"

"Tell him Amber Bradshaw. I'm here on behalf of Miss Irene Morand."

The receptionist was dressed casually in jeans, a plaid shirt and open-toed sandals. When Amber caught a glimpse of herself in a mirror, she saw a virtually identical outfit. She shook her head, smiling ruefully. Less than a month on the farm and the stylish young woman she had been in Chicago was in total eclipse.

"Mr. Rochet can see you now," the receptionist said when she reappeared. "It's the last door at the end of the hall."

Amber walked down the hall toward the back of the building. Sunshine flooded the hallway from a large window at the end of the corridor. She turned her thoughts away from all the things that were happening in her life, knocked on his door and opened it saying, "Mr. Rochet?"

"Come in," the man said, as he stood up to greet her. Smiling, he smoothed his dark hair back from his forehead. Must be ambitious to be President of a bank so young, Amber thought and suppressed a grin. Good looking, too.

"What can I do for you? Miss Bradshaw, is it?" He spoke with what Amber thought was a French Canadian accent.

"Yes, I'm Amber Bradshaw, Miss Irene Morand's grandniece. I'm here to renovate the Morand farmhouse prior to its sale. I'm sorry to tell you that Miss Irene's suffering from congestive heart failure."

"I knew she was in the nursing home. Is her condition stable?"

Amber took in a shaky breath. "Sadly, the doctor said she has only a few months to live. It's already getting hard for her to talk, because of the coughing." She felt tears prick her eyelids and her chest tightened at a sudden surge of loss.

"That's awful. Poor woman. Thank you for letting me know. I'll go visit her. She will need to sign some papers and identify someone to manage her money. I'll call Allswede, too. He's her attorney and has her last will and testament. She may wish to make some changes to her dispositions. Eventually, we will need her executor to distribute her assets to her heirs."

"Now you just slow down a minute here," Amber said, feeling a spurt of anger. "My Aunt Irene is a long way from giving up. She just might beat this thing. Her nurse told me there's even a surgical option that could help, although apparently her doctor isn't sure she would survive the procedure. I was just at the Nursing Home and told her the caretakers for the farm want to get the Morand Dairy going again. She told me to use her money to fund the project. I asked her how much and she said to use it all."

"Well, I can hardly release any of her money without signature authority, if that's what you're asking," he said, frowning. "And I thought Ms. Morand was selling the land to the Framingham Group? Should she invest anything such a short-lived operation?"

"I honestly don't know, Mr. Rochet," Amber said, sighing. "Originally, all I was planning to do was get the house fixed up and listed with a realtor. I'm headed back to Chicago in a few months."

But remembering Aunt Irene's hopes for the dairy and Claire's needs for help, she had a sudden sense of being out of her depth, treading water with no possible way to make it to a rapidly vanishing shore.

THAT EVENING AMBER REACHED for another page of Ina's journal. She wondered what early married life was going to be like for Ina.

Ina Morand Journal Entry
Summer, 1916

I haven't written in my Journal since the wedding. The first months of my marriage saw so many changes, I rode a wave of excitement. I had never been beyond Timisoara, the village where I was born. The passing countryside and all the little towns and villages entranced me. When we reached Bucharest, Frank found us some rooms to rent in a big old house. From the windows above the parade ground, I could watch him drill his blue-uniformed soldiers in handling their long shining rifles.

Some nights Frank brought soldiers home to eat dinner with us. His brother, Charles, and his wife Alene visited often. The men toasted each other and drank white vodka. I began to feel I had made a good bargain. It lasted only until I ran from the dinner table one night and vomited up everything in my stomach. Alene ran after me and wiped my face with a towel afterwards. Beads of perspiration decorated my forehead.

"You are pregnant," she told me.

"No," I whispered, horrified. I covered my mouth with my hand. I looked at myself in the tiny mirror. I was white as the towel. "I don't want to die, Alene."

"You won't," she said. "You are stronger than anyone I know." We looked at each other for a long time, each of us remembering some friend we had lost to childbirth.

She said she envied me. She and Charles had been married for three years with no child. I was so furious with my body's betrayal, I said she could have mine.

Before I became pregnant, I thought I might leave Frank and return to my parent's farm someday. Now it was different. Having a child meant I would always be tied to him. The thought left a sourness in my mouth.

Amber set the page down and took a shaky breath. Family history seemed about to repeat itself and she feared she would become an unwilling mother once again, this time to Claire's child.

TEN

A MBER WAS WALKING IN THE DIRECTION of Aunt Irene's carriage house the following afternoon carrying a sack of bird seed for Aunt Irene's wrens, when she spotted Claire lying in the hammock stretched between the cottonwood trees. The sound of the leaves moving against each other had lulled her to sleep. Her sister looked so lovely lying there, her blond hair fanned out on the striped hammock. The long shadows below the old trees were deep, almost purple. The grass felt cool beneath her bare feet. A bluebird arched through the air, landing in the honeysuckle shrub and Amber heard the tiny peeps of her newborns.

Where was the baby? Amber wondered. Looking around she spotted Minna in her baby seat at the base of the tree, sitting in direct sunlight. She was blinking her eyes against the glare and her little face was flushed. When she saw Amber and Cam, the baby kicked her feet excitedly. She followed the dog's every move with her eyes. The dog raced over, leaned down and licked the baby's hands and face.

"Stop that, Cam," Amber said, looking severely at him. Those doggy kisses were not given out of love. Cam, who was *always* hungry, was hunting for cracker crumbs. She set the birdseed down and picked up the baby, noticing how warm she felt. Feeling irked with her sister for letting the baby get overheated, Amber removed Minna's socks and sweater.

She carried the baby across the lawn to see the kitchen garden. When Amber first arrived at the farm and saw the garden, its well-weeded status was a surprise. Hunter told her that he and his father had put in the vegetable garden for Aunt Irene each spring and weeded it all summer.

If her condition had improved sufficiently that she could return to the farm, they didn't want to have her see the garden a weedy tangle. Toward the back of the large bed, she noticed some strawberry plants, the red berries ripening nearly out of sight beneath bright green tops.

Strawberry jam, she thought, seeing a sudden image of Mrs. O'Brien and her mother making jam when she was a little girl. I should see if Aunt Irene has a recipe for strawberry jam. Maybe I could make some as a thank-you gift for Emma and Mrs. Worth.

Continuing around the yard, she carried the baby to see the flower garden. It consisted of four large squares set two-by-two with grass paths bisecting the dark brown earth. It was something else Hunter had tended lovingly for Aunt Irene's return—a return that would probably never happen now. Ina Morand probably dug these flowerbeds nearly a hundred years ago, in a raw country far from home, she thought. Leaning down, she picked a single blue iris, furled like a flag. With Minna on her hip and the flower in her other hand, she walked into the house.

Minna was starting to fuss, and Amber talked quietly to her while she put the iris in a pewter bud vase. She warmed the baby's bottle and settled in the window seat to feed her. The sunshine lit Minna's pale curls. Amber heard the connecting door to the summer kitchen slide open and Claire walked in. She looked sleepy with sun-warmed cheeks, sensual half-open eyes, and tousled hair. She smiled at Amber and Minna.

"Thanks for getting her," she said. "I must have fallen asleep. For some reason, I remembered that hammock between the cottonwood trees. I was very small the last time I was here, but I remembered."

"Claire, I talked to Dad yesterday about his knee replacement. It's a major surgery and I want you to consider driving home to see him. Think how much it would mean to him to see his first grandchild." When Claire didn't respond, Amber said, "I made some sun-tea and cookies earlier. Want some?"

Her sister raised her eyebrows. "I didn't know you could cook," she said, looking dubious.

"Don't be too impressed, it's just pre-made chocolate chip cookie dough from the store. All you do is break it into pieces and bake it. Luckily the oven of this old stove has been converted to bottled gas, unlike the *burners*. Ryan is still stalling on connecting them to electricity. The worst of it is, I'm starting to think arguing with him isn't worth my effort since he just does what he wants to do anyway," she said grinning ruefully.

"Cookies and ice tea sounds good," Claire said. Carrying the snacks, the sisters went outside to the front porch and sat down on the porch swing. They settled the baby in her seat between them.

"Dad would be so happy to see you, Claire-Bear," Amber said gently.

Sitting side-by-side they gazed at the winter wheat field on the other side of the dusty road that ran in front of the house. The wheat, which had been lime-green when Amber arrived, had already begun to yellow. According to Hunter, when the field turned gold it would be threshing time. *Fields of gold*, she thought, smiling at the image and remembering the old song.

The afternoon darkened and thunderheads formed. Heat lightening laced the clouds and they crackled like crumpled paper. There was a sudden burst of warm summer rain. Claire stood up and ran out into the lawn. She spun in a circle, holding her hands out to feel the raindrops. The wind increased and the rain came down in a fine mist turning the wheat fields soft and dreamlike. Laughing, Claire ran back to the porch. She picked Minna up and twirled her around, humming an old lullaby. It sounded to Amber like one of those songs girls sang to soldiers going off to war. She felt a lurch inside, wondering if the song meant Claire was going to leave and if she did whether she would she take baby Minna with her . . . or leave her behind.

I would deserve it if she did, Amber thought.

After climbing out of the water, she had waited, lying flat in tall grass for hours afraid the laughing boy would return. Her backpack was close by. She pulled out the bottle and drank the rest of the whiskey. The sun was warm and the liquor made her feel sleepy. Waking later, she felt a slickness between her thighs. She touched herself. When she looked at her fingers, even in the dying light, she could tell they had blood on them. Could the sniggering boy have done something to her while she slept?

Finally twilight came down. It was dark enough that she could go home. Dashing from tree to tree, she was almost home when she realized the dog wasn't with her. She whistled for him, but there was no response. She had to get in the house and get some clothes on, then she would come back and look for him.

But it had turned out not to be that easy.

LATE THAT AFTERNOON A FURNITURE DELIVERY TRUCK pulled into the driveway. Amber had ordered furniture for the downstairs several weeks earlier, knowing staged homes sold faster. The refinished chestnut floors in the living and dining room shone, and the shiplap on the walls were freshly painted a warm dove gray, another battle she had lost, but the color did look good. Ryan had taken the original light fixtures from the 1920's and had them cleaned and re-wired. They cast a beautiful soft light on the golden floors, but other than the piano, there was no furniture in either the dining or living rooms.

Amber had managed to keep Ryan out of the selection of furniture by ordering it on line—without consulting him. She'd selected a slate blue sofa with pewter studs outlining the curve of the arms, two gray armchairs and a glass-topped coffee table. So there, Ryan Amherst, she thought.

The men placed the couch and chairs in the living room. When the drivers went back to the truck for the dining room table and chairs, Amber unrolled an area rug Ryan found in a local antique store. It was braided wool and had an edging of purple twining flowers. The color would be visible through the glass of the coffee table. She would go out after dinner, pick some lilac branches and put them in a vase on the coffee table.

"Amber, the furniture you bought is lovely," Claire said. "You have such a wonderful color sense."

"Thanks," Amber said.

Once the drivers departed, Amber looked around with a feeling there was still something missing. The living room was beautifully proportioned, a large light-filled space with a soaring vaulted ceiling, but it looked sterile. She knew why. There was no art on the walls. She needed a painting for over the fireplace, one for over the piano and something for the dining room. Remembering Hunter saying he had gone to art school, she decided to ask his advice about what to hang on the walls. Perhaps that would interest him, in the art even if not in me, she thought. Or, maybe he'll know what the Morands had here originally.

Amber was sitting at the tin-topped kitchen table after dinner going over the remodeling budget when her sister entered the room.

"I've been thinking about what you said about Dad. You're right, I should go see him." Claire took a somewhat shaky breath.

"That would be wonderful, Claire." Amber smiled, feeling a rush of love for her sister. "Do you want me to come with you? Maybe we should both go."

"No. I need to go by myself. There's something I have to do while I'm there. Can I leave Minna here with you for a few days?"

Amber ran her fingers through her dark curly hair while she considered. She didn't answer right away, feeling a rise of resentment.

"Please, Amber. I will only be gone three or four days. I don't want to take Minna into a hospital and expose her to all those germs."

"If it's just for a few days, I guess that would be okay," Amber said, but she felt a twinge of apprehension. "I love Minna, but she's your baby, Claire. You need to take responsibility for her. I'm only her aunt. You are her *mother*," Amber tipped her eyes up toward her sister.

Claire looked down, "You don't have to tell me. I know." Her voice trailed off. Her cheeks were flushed.

"I don't mean to make you mad, Claire, but I have so much going on here with the remodeling and visiting Aunt Irene. When are you going?"

"Pretty soon."

"Okay, but you *have* to come right back afterwards. Minna needs you." Amber looked intently at her sister who nodded. As Claire walked from the room, she thought, I need you too, little sister.

WHEN AMBER WENT TO BED THAT evening, she reached for the last few pages of Ina's journal that Aunt Irene's brother had translated. She wanted to read about the birth of Ina's child—the infant who grew up to become her great Aunt Irene.

Ina's Journal
October, 1916

The months have gone by and my belly is as round as a melon. Frank rubs my stomach and shows me off to the younger soldiers, pride in having made a child shines on his face.

"I've made a son in her," he often said. I felt as if I had been raped.

As spring began, I started having nightmares about childbirth, blood and dying. I woke screaming, heart pounding. My dreams spilled over into my days. I despised how I looked. I had always been proud of my slim figure and the way men looked at me. Now the young soldiers turned away and old men looked fatherly and patted me on the shoulder. I wasn't a woman any more. I was a vessel and I hated Frank for what he had done to me.

I woke one morning to wetness in the bed. I poked Frank in the shoulder.

"Get the midwife," I said.

It took hours and I thought it would never end. But in the morning, she emerged from my body, white, calm and not even crying. I hadn't wanted to be pregnant, but seeing her, I was knocked sidewise, pierced with love.

"Give me the baby," I demanded. The midwife moved back at my fierceness but handed me the infant.

I looked down at this tiny person, so helpless, so perfect. She opened her bright eyes and looked right at me. A stab of love so strong it made me weep, ripped through my body.

"You are mine," I told her. "All through this pregnancy, I never knew, but it was you I wanted all along." It seemed this baby and I had known each other for centuries, through all the eons of time.

ELEVEN

THE SOUND OF A CAR ENGINE STARTING woke Amber. She glanced at the clock; it was five a.m. She sat up and rubbed her temples, feeling a headache coming on. Was that the sound of Claire's car? She squeezed her hands into tight fists, clenching her teeth.

"Claire," she yelled, but there was no answer. She walked through the bathroom that now connected the two upstairs bedrooms, feeling the cool gray and white marble flooring on her bare feet. A horrible feeling struck her then, a sensation she hadn't known since the years Claire was a teen-ager. Some mornings she would wake to find Claire tiptoeing back into their room having been gone all night. Amber felt the past merge with the present. It was happening again.

Walking into the second bedroom, Amber saw the mattress on the floor where her sister slept. Claire's pillow was indented but the bed was empty, sheets and blankets in a white tumble. Minna was lying in the antique cradle. The baby opened her eyes and looked straight at Amber. Standing beside the small one, Amber leaned down to rub her tummy, soothing her until the baby closed her eyes again.

Claire didn't tell me she was leaving, she thought, and despite the promise she'd wrested from her sister about her return, felt a pulse beat fast in her throat. She walked back to her own room and sat on the edge of the bed, looking out at the sky through the sheer curtains. She gazed down at the hammock moving back and forth between the two towering cottonwood trees. When the rising sun shone through the trees, a brief hope rose inside her, warm as a flare in the dark. Claire wasn't running off with a boy this time. All that irresponsible behavior was just teen-age stuff, Amber told herself. Having baby Minna made my sister grow up. She'll do the right thing from now on.

She walked downstairs to the kitchen, hoping Claire had left a note. There was no note though, not in the kitchen or on the dining room table or written in chalk on the little blackboard in the summer kitchen. Knowing her sister was always short of money, Amber checked her purse. Her money was gone, but so was the address of the hospital where their father was getting knee surgery. Claire had taken it. She had definitely gone to see their father.

Opening the backdoor to let the dog out, she watched Cam dash happily out into the sunshine. The morning was cool and the sky a cloudless blue. The air had a lemony clean scent. Reflected light danced on the leaves of the cottonwood trees. The rising sun gave the wheat fields a near-fabled radiance. Normally, Amber would have relished the perfect weather, but a nagging intuition stayed with her, a sense of dread she couldn't quite shake—as if she had seen her sister for the last time. When she went back into the house, Amber dialed the hospital and got the number of her father's room. When it rang, a woman's hurried voice answered.

"I'm trying reach Mr. Bradshaw, or his friend Mrs. Miller. Are either of them there?"

"This is his nurse. He is getting some medical tests prior to his surgery. Can I take a message?"

"Please tell Mr. Bradshaw that his daughter, Claire, left the Morand farm early this morning. She is coming to see him." Amber took a deep breath and crossed her fingers that the hospital really was her sister's destination.

Amber heard the baby murmuring and went upstairs to get her. The baby's smile was so much like Claire's, heartbreakingly sweet. The first time the baby smiled at her, she was startled. It was as if she saw the person break through the softness of babyhood. She picked her up, changed her and carried her downstairs. She was sitting in the kitchen window seat giving Minna her bottle when Ryan arrived. He said he was going to start working on the main floor bathroom. Unsurprisingly, they had argued about its design. Ryan wanted to keep the old clawfoot tub and the sink attached to the wall. Amber wanted a more modern look, but ultimately Ryan's passion for the room as it would have been in 1920 prevailed.

"You have to promise me this design is going to attract buyers," she warned him.

"Lots of people like the authentic look," Ryan said. "Or you could just admit that you aren't really going to sell it." Amber felt like strangling him.

A FEW MINUTES LATER SHE HEARD HIM call her name. She walked into the bathroom, carrying the baby.

"Take a look at what I found," Ryan said. He had been ripping up the old floorboards in the bathroom and discovered an iron ring. "It's a trap door," he said, surprised and merry. He lifted the hinged piece of board, revealing a stone staircase that led down into a cellar. "How about that?"

He's found the cellar, she thought, a pleasant warmth spreading through her chest. "Go see what's down there, will you?" She handed him a flashlight and he descended the stairs. He came back up only a few minutes later.

"Turns out there's quite a big cellar under the house. This seems to be the only entrance. Looking at the stone walls, I think you might need to have them re-pointed. I saw one stone with hardly any mortar around it. I jiggled the stone out and saw something in the hole where the stone was. Do you want to come down and see?" Ryan asked.

"OMG, I sure do. Just let me put the baby down." Amber felt a curl of excitement as she buckled the baby into her seat, walked into the bathroom and descended the damp steps into the stone-sided room. At the back of the room there was a shelving unit holding some old canning equipment and a camping lantern. The floor was made of tamped earth, it smelled cool and clean. There was a good earthy tang to the air.

Ryan trained the flashlight on the opening with the missing stone. The light hit something deep inside that looked like an animal pelt.

"Keep the flashlight on it," Amber said. Her hands tingled as she reached into the hole and pulled out the fur-clad bundle. She had to tug hard and felt a momentary hesitation, as if the packet wanted to stay where it was. She persisted though, and when it came free noticed it was tied with old leather lacing. "Let's take this upstairs so we can see it better."

Once back on the main floor, she untied the laces and opened the folded leather wrapping. Inside was a small book. She trembled all over, feeling a rush of pleasure.

"That looks valuable. You could take it to the antique shop in Appleton. They might know how old it is," Ryan said smiling.

"It must be Aunt Irene's mother Ina's journal," Amber said, feeling almost primally drawn to the ancient object. She opened the book carefully trying to decipher the hand-writing before realizing why she couldn't read the words—the journal wasn't written in English.

"What do you want to do with the trap door," Ryan asked. "Shall we just cover it over?"

"No. I might want to be able to get down there again. There could be other things left by the original settlers. Could you install a hinged panel in the floor so I can access the cellar?"

"Yes, Boss," Ryan said, teasingly. "I'll get a lock too. It will have to be one of those flat ones with a combination lock. I think you can pick your combination for those. Probably a 4- digit number. What about the year the farm was established? It was 1918 wasn't it?"

"Yes it was. That will be good, Ryan."

"I'll have to order the lock, but when it arrives, I'll write the combination on the bulletin board in summer kitchen. Once the bathroom is finished, I would hate to think that someone could leave the door open and you or the baby could fall in."

For a moment, the back of Amber's neck tingled.

When she put Minna down in the little antique cradle for her nap that afternoon, she could see that the baby was already getting too big for it. Her arm stuck out through the bars. After quietly letting the dog in with the baby, which was what he insisted on recently (despite Amber's ineffectual protests), she walked downstairs to the living room with its empty dove gray walls. They cried out for art. Hoping he would know what Ina originally had hung on the walls, she called Hunter.

"Hello," he said.

"Hi, Hunter. It's Amber. I'm going to order art for the walls in the main floor rooms. Because of Ryan, I have to make it appropriate to the era of the house, but I had a thought. Do you remember what was on the walls in this house in the old days?"

"There were some old black and white photos of the barn and the huge horses that pulled the grain wagons. They were hung on the wall above the fireplace mantle. I have no idea where they are now. Possibly the attic," he said.

"Okay, thanks." Saying good-bye, she felt a bit disappointed that Hunter hadn't been more interested. She had hoped to connect with him around art, but impatient to get the rooms finished before listing the house for sale, she reached for the phone again.

"Hillside Gallery," Amber heard Cassidy's professional voice say.

"Hi, Cassidy, it's me."

"Well hello there, my supposed best friend. I wondered what had become of you. Are you ready to stop being a country bumpkin and come back to city lights yet?"

"Not yet, Cass, but I have big news. My sister, Claire, showed up. I hope you're sitting down because she's had a baby. Little Minna is just so darn cute. Anyway, she left this morning to visit Dad who is having knee surgery. I'm keeping baby Minna for her while she's gone. I made her promise to come back."

"I'm not surprised to hear she has shown up," Cassidy's voice was quietly thoughtful. "I remember how many times you got called to the school because of some issue with her. Your father was always too busy working to go. I certainly hope she's going to keep her promise this time."

Amber swallowed, feeling her heart squeeze tight and finding it hard to breathe. "Me too. Changing the subject, on the remodeling front I've finished the main floor, but the walls are empty."

"Hence the call, I suppose," Cassidy laughed.

"I need art for the living room and the dining room. I'd like to get something for baby Minna's room, too. How is the gallery doing? Does the boss miss me?"

"We are swamped and because you sweet-talked Kurt into keeping your job open for you, he isn't hiring anyone. He says you will be back by the end of the summer and is just loading me up. Thanks a lot, Booger."

"Sorry, Cassidy." Amber said and hesitated, reminded of how fast the time was passing and how much she still had to do before listing the house. "Apparently, there were black and white photos hanging on the walls here originally, I'd like to find them but if they don't show up, I want the house to look finished."

"What are you envisioning on the walls?" Cassidy asked.

"My contractor, Ryan, will *murder* me if I get anything modern, so I went on-line last night and found a few pieces I think would work. I'd like Paul Ranson's *Apple Tree with Red Fruit* for above sofa. Luckily, Ranson died in 1909 so his art is officially antique."

"I've always loved that piece, the apple tree in the foreground above the soft green valley surrounded by misty mountain ranges. Very nice. What else?"

"Above the piano in the living room, I want a painting by an artist named Eugene Iverd. He was an American illustrator. His work is from the same era as Norman Rockwell's. He did a lot of magazine covers, mostly portraying children playing games and dreaming of their futures. The one I want is unusual for Iverd as it features old men. The title is *The Old Masters*. It depicts a violinmaker in the foreground assembling a violin and a master violinist standing behind him, just putting his bow to the instrument. It's done in black and whites, except for a red potted geranium in the window."

"That last one will be hard to find, but I'll try. What do you want for the dining room?"

"Now don't laugh, but I found James Audubon's Opus, Birds of North America, in the bookcase. His work was amazing and since he died circa 1850, Ryan will be okay with it. I want number 277, it's the one labeled Barn Swallows. I've seen swallows nesting in the barn."

"I recall a time when you would call women who chose such things, Bird Nerds. Have you gone native up there?"

Amber laughed. "I'm surprised at myself, but there's something about being here among the quiet fields and trees that relaxes me."

"Becoming quite the rustic Bird Nerd, are we?"

"Let it go, will you, Cass?"

"Just kidding. Any good-looking guys in the country?"

Amber laughed. "There are two men I've met here, Hunter, the care-taker for the farm and Marc, who is the President of the bank. I like them both, although I'm surprisingly drawn to Hunter. He isn't my usual type, but I find myself . . . wanting to touch him." She giggled.

"Well, well, well, this must mean you are finally over that loser Brock," Cassidy said.

"I'm getting there, but since neither Marc nor Hunter has asked me out, maybe they already have girlfriends. Besides, with Claire gone, I'm busy taking care of baby Minna and visiting Aunt Irene as well as fight-ing a losing battle with my contractor, Ryan, who wants the house to look like it did a century ago."

"How's that going?"

"It's a constant struggle and I fear he's winning. I keep asking him if all this authentic renovation is going to attract buyers. He says since I'm not going to sell the place, it doesn't matter."

"That's ridiculous. Can't you just fire him? Get someone new?" Cassidy asked.

"It's way too late for that," Amber said. "I care about him now and actually the house does look great. Anyway, the last piece I'd like is John

Singer Sergeant's painting called *Carnation, Lily, Lily, Rose*. He's an oldie too, died in 1925. It's for Minna's room."

"Sweet. That's the one of the little girls wearing white linen dresses in the garden under glowing Japanese lanterns and night-ripened fruit. I'll get started hunting these down. So, when are you coming back? Sorry to put you on the spot, Amber, but the boss keeps asking."

"I'm not sure yet. Is it okay if I let you know next month?"

"If you must," Cassidy said, but there was a smile in her voice.

After they said goodbye, Amber asked herself again what she was going to do once the house was finished. When she returned to Chicago, would Claire and Minna live with their father? Would he be up to having the two of them there? Aunt Irene, temporary motherhood and Ryan's plans for the house were all she could deal with at the moment. At least I trust motherhood is temporary, she told herself, but wondered if her long penance for the day she disgraced herself wasn't over and would now include raising Claire's child. Try as she might, she was unable to stop the memories of that awful day crowding sharp-edged and painful into her mind.

By the time she reached the edge of the woods beyond their house, it was fully dark. She peeked around a tree. A crowd of people were standing in the driveway. There was a police car with a rotating light. She saw her father and the O'Briens. All the O'Brien kids were milling around. She didn't see Claire, but she was sure to be with them. Then she remembered, like a stab in her chest. She was supposed to have walked Claire home after school. Mrs. O'Brien, who usually picked Claire up, had a doctor's appointment. Amber's heart sank and she started to cry.

A second police car drove up with its siren blaring and everyone turned to look at it. While they were distracted, she made it into the back door of the house and dashed down into the basement, breathing hard. She had done some laundry the previous day and her clothes were in the washing machine, clean but cold and wet. It was a struggle pulling them on. She felt as if she had dressed herself in wilted lettuce.

Running back up the stairs, she opened the door into the kitchen where she encountered a young police officer sitting at the table. He looked up and said, "You must be the older daughter, Amber's your name, right? Do you know where your little sister is? Nobody can find her. Or the dog either."

She begged God to die right then—of humiliation and shame. In the years to follow, whenever she heard the sound of a police siren, it recalled the Day of Disgrace and her unending remorse.

TWELVE

A MBER WAS POURING HERSELF SOME ICED-TEA and munching on a cookie in the kitchen when she heard baby-talk coming from the monitor. Minna was waking up from her nap. When she walked upstairs to get her, the tyke was lying on her back smiling and waving her arms excitedly. She's always so glad to see me, Amber thought, feeling a tug at her heart. She pulled her cell phone from the back pocket of her jeans and took a picture of the baby. She clicked on Cassidy's number and sent her a quick text saying, "Look at how cute this kid is," and attached the picture.

Then she impulsively forwarded the picture to Mrs. Joanna Miller, her father's unexpected girlfriend, with a message saying "Call me ASAP please." She wanted an update on her father's surgery and to know if they had gotten the message that Claire was coming. The phone rang almost immediately.

"Hi Mrs. Miller. How's Dad doing?"

"They just took him into surgery. Should be out in another couple of hours. Whose baby did you send me the picture of?"

"Are you sitting down? I have some very big news. Claire has been here at the farm with me for about a week and she's had a baby girl named Minna."

"Oh, my . . . Well, she's very cute, thanks for the picture. Hearing that Claire's had a baby might not be the best news your father's ever had, but I have no doubt he will adjust to being a grandfather. Once he gets over the shock, he'll probably just dote on her."

"I left you a message earlier and wanted to know if you got it. Claire left the farm early this morning on her way to see him. It's about a nine hour drive, so she should arrive sometime tonight."

"Your father will be thrilled. As soon as he can travel, he suggested we come to the farm for a visit. Would you like that?"

"Oh, I sure would. You've just been a Godsend, Mrs. Miller. Dad and I are both so grateful."

"We've gotten close, your Dad and I. I'll call you with the results of the surgery as soon as I talk with the doctor after the procedure. And I'll let you know when your sister arrives."

Mrs. Miller called several hours later. The surgery had gone perfectly but Claire hadn't shown up. Amber continued to check her phone all day, waiting for a call or text about her sister, but heard nothing.

Minna woke her several times that night. She was fussy and wouldn't take a bottle. Amber changed her and rubbed her little back but she wouldn't settle. The baby felt warm and Amber wondered if she had a temperature. She didn't have a thermometer and fear caught like a stone in her throat. Finally, the baby slept, but uneasily, whimpering from time to time. Cam refused to lie down, standing sentry in the corner of Minna's room.

"Come here, Cam," she hissed at him. He refused to budge. I can't even get my dog to mind. No wonder Ryan is winning.

WHEN AMBER WOKE EARLY THE NEXT MORNING she checked her phone immediately. No message or missed calls, no texts. Claire should have arrived at the hospital the previous evening but since she hadn't received a message from Mrs. Miller, she must not have arrived. Where had her sister gone for an entire night? What was the errand she said she had to do?

When she got Minna out of bed, Amber thought she still felt warm. At nine o'clock, she called the family physician's office in town hoping to get an appointment.

"Are you a new patient?" the receptionist asked.

"Yes. I have a sick baby."

"We will work her in today then." The receptionist got some general information and said, "Bring her birth certificate with you. And don't give her any fever-reducer after noon. We will need to get a temperature that hasn't been lowered by medication."

"Thank you," Amber said, relieved to have the appointment. I am an idiot, she thought. Why didn't I think to give the baby something to bring the fever down? Probably because I don't have a clue what to give or how much. She went through the baby's diaper bag and to her relief saw a paper in a little folder entitled, "Certificate of Live Birth." She put the document in her purse so she wouldn't forget to bring it.

Amber buckled Minna in her car seat after lunch, glad Claire had remembered to transfer the seat. She arrived at the family practice office shortly before the time for their appointment and after filling out some paperwork, a nurse led them to an examining room. Nurse Andrews was a large woman with a pleasant face. She wore her gray hair in a bun at the back of her neck. She had an air of confidence that made Amber feel even more aware of her maternal inadequacies.

"Glad you brought her in," Nurse Andrews said. "Her temperature is close to a hundred degrees. Did you remember her birth certificate?"

Amber pulled the folder from her purse.

Looking at it, the nurse said, "She was long for a newborn. Must have a tall father." She smiled and entered the information into the record. When she handed the document back to Amber, the paper was unfolded. Scanning the document, Amber read: Cosmina Grace Morand, d.o.b. November 1, weight seven pounds, eight ounces, twenty-three inches long. She smiled, noting that her sister had given the baby the middle name of Morand and the last name of Bradshaw. Looking at the section where it listed the parents, the father was listed as J.J. Stryker. Inside the folder was a note in her sister's distinctive handwriting.

"Might be a while before I can come back. I have things I need to do. Keep the baby safe. If anything should happen to me, I know she's in good hands with you." The note was signed with Amber's nickname for her sister. "Claire Bear."

Amber felt suddenly light-headed, ambushed by a premonition she would never see her little sister again.

"Now don't you pass out on me," Nurse Andrews said, her blue eyes snapping, "Give me the baby and sit in that chair. Put your head down. You don't need to be so worried about this one. She's a strong little tyke."

As Amber felt the dizziness diminish, she raised her face to the worried nurse. "I'm okay now. It's just . . . the baby hasn't been sick before."

"First time mothers," Nurse Andrews said, shaking her head and looking amused. "The doctor will be in shortly." She handed Minna to Amber and left the room.

Alone in the examining room, Amber couldn't shake the trepidation that made her stomach roil and her head pound. She re-read Claire's note, crumpled it up and threw it in the trash, then a sudden sense of unease made her reach into the wastebasket and pull it back out.

The door opened a few minutes later and a red-headed man in a white coat walked in.

"I'm Dr. Logan," he said holding out his hand and smiling.

Amber shook his hand and introduced herself. The doctor examined the baby and said Minna had an upper respiratory virus and would be feeling better in a day or two. He reached into a cabinet and pulled out a bottle of purple liquid. It had a dropper and he squirted a few drops in Minna's mouth. He gave Amber the bottle, showed her the dosage and asked her if she had any questions.

"I'm sorry, I just can't think of anything right now," Amber said.

"I wondered if you might like a pamphlet about caring for infants. I get the sense that Minna was unexpected?" The doctor tipped his head to one side, looking at her kindly.

She nodded thinking, you don't know the half of it.

Carrying the baby out to the car after the appointment and buckling her into the car seat, Amber found herself trembling. She drove very slowly out of town. When she turned onto Morand Road and saw the luxurious winter wheat fields, she felt calmer. Glancing in the rear-view mirror she saw Minna sound asleep and a warm swell of tenderness engulfed her. She remembered her father saying, "The only beings who are evolved enough to give pure love are dogs and babies."

"Somehow we are going to make this work, with or without your mommy," Amber whispered. When they drove up behind the farmhouse, Amber lifted the baby tenderly from her car seat, feeling protective of the innocence and vulnerability of the little one.

IN THE LATE AFTERNOON, AMBER DECIDED to take Minna to the barn for her first viewing of the calves. The sunlight was gold, the air warm and dreamy. The dog came with them, running in huge circles. When they reached the calf paddock, Minna's eyes opened wide. She lowered her little head and looked straight down on the calves, intent and serious. The baby's hair was getting thicker, Amber noticed. She had one tiny golden curl at the nape of her neck.

Hunter looked up from feeding the calves and smiled. "Who is this little person?" he asked.

"This is Minna, my sister's baby. Our father is having knee surgery and Claire left to visit him."

"Can I hold her?" he asked, smiling at Minna.

"Only if you wash your hands really well first. I mean it, Hunter, really wash your hands thoroughly."

"Of course," Hunter said. He disappeared into the cement block building where they kept the pails and refrigerated milk. When he returned, Amber handed Minna gently to Hunter. She wondered if the baby would protest, but the little flirt beamed right up at Hunter's handsome face.

"I wanted to tell you some big news, Hunter. Aunt Irene is interested in re-establishing the Morand dairy. She's willing to fund the project, but as you know she promised to sell the land to Framingham. That could still be a problem, but she had me go and talk to the banker because she wants to get the dairy operational again."

"That is so great," Hunter said with a wide grin.

"Until I find out how much Aunt Irene has to invest in the project, please hold off on bringing the cows back from Lundgren's. And keep in mind that the project might be pretty short-lived."

"You're probably right, but I'm keeping my hopes up," Hunter said, but a brief shadow crossed his face.

"Should Aunt Irene cancel the Framingham deal, I was reading about a new system that allows cows to practically milk themselves. Do you know about this?"

"We would love to have it. Most of the bigger farms around here have installed it. You have to walk the cows into the stalls and attach the machine to their teats. The machine then takes over. The milk runs through tubes into a large stainless container. Each cow wears an electronic collar that measures their milk production. It's a wonderful system. Expensive though."

"How much does it cost?"

"About a quarter of a million dollars. That system aside, with three hundred acres in hay and oats, you could easily produce all the feed necessary for a herd of eighty to a hundred cows. If you sold half the hay, you would make enough to cover your living expenses with some left over. That's if you ended up staying here." He smiled and the summer sunshine lit his clean features.

Amber felt taken aback. If she ended up staying on the farm, Hunter had said. Until that moment, it had not occurred to her that she could decide to stay—to live permanently at the farm. Ryan kept saying she was going to keep the house, but keeping the farm was a totally different proposition. She took a breath, "Mr. Rochet from the bank was going to talk to Aunt Irene and have her sign the papers to release some funds to start the dairy again."

"This will mean the world to my father."

"Hunter, you know I go into town to see Aunt Irene almost every day, right? Would you like to go with me tomorrow? Maybe we could get lunch afterwards?" She looked up at him hopefully. His smile wavered and he rubbed his hand through his hair. He seemed to be struggling to find an answer.

"Maybe another time," he said softly, handing the baby back to Amber.

Hunter's lack of interest felt like a burn on her face. That's it. I'm never going through this again, she thought. She was too raw from Brock's rejection and ending their relationship so painfully to risk approaching Hunter again.

She was walking back toward the house when her cell phone rang.

"Hello," she said.

"Miss Bradshaw?" the man's voice asked.

"Yes."

"My name is Fred McMillan. I represent the Acquisitions department of the Framingham Group and I would like to meet and go over what we are offering for the Morand farm. We would like to take ownership soon. When we called the owner, a Miss Irene Morand, she said to contact you."

Amber took a deep shaky breath and said, "I'm coming into Apple River Falls tomorrow around lunchtime. I could meet with you then. Do you know the town? There is a place called Sunshine Café on Main Street. It's just a block east of the light at the four corners. Will that work?"

"Certainly. Can you bring the original deed to the property with you?"

Amber hesitated. Although she had the deed to the house, she hadn't seen hide nor hair of a deed for the farmland. "I'm not sure where it is, but I'll look."

"All right. See you then."

Clicking off the phone, Amber felt her stomach tighten and swallowed hard. Decisions about the farm were coming to a head.

THIRTEEN

THE PHONE RANG EARLY THE NEXT morning. Busy changing Minna, Amber could only glance at the screen, hoping it was her sister. But it was Mrs. Miller's number. She touched the "will call back" button on her phone.

"We better get you fed little one." She gave Minna her a bottle, burped her, cuddled with her for a minute and then pushed redial.

"Hi, Mrs. Miller."

"Amber, I think it's time you called me Joanna, don't you? I have some news about your sister."

"Did she get there?"

"Yes, Claire finally arrived this morning at dawn. She woke your dad and told him about the baby. She kissed him good-bye but left before I got there. I'm very glad you told me about the little one yesterday. I was able to prepare him for the news."

"I'm so sorry she didn't stay longer, Mrs. Miller, I mean Joanna," Amber said, feeling frustration mounting at her sister who had vanished for twenty-four hours, finally appeared at the hospital and then hadn't even stayed long enough to thank Mrs. Miller who had done so much for their dad. "Claire left me a note saying she said she had some things to do before she would be back, but she hasn't been in touch with me since. I'm really worried."

Mrs. Miller took a quick breath. "Oh, Honey, I'm sorry. I'd have liked to talk to her, too."

"I'm glad she saw Dad at least. It must have raised his spirits."

"It did. He's going to call you later," Joanna said.

WITH THE HELP OF THE MEDICINE she got from the doctor, Minna went down easily at her normal bedtime that night. Afterwards, Amber walked out to the front porch, enjoying the summer sounds in the evening twilight. She had put up a hummingbird feeder and the miniature birds her sister always called flying jewels darted in and out, taking minuscule drinks of the sweet nectar. She sat down on the porch swing to watch the sun go down over the yellowing wheat fields. The light was fading, turning the fields hazy and insubstantial. As the sun went down behind the trees, bands of shadow stretched across the yard.

Just before dark, she heard Ryan's truck pull into the driveway. She heard voices and the sound of knocking on the back screen door.

"Amber, where are you?" Ryan called.

"I'm on the front porch. Come around to the front."

When Ryan appeared, he had a woman and a little boy about a year older than Minna with him. "Amber, I would like to introduce you to my wife, Megan, and this is our son, Connery."

"It's so good to meet you," Amber said, pleased he had brought them over.

"I've been bugging Ryan for weeks about meeting you," Megan said. "I wouldn't let him off the hook tonight."

Megan looked like the all-American girl. She had hair the color of dark honey and freckles sprinkled across her face. Her eyes were a greeny hazel. She wore her wavy hair pulled back with a hairband. The style suited her. Amber put her hand down on little Connery's head feeling the springiness of his curls. He was adorable, shy with his father's dark blue eyes.

"Your little boy is just darling, Megan."

"Thank you," Megan said quietly.

"I wanted to show Megan your house. I've won her over to the beauty of historic renovation," Ryan said, his voice full of pride in his work. Megan pursed her lips, glancing obliquely at Amber who suppressed a grin. Clearly she and Megan had the same issues with Ryan's century old design aesthetic.

"Take a look around," Amber said. "I'll find something for us to drink. When you're done with the tour, I have a question for you, Ryan."

When the family got seated on the front porch, Amber offered them iced tea. She even managed some Kool-Aid for little Connery, feeling proud she had some. Megan poured it in a sippy cup she kept in her purse—she was clearly an organized mother—and he downed it happily. They ate the last of the chocolate chip cookies.

"I discovered an antique buffet cabinet yesterday. It had been stashed in the cupboard under the staircase. I dragged it out, but it's locked. There might be some important papers in it, hopefully the deed to the farm. Take a look, will you? It's in the dining room."

Ryan went inside to see the sideboard. When he came back out he said, "That is a lovely old piece. It's made of solid cherry. Hope we can get it open. Chris, my carpenter, has a bunch of keys we can try."

Turning to Megan, Amber had a sudden thought and said, "I have to go into town tomorrow to meet with the Framingham representative and see Aunt Irene. I was planning to take Minna with me, but it would be an easier errand without her. I hate to ask you since we just met, but could you possibly baby-sit for a couple of hours?"

"Where's Claire?" Ryan asked.

"She left to see our father. He's having knee surgery."

"I would love to take care of her while you have your appointment," Megan said in her soft voice. "I run a day care out of my house."

"Thank you so much. I'll bring her to you around eleven tomorrow. Could you come upstairs so we can peek in on her?"

They walked upstairs to see Minna sleeping in the antique cradle. One of her little feet was poking out between the slats.

"I know I need to buy a full-sized crib," Amber said, noting Megan's concerned expression.

"Better get one soon," Megan said, looking at Amber. "If she pulled herself up, she could topple that cradle right over. I love going to garage sales, I'll keep an eye out for a crib for you."

LATE THAT EVENING, AMBER REACHED for another page of Ina's journal. Now that she and Ryan had found the journal itself, she would eventually be able to read how Ina's story ended. *If we can find someone to translate it, that is,* she thought and wondered where they would ever find such a person in the little village of Apple River Falls.

Ina's Journal
January, 1917
    It is late and I'm sitting at the desk in my nightgown with a red wool shawl over my shoulders. The kitchen fire has burned down to embers. It's been two months since I wrote in my journal. Frank doesn't understand why I need to record my life. He's sleeping, so I can scratch these words without angering him. The baby sleeps too, blessed happy child. She grows as easily as a flower.

I ran out of ink some time ago. When the wind blew walnuts from the trees onto the paths of the park along the river, I took the nuts to our apartment and hammered the shells into bits. I boiled them for a long time in a pan. When I poured the dark brown liquid through my wedding stockings and added salt and vinegar, the liquid made a brown ink. As I write, my words sink into the parchment. What's left when the ink dries is a stain in the shape of invisible words. Sometimes I think I'm not real any longer either, just a stain in the shape of a woman.

Poor, poor Ina, Amber thought. What an appalling way to think about oneself. She felt a shiver cross her shoulders.

FOURTEEN

IT'S BEEN THREE DAYS SINCE CLAIRE LEFT THE FARM, Amber thought, feeling a mixture of irritation and apprehension. Her sister hadn't answered any of her calls or texts. It brought back the many times she would try to reach Claire while she was away at college, the months she now knew her little sister had been dealing with being pregnant and alone.

Taking a deep breath, Amber picked up Ina's journal to take with her into town. After she met with the Framingham representative she would show Aunt Irene the journal and prove to the old dear that she was capable of meeting a challenge. She arrived at Ryan and Megan's house around eleven o'clock. At the entrance to their driveway, she saw a sign that said, "Megan's Muppets: Loving Day Care for your Child."

Megan had selected modern furniture for their home in bright colors, turquoise, yellow and orange. The walls and floors were done in historic paint shades, but the rest was clearly all her own. I have to ask Megan how she won that battle, Amber thought, feeling amused. Two small toddlers were playing with toys in a corner and Connery was running around wearing nothing but a diaper.

"Hi Amber," Megan said. "It's sort of a mad house around here. Good morning, little Minna, come to Auntie Megan," she held out her hands for the baby.

"Nobody other than her mother and me has ever taken care of her," Amber said, feeling a bit reluctant at handing the baby over.

"She will be fine. Don't you worry," Megan said. She smiled at Minna who grinned right back.

Amber was getting into the car when the dog came racing down the road and skidded to a halt beside the car.

"Cam, you are a bad boy. How in the world did you get out this time?"

The dog looked happily up at her, unrepentant. She loaded him in the car and he sniffed Minna's car seat. Then he gave a little moaning cry.

"You missed your chance to stay with Minna. You're coming with me this morning," she told him firmly. "So there, you big rascal."

WHEN THEY ARRIVED AT THE SUNSHINE CAFÉ, Amber tied the dog to an outdoor street lamp. She went inside and spotted a stocky man wearing a suit and tie. He wore a pin on his lapel that said Framingham, had a buzz cut and wore glasses.

"Mr. McMillan? I'm Amber Bradshaw," she held out her hand.

"Call me Fred. Thank you for meeting me."

"Sorry, I had to bring my dog. I tied him up outside. Can we eat at the outdoor tables?"

Fred agreed and once they were seated said, "The Framingham Group is offering a good price for the Morand farm, Miss Bradshaw. We plan to tear down the barns, the milking shed and most of the fencing. The commercial combines we use to harvest hay and wheat work best on unfenced land."

Amber felt a wrench at the thought of the big red barn coming down after nearly a century. How dear the old place has become to me, she thought.

"Did you find the deed to the property?" he asked.

"Not yet. My Aunt Irene owns the farm and she is in a nursing home in town. I'll go over there and ask her where the deed is, but she has expressed some reservations recently about selling the farm."

"Hold on a minute, we have an agreement with Irene Morand."

"A signed sales agreement?" Amber asked.

"No, but a signed Promise to Sell. I assure you in legal terms that it is enforceable."

"I am not an attorney, but I would think it could be revoked, couldn't it?"

"Not without lots of lawyer time," Mr. McMillan said firmly.

"Regardless, I don't believe my Aunt Irene has made a final decision about the property." Amber felt her anger rise and she clenched her teeth. She would not have this man take advantage of her elderly ill Great Aunt.

"Wisconsin leads the country in dairy farming, but our company does not do milk production. We just want the land for hay. The prices have risen sharply. It's a paying proposition for Framingham. We would appreciate your having Irene Morand sign off on the deed as soon as possible," Mr. McMillan said crisply.

"I will talk with her, Mr. McMillan, but I'm making no promises," Amber said frowning, irked with the man's continuing insistence. I might be losing battles with Ryan, but I'll be damned if I lose to this jerk from Framingham, she thought.

AMBER WALKED DOWN THE HALL TO Aunt Irene's room at the Nursing Home and opened the door. Aunt Irene was coughing and Amber noticed how thick her ankles had gotten. The fluid retention caused by her congestive heart failure was getting worse.

"How are you feeling today, Aunt Irene?"

Aunt Irene didn't answer, just shook her head. Amber handed her a glass of water. The coughing subsided a bit.

"I have some good news. My contractor, Ryan, found the trap door to the cellar. And hidden behind a loose stone in the cellar wall was a little leather book." She grinned.

Aunt Irene's eyes twinkled. "You found Ina's journal."

"Take a look." Amber pulled it out of her purse.

"I remember it," Aunt Irene said with a dismissive note in her voice. "Nothing wrong with my mind you know." Amber stifled a grin, pleased to see the feisty old woman was still with them.

"As you warned me, it's not written in English, so unless you can read Romanian, it will have to be translated," Amber said.

"Like a lot of immigrant parents, mine wouldn't even speak Romanian in front of me. Once we were in this country, they wanted me to be able to speak English fluently. But I mentioned the journal to Mr. Rochet when he came to see me. He has someone who works for him who reads Romanian."

"I'm frankly astounded," Amber beamed. "Who is it?"

"His assistant, Nate. He has family still living in the old country," Aunt Irene started coughing again and reached for the water glass.

"If you want this Nate person to translate Ina's journal, I going to make a copy first. I'm uncomfortable giving him the original. On another note, I just met with Mr. McMillan from the Framingham Group. Do you still want to sell the farm, Aunt Irene?"

"Not now," Aunt Irene whispered. She was still coughing.

"That's what I thought," Amber said. "I thought you wanted to re-establish the dairy, but Mr. McMillan said you promised to sell the property to them."

Aunt Irene shook her head. "Changed my mind. Woman's prerogative, you know." She managed a tiny shaky grin and Amber rolled her eyes and chuckled.

Just then, Aunt Irene's nurse knocked and entered the room. "We've been talking about the farm, Emma. Did you know Miss Irene wants to start the Morand Dairy up again?"

"I know," Emma said, smiling. "It's exciting."

"I will see what it's going to take to get out of this Framingham deal, but we will probably need to hire an attorney to fight it," Amber said.

"Just wanted to check her blood pressure, but I'll come back later," Emma said. "When Mr. Rochet was here, Miss Irene signed her entire account over to you, Amber. She wants you to use it to get the dairy operational." The door swished silently as Emma left the room.

Amber looked at the frail old lady and her heart contracted in pity. "Thank you, Aunt Irene. I promise I will live up to your faith in me. Don't you dare die on me now," her voice turned fierce. "When everything is done, I will bring you out to the farm so you can see the barn, the calves and everything I've done with the house."

With great difficulty, Aunt Irene raised herself on her elbows and whispered, "To run a dairy, you will need help. I was wrong about you being a wimp. You have guts, Girl, but it's too big a job to do on your own. I ought to know. Did it alone for decades," she smiled weakly, but the effort had cost her dearly. She laid back and closed her eyes.

It seemed to Amber that Aunt Irene's fierce personality was shutting down, like a generator losing its power source. Life was draining out of her. Amber bent to kiss the old woman's forehead, tasting her own tears. Wanting to be able to read Ina's journal to Aunt Irene before the old woman's time ran out, Amber walked up to the front desk to see if Mrs. Worth knew where she could make a copy. The translator would have to work from that—the original of Ina's journal was never leaving family hands.

FIFTEEN

After making the copy of Ina's journal at the local Library and walking to the bank, Amber tied Cam up to a street lampost and went inside. She greeted the receptionist and a teller showed her into Mr. Rochet's office.

"Hello there, Miss Bradshaw," he said, smiling warmly and holding out his hand to shake hers.

"Hi, Mr. Rochet," she responded.

"Please call me Marc," he said.

"Only if you will call me Amber," she said and he smiled, glancing quickly at her left hand. She wondered if he was checking for a ring. "I have two things I wanted to talk to you about. First, Aunt Irene has made a decision. She definitely doesn't want to sell the farm now. She wants to re-establish the Morand Dairy. And second, she said you had an assistant who could translate an old family journal written in Romanian. Is he here?" she asked.

"It's Nate Bogdan. He's off work today but I can send him out to the Morand farm to get the journal if you like."

"Thanks. That will be fine. Can you tell me how much Aunt Irene money has in her account? I was told she signed the papers to make me a signatory on the account."

"Actually," he paused and smiled. "I have a question. If you're not dating anyone, I'd like to take you to dinner Friday night and we can talk about the money then. Are you available?"

"Well, that certainly took me by surprise, Marc," Amber paused. It seemed too soon for him to ask her out. She was taken aback by his invitation, but then felt a simmering rise of satisfaction. Why was she hesitating? A gorgeous single guy with a delightful French accent had just asked her out on a date. "You can pick me up at seven. You know where the Morand farm is, I presume? Have you already thought of a restaurant, Marc? Will we be going somewhere casual or should I wear a dress?"

"By all means wear a dress. This is an occasion." He smiled and Amber felt her cheeks warm.

Amber left the bank feeling cheered. It was nice to feel appreciated as a woman. Then she recalled asking Hunter to go with her to visit Aunt Irene and afterwards out to lunch. He had declined and seemed discomfited, as if he really didn't know how to respond.

And the first man to ask a girl to the dance, gets the date, she thought, shaking off the regret she felt about Hunter's lack of interest. Tall, dark and ambitious Marc Rochet was much more her type anyway. When she and Cam got back to the car, however, she remembered the pathetic state of her wardrobe. She had brought only jeans, T-shirts, underwear and nightshirts to the farm. Then she remembered the new dress she bought just before she left for the farm. She called Mrs. Miller from the car.

"Hi Joanna, how's Dad doing?"

"He's doing well, but he's asleep right now," she whispered.

"To my surprise, I have a date on Friday night and would like to wear this little black dress I bought before I came up here."

"A date, hmm?"

"Yes, the dress is in my closet at the house. Still has the tags on it. I assume you have a key?"

"I've had a key to your house since you were ten," Joanna said, dryly. "I was friends with your mother for years you know."

"Oh, of course. Could you possibly Fed Ex the dress to me? The address is 866 Mains Crossing, Apple River Falls, Wisconsin."

"I'll send it overnight. Is Claire back yet?"

"Not. I have absolutely no idea where she is," Amber said and felt a rising swell of despair. Despite repeated calls and texts, neither Amber, Joanna nor her father had heard anything from Claire since she left the hospital.

Mrs. Miller's voice interrupted her thoughts, bringing her back to the present. "Amber, are you still there?"

"I'm here," Amber said softly.

"I thought we got disconnected for a minute. Anyway, I just wanted to remind you since you have a baby now, you're going to need a baby-sitter before you can go on a date."

"Right," Amber said, feeling dismayed. She hadn't thought that far ahead. She took a shaky breath, wondering if getting a baby-sitter for Minna was just an omen of things to come.

The package from Mrs. Miller arrived the next day. Amber opened it and found not only the dress but also a bra, panties, nylons, her malachite jewelry and a large green paisley shawl. Her thoughtful neighbor had even included Amber's sling-back heels.

"Bless you, Mrs. Miller," she murmured and dialed Megan for baby-sitter names.

Megan's pick as the area's most reliable baby-sitter was a girl named Lizzy Swenson. She gave Amber her phone number and address adding, "Lizzy's seventeen and has her driver's license, so you won't even have to pick her up."

"You're sure she's dependable?" Amber asked.

"Lizzy has been taking care of Connery since he was six weeks old. She's the best. Stop fretting, Miss Worry Wart, Minna will love her."

When she said good-bye to Megan, Amber again checked her cell phone for any messages from Claire. *It's not the first time my sister has gone missing*, Amber thought as the memory came surging back.

All the local police officers and many of the men from the neighborhood searched for Claire that night. It had turned cold and everyone feared if Claire was outdoors, she might die of hypothermia. Officer O'Brien suggested bringing Claire's pink baby blanket with them. If they located the dog, her scent would be on it. Her father told Amber to keep calling Sam, certain he was with her sister. Assuming Claire had left Kindergarten when Amber failed to show up, she had already been missing for eight hours. They started their search at the elementary school.

"Here Sam, here Sam," Amber's thin reedy calls seemed impotent and pitiful in the total darkness.

The searcher's flashlights swept the ground in huge arcs, calls rang out again and again, piercing the night. Many hours later, having come up empty, the men stopped. They would start again in the morning, they told Amber's father. They were walking back toward their vehicles when she called Sam one last time and heard a faint bark. She ran toward the sound, stumbling, calling and sobbing. When the dog barreled up to her, she fell to her knees and hugged him desperately. Wrapping the blanket around his nose, she kept repeating "Sam, find Claire," until he took off barking into the night. She tried to follow but her legs just went out from under her. Scrambling to her feet, she ran unsteadily after the search party that had quickly reassembled.

Officer O'Brien found Claire hiding in a hollow under some bramble bushes half an hour later. Amber was right behind him when his flashlight lit her little white face. Claire was crying and holding out her arm. It was bent at an unnatural angle. "I was waiting and waiting for you to come and find me," she said and Amber's heart broke in two.

Claire had been taken to the hospital in the ambulance that night for surgery on her broken arm. Their father went into rehab the next morning. Mrs. O'Brien offered to have the two girls live with them until their father returned. Amber's guilt for failing to get Claire from school still weighed on her heart like a boulder. And where was her sister now, she wondered.

FRIDAY AFTERNOON AMBER ADDED a capful of French lilac bath oil to the water steaming into the old claw-footed tub. It dissipated slowly, sending a luscious scent into the air. She stepped into the warm water and rested her arms on the side of the tub feeling like a pampered princess. When the bath water started to cool, she reluctantly got out and dried off. She had washed her hair earlier in the day, rinsing it with rainwater collected in the old rain barrel, feeling like a real native. She ran a brush through her dark curls. She laid the dress, jewelry and shawl on her bed but didn't put them on, knowing she would have to feed the baby before she left.

When Minna woke up from her nap, Amber changed and fed her. She tickled her and blew on her tummy. Minna giggled. She put the baby in her little seat, placing her on the floor where she could see the fully-restored dining room chandelier. The afternoon sun lit the crystals that made tiny prisimatic rainbows in the air. Tipping her little face all the way back, Minna gazed up at the chandelier, kicked her feet and gurgled.

Lizzy Swenson knocked on the door at 6:30. She was petite, had white-blond hair and wore glasses with dark rims.

"Hi, Lizzy. Thank you for coming on such short notice. This is baby Minna," Amber said gesturing to the baby in her little seat.

"Oh, she's so cute," Lizzy said as she knelt down on the floor and played peek-a-boo with Minna and who giggled.

"She will need a bottle later. Minna knows a little sign language and when she closes and opens her fist, it means she's hungry. The bottles are in the fridge. Just put one in the microwave for twenty seconds. Oh, you might have trouble finding the microwave. It's hidden behind cupboard doors beside the antique range," Amber said. Having the microwave was the one of the few battles she had won with Ryan, although even that was a compromise, since it was completely out of sight.

Leaving Lizzy and Minna together, Amber went upstairs to finish dressing. Her little black dress had a tight embroidered bodice and a skirt that flared below the princess waist. She slipped it on, appreciating the silky feel. When she came down in her dress and green jewelry, she felt confident she looked her best.

"Ms. Morand, what time do I give the baby her bottle?" Lizzie asked.

Amber beamed at the teenager calling her Ms. Morand. "Call me Amber, Lizzie, and you can feed her at seven-thirty or sooner if she uses the sign for hungry. Put her in the cradle upstairs at eight o'clock. The dog can go in the room with her. If you don't, he'll just scratch on her door until you let him in. It was ridiculous, Camelot clearly loved Minna more than he loved her. Irritating mutt. "Here's my cell phone number, Lizzie. Please enter your number in my phone contacts. If you need me, just call."

Still feeling a twinge of concern at leaving the baby with a teenager, even given Megan's unreserved recommendation, Amber watched surreptitiously as Lizzy correctly entered the contact numbers. You're being ridiculous, she told herself. You aren't even Minna's mother. But she took a quick indrawn breath thinking, not yet anyway.

WHEN MARC ROCHET DROVE INTO THE DRIVEWAY, Amber walked outside, very aware of his eyes that subtly looked her up and down. It had been a long time since she had felt the warmth of masculine admiration and it felt very good. Marc got out of the driver's seat and walked around to open her door.

"Good evening," he said.

"Yes, it is a lovely evening," she answered, feeling her lips soften in a smile.

They drove to Spencer's Grove. On the way, they passed fields rich with ripening grain. Distant Angus beef cattle looked up from fields when they passed, so stocky they could have been furry black bears. At the next farm, a farmer and his Border collie were driving black and white Holstein cows into the barn for milking.

Marc took them to a lovely restaurant on the Apple River. The host asked if they would like to dine al fresco and Amber nodded. They were seated on a flagstone patio so close they could hear the sound of the rippling water. The scent of moving water tumbling over rocks was so clean she could almost taste it. As the sun dipped in the west, they enjoyed the pink clouds that graced summer's twilight.

After ordering their meals, Marc said, "I thought we should be together for this."

"It is good news?"

"Very good news," he smiled.

"Let's wait a bit then," Amber said, touching his hand. "We can talk business later." She wanted to delay the decisions she knew she was going to have to make. For a little while, she wanted to be a young woman out on a date with a good-looking guy. Marc nodded, looking pleased. The classical tones of Beethoven's Pathetique Symphony drifted out to the stone patio,

"As you know, my mother's family came from Romania," Amber said. "Where does your family come from, Marc?"

"We are French Canadians from Montreal, thus the French accent. My father owns an accounting firm and my mother taught high school English until her recent retirement. She's working on a novel about Quebecois history."

"Did you always want to be a banker, Marc?" Amber asked.

"No, I love history and originally intended to teach, but my father encouraged me to take a business major in college. I was offered a job with a bank right out of college. What about you, Amber?"

"I graduated from the Art Academy in Chicago and took a job with Hillside Gallery. I'm on leave from there for the summer to fix up the old Morand place. Are you an only child, Marc?"

"No, I have a younger sister, Daphne, who is in her first year at university. I know she would enjoy meeting you. She's interested in interior design and I'm aware you have been renovating the Morand farmhouse."

"If Daphne comes for a visit, I'd be happy to show her what I've done."

"I realize we're sort of mixing business and pleasure here, but I wanted to be sure to tell you that Irene Morand has over three hundred thousand dollars in her savings account," Marc said.

"Wow. That is huge! With that much money we could clean and insulate the barn, bring back Irene's cows from Lundgren's farm and buy the self-milking system."

"I wonder if you should, Amber," Marc's face was thoughtful. "If you intend to return to Chicago when the house is sold, who would run the dairy? And don't forget you'll will need some of the money for an attorney to get out of the deal with Framingham. If Framingham is able to prevail, Irene's funds would be wasted."

"My Aunt Irene wants to re-start the Morand Dairy. I told her she needed to get better so she could come out and see everything I've done. I know it seems crazy, I have doubts from time to time myself, but I feel I owe it to her to realize her last dream," Amber said clenching her fists in her lap and feeling a surge of determination.

"Steve Allswede is the attorney of record for the property. You will want to talk to him if you are going to try to legally decline the Framingham offer."

AFTER DINNER, AS MARC DROVE THEM SLOWLY to the farm in the deepening summer twilight, Amber glanced out the car windows smiling. Her eyes crinkled around the edges. "I just had a thought," she said.

"What is making you smile?" Marc asked.

"I was thinking how thrilled Hunter will be about having the money to purchase the milking equipment."

"Is this Hunter guy someone you're seeing?" Marc asked, frowning.

Amber hesitated a moment, not wanting to mislead Marc. She had been very attracted to Hunter from the first day she saw him, but he didn't seem to have any romantic feelings for her. "No, Hunter and his father are the caretakers for the farm."

"Just checking. I like to know my competition," Marc grinned.

"This is only our first date, Marc," Amber said, feeling a bit pushed. "But for the time being, your only competitors are Cam and Minna. Cam is my Afghan hound and Minna is my sister's baby. My sister, Claire, went to visit our dad who's having surgery. She left baby Minna with me while she's gone."

"I think I can prevail over a dog and I'd like to meet the baby," Marc told her.

Amber didn't invite Marc inside when they reached the farm, only thanked him for a lovely evening. He walked around the car and opened the door for her. They walked up to the back door of the summer kitchen together. She reached to open the screen door, intending to simply wish him good night, but he pulled her into his arms. He kissed her passionately and although initially startled, she found herself responding.

Marc was a lot like her former boyfriend, Brock, she realized seeing his red taillights as he drove off. He was ambitious, good-looking and financially successful. It had been a wonderful evening, but she still felt he was rushing things.

Getting into bed that night, Amber reached for the last page Aunt Irene's brother had translated from Ina's journal. Once she gave Marc's assistant, Nate, the copy of the journal she hoped it wouldn't take him too long to finish his translation. She was gripped by Ina's story.

Spring, 1917
Ina's Journal

Since baby Irene's birth, my husband has become a ghost. He is disappearing from our lives. I am furious. I grip the pen so hard my hand trembles as I write this and cuts the paper. Frank leaves every evening and sometimes doesn't come home until two or three in the morning.

When I asked him where he went, he said to his brother's house. I didn't believe him. At first, I thought he was visiting the injuratura women, the shameless ones who follow the soldiers, but he clasps me so fiercely against his body when we get into bed, his hands make bruises on my shoulders. I am afraid he will make another baby inside me. I wash myself out with vinegar every night. Little Irene is still an infant, and I never want another.

Two days ago, Frank took my wedding jewelry out of the fabric roll and put it in his jacket pocket. He wouldn't tell me why. I begged him not to take it. I grabbed his jacket and held on to him to keep him from leaving. He knocked me down. I fell on the hard floor landing on my knee. I screamed at him to come back. He didn't even turn around. When I checked my knee, it was bleeding from the rough boards. I limped over to the window to see where Frank went. Then, the worst thing of all happened. He hooked my little spotted dog on a chain and dragged her howling out of the yard. I crumpled to the floor, crying so hard I didn't hear the baby wailing.

"Despite the useless mutt loving Minna more than me, it would kill me if someone took Cam away," Amber whispered aloud into the warm summer darkness. She gazed out the window at the sky. The clustered stars were thick as wildflowers in a mountain meadow.

SIXTEEN

MARC CALLED THE FOLLOWING AFTERNOON. "I don't have time to talk very long, Amber. Just wanted you to know I'm sending Nate out to pick up your great great grandmother's journal."

"I'm not giving him the original, Marc. I made a copy for him to work from."

"That's fine. He will be there soon."

"I'll watch for him."

A silver Honda Accord drove into the driveway half an hour later. A slim dark-haired young man got out. He was holding tissue-wrapped flowers in his hands. Amber walked outside to meet him.

"Miss Amber Bradshaw?" he asked.

"That's me," she said.

"I'm Mr. Rochet's administrative assistant, Nate Bogdan. He sent these for you."

Marc had sent a bouquet of red Mexican sunflowers, blue balloon flowers and white babies' breath wrapped in green tissue paper. The little card read, "Thank you for a memorable evening."

"It's nice to meet you, Nate. Please thank Mr. Rochet for me," she said reaching for the flowers.

"I will. He said you had a journal you would like me to translate?"

"I made a copy for you to work from. Come inside and I'll get it." They walked into the house together.

"What a wonderful old house this is. Mr. Rochet told me your relatives came from Romania during World War I. Mine did too. Oh, would you mind if I used your washroom?" he asked.

"Not at all. It's just through there."

When Nate came out of the bathroom, Amber handed him the copy of Ina's journal she had made at the Library.

"I noticed that you have a trapdoor in the middle of the bathroom floor," Nate said. "Where does it lead?"

"To an old stone basement," Amber said, but felt troubled. She wondered why he would have noticed. He would have had to move the cotton rag rug aside to see it, although perhaps the rug had simply shifted. Handing the copy of the journal to Nate, Amber felt a reluctant pang, as if she were giving away her family's history. She had the original though, she reminded herself, glancing at it lying on the kitchen island. "How long do you think it will take you to do the translation?" she asked.

"Provided I can read the handwriting, I will have it for you in a week. Would $500 be fair?"

"Fine, Nate. Thank you."

Watching Nate's car pull out of the driveway, Amber thought for the hundredth time about her sister. Where was Claire? Why did she insist on going to see their father alone and what was the thing she had to do before she could return? She wondered if she should turn her in as a missing person but knew the police didn't search very hard for adults. Adults had the right to go where they wished.

The phone rang just as Amber was putting baby Minna to bed for the night. She saw her father's cell phone number and picked it up saying, "Hi, Dad."

For a moment all she could hear was a woman sobbing in the background and then her father's stricken voice saying, "Amber, we have had a visit from the police." He could hardly continue. His voice was choked with wretchedness. "Your sister has been critically injured in a car accident. She's been taken to a hospital in southern Michigan. We are driving there now.

Amber felt a stab of anguish so strong she was bent almost in half. "Should I come, Dad? I can grab Minna and leave right now."

"No. I don't think so, Honey. You and the baby shouldn't be on the road when you're so worried. We will call you as soon as we know anything. Joanna is here with me. Sorry, but we need to go. The police are asking us some questions."

Amber touched the "end call" button and took a deep shaky breath.

Claire, my little sister, please hang on. Don't leave us. Minna needs you. As do I. She started to cry.

IT WAS THREE IN THE MORNING when the phone rang again. She hadn't been able to sleep at all and had tried to reach her dad a dozen times with no answer. Her throat was raw from crying and fear consumed her.

"Our baby is gone, Amber," her father's voice was barely audible. "They took her into surgery to try to repair the damage, but it was just too extensive. Our sweet Claire is gone." Amber could hear harsh wracked sobs from her father and then Mrs. Miller picked up the phone.

"I'm so sorry, Amber," she whispered. Amber could hear the sorrow in her voice as she said a sad good-bye.

When the call ended, Amber looked around with a sense of unreality, as if time itself had been dislocated. It couldn't be true. Claire couldn't be dead. She had a baby who needed her, a sister who loved her.

Claire's note had read, "I don't know when I'll be back," but now Amber did. Her little sister, the blithe spirit of the family, wasn't coming home ever again.

AMBER MANAGED TO FEED AND DRESS MINNA the next morning, but that was all she could accomplish. She had hardly slept and couldn't even get out of her pajamas. She poured some cereal and milk in a bowl for her breakfast, but walking into the kitchen later saw the cereal bowl still sitting on the counter and poured the soggy mess down the disposal. She just kept looking around the house with the feeling she was living in an illusion. Vibrant, fun-loving Claire, could not really be gone. It seemed impossible to envision a world without her sister in it. She dialed her father's phone.

"Dad, I can't stop thinking about her," Amber choked back her sobs.

"I know, Honey. Me neither." His voice wavered.

"Did the accident happen in Michigan?"

"Yes. It was near a little town called Three Rivers."

"Was she conscious when the 911 people arrived? Did she say anything?"

"Not that they told me," he said. The sorrow made his voice thick. "Oh, Amber. It's so hard. Just tell me that she knew . . ." his voice broke off.

"That she knew? What do you mean, Dad?"

"That she knew I loved her. She knew didn't she?"

Amber wiped away tears. "Oh Dad, of course she knew. She always knew you loved her."

"I feel terrible about the fight we had when she left for college. To think that she went through an entire pregnancy and giving birth all alone. She must not have thought she could tell me. And now she's gone and I am . . . desolate. I can't forgive myself."

"Claire's death was not your fault, Dad. I thought about both of us coming to visit you. I should have insisted. Perhaps I could have saved her," Amber's voice broke and she choked back a sob.

"She wouldn't have let you come," her father said. "She told me she was going to see the baby's father. And if you and the baby had been in that car with her, all of you could have been killed."

"I tried so hard to be a good big sister," Amber cried.

"Sweetheart, you were always a wonderful big sister. It was wrong how much responsibility I put on you for Claire, even after I got sober. I feel terrible about it now. You must have resented her and me too."

"All I ever wanted to do was make it up to her, for the terrible day I forgot to pick her up from school."

"It was a long time ago and you were just a kid. You need to forgive yourself. What I did was far worse, turning to alcohol after your mom died. You have no idea how sorry I am, Amber."

"We have had many years now with you sober, Dad. I forgave you a long time ago."

"Thank you, Amber. At least the baby is there with you and you are both safe. All we can do now for Claire is to love her baby, the little part of her she left behind for us."

SEVENTEEN

A MBER WOKE THE NEXT MORNING to the phone ringing. She looked at the number blearily and let it go to voice mail. Her whole body felt heavy. She ached all over. Why am I so tired? She wondered. Then she remembered . . . the late-night phone call . . . her father's anguished cries . . . her little sister's face. It seemed like only a few moments ago that Claire and Minna had arrived at the farm. Now her sister was gone . . . forever. My little sister is dead. She heard the words in her brain, but they didn't register. It was as if the world had ceased to spin, had reversed its magnetic polarity and shifted off its axis—spinning out of the known universe through unending dark and cold.

She gazed out her open bedroom window at the enormous cotton-wood trees, watching the mist disappear as it rose through the branches. It all felt dreamlike, illusory. The dawn chorus of birds sang and the sun touched a spider web in the corner of the window lighting the dew drops. She swung her feet out of bed and put them on the cool floor. Looking at her small white feet with their pink toenails, she didn't feel like they belonged to her.

In slow motion, she stood up and peeled off her pajamas, letting them drop to the floor. They were soft cotton with a pattern of blue flowers and little birds but she had had no memory of where they came from. Looking around the room, Amber gazed at the spooled headboard on the bed, the tumbled blankets and the mirror over the dressing table. She dimly realized she was in her bedroom at the old Morand family farm, but when she looked in the mirror, she hardly recognized herself.

She seemed to have aged a decade. Her eyes were huge with dark blue circles. Feeling numb, she picked up her hairbrush and pulled it through her tangled hair with harsh strokes. Perhaps the pain would make her feel alive again.

Taking a shaky breath, she opened the top drawer of the dresser pulling out clean underwear and feeling the warmth of the morning light on her body. Then she registered a noise coming from the other bedroom. For a moment she couldn't for the life of her remember what made that kind of noise. It sounded like a kitten.

But I don't have a kitten, she thought, before she remembered. The sound was coming from Minna—the baby was waking up. Grief washed across her heart. She closed her eyes tightly as tears ran down her face. So many years of her life had been spent taking care of Claire, worrying about Claire, atoning for her failures with Claire. Why did I waste all that emotional energy when I should just have loved and treasured her? Now it was too late. Amber groaned aloud in pain.

LATER, HAVING REGAINED SOME MINIMAL CONTROL over her emotions, Amber pressed the button on the phone to hear the message from the call that had woken her.

"Miss Bradshaw, this is Nate. I have finished the translation of Ina Morand's journal. Mr. Rochet said for me to give it to Mrs. Worth at the front desk of the nursing home. I am just leaving there now."

The everyday voice brought her back to reality—her reality, the life of a woman who had her sister's baby to feed, dress and care for. While it was a struggle, she managed to get herself and the baby dressed at last, but felt as if she were playing a part on a stage, acting out someone else's life—a life that had ended in tragedy.

Amber was walking slowly out to her car carrying Minna when Hunter walked up. She was immensely relieved to see him. "Hunter, I'm so glad you're here. I've just had horrible news. My sister, Claire, Minna's mom, was in a car accident." Amber stopped talking and just looked at him. For a moment she swallowed, unable to speak, then she said, "Claire died in surgery last night."

"Oh my God, Amber, I'm so terribly sorry," Hunter said. His dark eyes opened wide and he looked shocked.

"I want to go see Aunt Irene, but I'm so shaky I'm not sure I should be driving," her voice trailed off. Driving into Apple River Falls suddenly seemed impossible. All she wanted to do was to go back in time to the day before Claire left the farm. Remembering encouraging her sister to go visit their father, she felt crushed. It was her fault that Claire was gone.

"Do you want me to take you into town?" Hunter asked, reaching out and patting her arm gently.

Amber managed to nod.

"I just need to stop and tell my father where I'm going. I always let him know if I leave the area." He touched her cheek, wiping away a tear.

"Oh, Hunter, I'm so sad," she said and started to cry again. Hunter took baby Minna from Amber's arms and carried her over to the car. He buckled the baby into the car seat. When he came back, he took Amber into his arms. They stood together beneath the cottonwood trees and all the time she was crying, he never let her go.

Grateful for Hunter's sensitivity, Amber's tears trailed off and the three of them got into the truck, drove down Morand road and turned left onto a grassy two-track. The lane curved back and forth through the trees until they reached a small log cabin. Mr. Freedman was outside, tending his vegetable garden. Hunter rolled down the car window.

"Dad, Amber and I are going into town to see Aunt Irene. We will be back in a couple of hours," Hunter said. "Okay?"

"Amber, do you want to leave the baby here with me?" Mr. Freedman asked.

"Another time," Amber told him with a tremulous smile. She just couldn't be parted from Minna. Not now, maybe not ever again.

WALKING UP TO THE DOOR OF THE NURSING HOME, Amber started to tremble violently and asked Hunter to hold Minna. She couldn't stop thinking about her sister, horribly injured and then dying in a cold operating room surrounded by masked doctors and nurses. She swallowed hard and turned her face away, her shoulders shaking. When she was composed enough to enter the nursing facility, she picked up the journal translation from Mrs. Worth at the front desk, but found herself unable to even greet the woman.

"Goodness Amber, are you all right?" Mrs. Worth asked with a worried frown.

"Not really," Amber whispered, and the three of them walked down the hall to Aunt Irene's room, leaving a concerned Mrs. Worth looking after them.

"Good Morning, Miss Irene," Hunter said, opening her door.

"Hello, Hunter, I'm so pleased to see you," Aunt Irene said and held out her hand. He squeezed her hand in return.

"We have the translation of Ina's journal to read to you," he said.

"What's wrong, Amber?" Aunt Irene asked, looking closely at her face.

"My sister Claire . . . was killed in a car accident last night," Amber managed, biting her lip to try to stop the tears.

Aunt Irene's eyes moved from Amber's face to the baby. "You mentioned your sister had a baby. Is this little one Claire's?"

"Yes. This is baby Minna."

"I remember your sister. The last time I saw her she was around four years old. Near-white hair, she had then. Such a spritely elfin girl. Always leading your mother a merry chase. It was a car accident, you said?"

"That's right." Amber said, feeling tears prick her eyes.

"I am very sorry for your loss, Amber," Aunt Irene said formally, reaching out and patting her hand.

"Thank you. I'm glad you remember Claire. She deserves to be remembered," she said, wiping her eyes. "I wanted to read you part of your mother's journal, but I'm afraid I will start to cry again. Could you start here, Hunter?" she asked, indicating the page. Turning to Aunt Irene, she said, "This entry is from a time shortly after you were born."

Hunter's deep voice began to read the words of Irene Morand's mother from a hundred years ago.

Spring, 1917

Last night, I swallowed my pride. I followed Frank when he left. He walked to his brother's house. He had told the truth and I was ashamed I had doubted him. I peered into the living room window. Baby Irene started to cry, and I ducked down into the shrubbery, rocking her in my arms until she quieted.

When I stood up again, Frank and his brother were sitting close together in front of the fireplace on the wood floor. Their living room had no furniture left. Alene came into the room. She screamed at both the men, her mouth open. Charles's face looked like a wolf's. He stood up and struck her. She stumbled against the fireplace, hitting her cheek against the split stone. She walked unsteadily out of the room, holding her head. I saw blood on her hand.

This morning I talked to Alene in the community garden. There was a large bruise on her cheek. I demanded to know what our husbands were planning. She said they were going to sell everything we owned and leave our country. We couldn't tell anyone. If we did, the Army would assemble a firing squad. They would both be shot.

When I got home from the market, the walnut table and high-backed chairs my father made for my wedding dowry had disappeared. I ran to our proprietor's apartment. She said my husband had sold them. When Frank finally came home at dawn, I screamed to know what was happening.

"After one more night mission, Charles and I plan to desert from the Army," he said.

For a moment I stopped shouting, watching shame spread across Frank's features.

"Desert from the Army? But you are razbonic, a soldier. What else are you?"

"I'm not going to be a soldier for much longer, Ina. After tonight, we are leaving here."

"Where are we going?" I started to shake.

"It's better you not know." He looked down at the floor, turned and walked into the bedroom.

I felt a corrosive rage rise boiling inside me. I followed him into the bedroom where he was undressing. His neatly brushed blue uniform lay on the bed.

"I'll be back in the morning," he told me.

I won't be here then, I thought, but bit back the words. Whatever Frank is doing, I have made my decision. I won't go with him.

When he left, I packed my clothes and baby Irene's things. I paid a peddler to take me all the way to my parents' house in his vegetable cart. He drove me until we could go no further, there are already areas off-limits to ordinary citizens because of the Occupation I never thought would happen. The soldiers at the edge of the village demanded my papers. They talked a while between themselves but finally let me through. The peddler turned his mule around and left. I walked the rest of night under a cold moon. I reached Timisoara with baby Irene in my arms just as the sun came up, bright as a consuming fire. Like the burning resentment in my heart for what Frank is doing . . .

Hunter's voice trailed off.

"Thank you, Hunter. That's enough for now. I'm tired, but please come back tomorrow. All three of you." Aunt Irene said.

Amber kissed her on the cheek and lowered Minna so Aunt Irene could kiss her good-bye.

Her phone rang as they were driving back to the farm. "Hello," she said, her voice quiet.

"Miss Bradshaw, this is Nate. Did you find the Morand journal translation at the nursing home yet?"

"I did. Thank you. I left your check with Mrs. Worth."

"I wondered if I could see the actual journal sometime, the original."

"Why would you want to see the original? You have read every word from the copy I gave you." She felt an angry frustration breaking through her sadness.

Nate hesitated a moment before he said, "I forgot to check something and just remembered it. Okay if I stop out to see it?"

"Sometime perhaps, but not today. I'm not up to visitors today," Amber said. "Good-bye."

"Who was that?" Hunter asked when she hung up.

"Nate Bogdan. He's the person who translated the Morand journal. He wants to see the original of Ina's journal."

"I wonder why," Hunter said, frowning.

"Just what I was thinking," Amber said.

As they drove down Morand road past the yellowing winter wheat fields to the farm, a troubling thought crossed her mind. *Could something be hidden in Ina's journal that would unlock the family mystery? Did Nate suspect something about the missing treasure?*

EIGHTEEN

Amber set both the original and the translated copy of Ina's journal on the shining surface of the kitchen island when she and Hunter got back to the house. She sat down to give Minna her bottle.

"I need to get going. Would you like me to come back later?" Hunter asked. "You've had a terrible blow with Claire dying."

Amber took a shaky breath. "Yes, Hunter, please come back after you feed the calves this afternoon."

When the baby finished her bottle, Amber took her upstairs and put her down in the cradle. She told herself for the hundredth time that she needed to buy a full-sized crib. The temperature outdoors was in the 80's and it was uncomfortably warm in the room. Minna sat up, held out her hands and started to cry.

"Are you too hot, baby?" Amber reached down for the little one, feeling a lurch of recognition. Minna looked so much like Claire as a baby. "Maybe it would be better for you to take your nap on my bed." Her room was shaded by the cottonwoods and much cooler. She walked into her room carrying the baby and laid her down on her side, gently placing pillows all around her small body to keep her from rolling off the bed. Cam jumped up on the bed and lay down beside Minna.

"Stay right there, Cam," Amber whispered. She had given up trying to keep him away from the baby, and his long body would shield her from rolling off the bed. She opened the window to catch the slight breeze. Leaving the room, she closed the door softly, making sure it latched so the dog couldn't leave.

While Minna napped, Amber knew she couldn't just sit in the house remembering Claire, it only deepened her remorse. She pulled herself together, deciding to search the cellar. Perhaps there were other treasures Frank and Ina had hidden, possibly the icon Aunt Irene wrote about in her notebook. Amber found her flashlight and pulled up the newly installed trapdoor in the bathroom floor. Remembering the password, she entered the numbers 1918. For just a moment she felt uneasy walking down the steps into the darkness, but shook her head, dismissing her fears.

She was working her way around the cellar checking for loose stones when she heard someone's footsteps above her. "Ryan? Is that you? Hunter? Is someone there?" she called. Nobody answered. The sound of footsteps stopped and she walked over to the bottom of the stairs. She was starting up the stairs when suddenly, as if someone blotted out the sun, the trapdoor to the cellar clanged down. Then, to her horror, she heard the distinctive click of the lock closing and heavy footsteps walking away. The back door of the summer kitchen slammed shut. The damp walls closed in. Claustrophobia threatened to overwhelm her. She climbed up the stairs until her head bumped against the trapdoor. Despite pushing hard, it didn't move. Some maniac had locked her in the cellar. The horror of the situation made her heart race.

"Cam," she screamed. "Cam." She heard the dog start barking. Then she remembered. The bedroom door was latched, he couldn't get out. Still she continued calling. It kept the dog barking. Then she heard Minna start to cry. Hunter hearing the dog and coming to investigate was her only hope. A half-hour later she heard the sound of Cam jumping down from the bed, his claws clicking on the bedroom floor, scratching at the door, uselessly trying to get it to open.

The battery on her flashlight was fading. Soon she would be in complete darkness. Her wristwatch's fluorescent dial showed 3:40. Hunter would be at the farm by 4:00 to feed the calves. Forcing herself to do it, Amber shut off the flashlight. If Hunter forgot to stop by the house and she was trapped for a long time, she wanted to conserve power.

A few minutes later, she heard baby Minna start to cry. Amber sat on the bottom step in despair, her face in her hands, weeping in rage. Then she heard a hard thump. Minna's cries stopped suddenly and then she wailed louder than ever. Amber felt a sick thud in her stomach. The baby had fallen off the bed. She could have broken her little arms or legs, even have a head injury. She couldn't stop her tears thinking that she had failed again and this time she had injured Claire's baby.

IT SEEMED LIKE HOURS LATER when Amber heard boots on the floor above her and Hunter's voice calling her name. "Hunter," Amber screamed. "I'm trapped in the basement. Help!"

Footsteps came closer and she heard Hunter's voice. "Amber, where are you? Are you down in the cellar?"

"Yes. Let me out!" she yelled.

"Hang on. What's the combination to the lock?"

"It's 1918," she called loudly. "Hurry!"

In only moments, she heard the lock click open. The trapdoor was lifted and Amber saw Hunter's worried face looking down at her. She climbed out, her chest heaving, gulping air, grabbed hold of his shoulders and kissed him hard on the mouth. Pushing past him, she raced upstairs and opened the door to the bedroom. Cam was standing beside Minna who was sitting on the bedroom floor.

Amber bent down to pick up the baby who seemed remarkably unfazed. Her face was wet with tears, but seeing Amber she smiled. Setting the baby on the bed, Amber checked her over carefully. There was a bruised bump forming on her forehead. It didn't look serious, but she would have the doctor check her as soon as possible. She carried the baby downstairs, holding tight to the railing. Her hands were wet with sweat and she took the stairs slowly, afraid she might trip and fall.

"Did you see anyone when you got here, Hunter? Any cars?"

"Sorry, Amber. Most of the time I was in the milking shed. That building is pretty soundproof and doesn't have windows. I didn't hear Cam until I was out in the barnyard. It's a good thing your bedroom window was open, otherwise I would never have heard him."

Amber put Minna down in her baby-seat. She felt chilled and started to shake, knowing she was going into shock. Reaching for Hunter she said, "Thank you my friend, thank you so much. You are my hero," and she hugged him. Hunter's body felt so warm and strong. She raised her face to kiss him again, but as her lips touched his, he pulled back slightly. She looked up at him seeing a pained expression on his face. Feeling hurt and confused, Amber said, "Sorry."

"No need. Come into the living room. We should talk about who could have done this to you. I'll bring Minna."

They talked for a while with Minna sitting in her baby seat, before Hunter glanced at the clock. "I think you should call the Sheriff's office. Would you like me to stay until they get here?" he asked. Amber shook her head. "Are you sure?" When she nodded, he reached out for her and hugged her.

It was a gentle hug, though, not an embrace a man would give a woman he was attracted to, she thought sadly.

After Hunter left, Amber felt herself descend into a whirling dark despair. Claire was dead. Minna could have died and was now her responsibility. Hunter didn't want her. Aunt Irene was dying and some debased criminal had locked her in the cellar. She started to sob and was unable to stop crying for a long time. When she finally got herself under control, she dialed the Sheriff's office. It wasn't an emergency, she told the dispatcher, but she needed to talk to an officer. Somebody had locked her in the basement.

"You're sure the cellar door didn't just shut on its own?" the woman asked, in a dubious voice.

"Very sure. I heard someone walking above me and then the trap door slammed down. I heard the click of the lock. When my neighbor, Hunter Freedman, heard my dog barking and came to check on me an hour later, the padlock on the trap door was still locked."

"I'll send Deputy Foxcroft out," the woman said.

Amber thanked her and walked into the living room, carrying the baby. Although she was still shaky, she couldn't make herself put her down. She sat at the kitchen island with Minna in her lap. Doubting her eyes for a moment, she looked again. But there was no question. To her horror, although Nate's translation was right where she had left it, the original leather journal written by Ina Morand a hundred years ago was gone.

NINETEEN

A WHITE PATROL CAR PULLED IN behind the house an hour later. The heavyset man who got out of the car was wearing a brown Sheriff's office uniform. Amber walked out to greet him. Minna was sound asleep, cuddled against her chest.

"Deputy Dwayne Foxcroft, responding to your call," he said.

"Please come in. I'm glad you're here." They walked inside and Amber asked him if he wanted some coffee. He nodded and she poured him a cup. "I need to put the baby in bed. I'll be right back," she said. She walked back into the kitchen only moments later.

"Tell me what happened," the Deputy said, pulling out his notebook.

"Someone locked me in the cellar. There's a trap door in the bathroom that pulls up to access the stairs that lead down into the basement," she said. "I'm sorry, but I can't go into that room with you just yet. I'm still too shaky. The lock is on the floor."

"I'll take a look," Foxcroft said. When he came back into the kitchen, he was wearing gloves and had the lock in a plastic evidence bag. "Okay, run through what happened for me," he said, looking at her intently.

"The baby was napping upstairs on my bed. While she was sleeping, I thought I'd take a look in the cellar for anything the original settlers might have left down there." She paused, and swallowed, taking a deep breath.

"Go on."

"When I was down in the cellar, I heard someone walking on the floor above me. I thought it was my contractor, Ryan Amherst. I called out, asking who was there. I started up the steps when the trap door closed above my head and I heard the lock snap shut. Sorry," she said trying to control the quaver in her voice. She wiped her eyes.

"How long were you down there, Miss Bradshaw?" Deputy Foxcroft asked.

"Over an hour."

"Well, no harm done, right? You said the baby was okay and there was nothing taken?" the Deputy said cheerfully, closing his notebook with a snap.

Amber felt a burn of anger at his dismissiveness. Her voice was cold when she spoke. "I am going to have Dr. O'Brien check the baby, so we'll know for sure. She seems fine, except for a little lump on her forehead. But, there *was* something taken—a small leather journal."

"What was in this journal?"

"The journal was written in the Romanian language by Ina Morand, my great great grandmother. Nate Bogdan, the bank president's assistant, translated the journal into English for me. Hunter Freeman took me into town this morning to pick up the translation. On our way back home, Nate called asking if he could see the original journal. He did the translation from a copy. I found his request a bit suspicious. When Hunter and I got back to the farm, I set both the original and the translated copy side-by-side on the kitchen island."

"So to your knowledge this guy, Nate Bogdan, never arrived here?"

"That's right."

"So other than yourself, Hunter Freedman was the only person who knew exactly where the original of the journal was. He brought you home, you said, so he saw you put it on your kitchen island."

"He would never have done this," Amber said, outraged by the Deputy's conclusion. Trying to lower her voice she said, "As I said, Nate Bogdan works for Marc Rochet, President of the bank in town. You should check on his whereabouts during the time I was in the basement."

The officer hesitated, frowning. "Mr. Rochet is an important man in this town. I wouldn't want to accuse his assistant of anything untoward without more proof," Deputy Foxcroft said.

"Just call, will you, please?" She felt an upwelling of rage at his stalling. Blood pounded in her ears.

"Is this journal valuable? I can't see why somebody would steal an old journal."

"As I told you, the journal was written by my great great grandmother, one of the original settlers in this area. It records her trip to the U.S. when she and her husband fled Romania at the outset of WWI."

"You aren't answering my question," Foxcroft said. "Is it valuable?"

"It certainly has historic value and it is priceless to me. Since Nate Bogdan was the person who wanted to see the original, you need to check on him. Call the bank now, please."

"Hang on and I'll call." He talked on the phone for a bit, hung up and said, "According to his personal secretary, Mr. Rochet was on his way to Minneapolis when this happened. His secretary said Nate was at work this morning, but since his office is down the hall from her desk, she couldn't say for sure whether he left at any time. He's there now. I'll go by and speak with him. Unfortunately, finding fingerprints on the lock is a long shot. Since it's a metal lock, whatever is there is probably smudged, but I'll have it checked. And I'll talk with Hunter Freedman too."

AT ABOUT TEN THAT NIGHT, Amber heard a tentative tap on the summer kitchen door. She went to see who it was, heart thumping. She felt her whole body relax when she saw it was Hunter. He looked at her intently.

"Can I come in?"

"Of course, please do," she moved away from the door holding it open. He had a bag of groceries in his hands and a package wrapped in brown paper under his arm.

"I brought you some food, in case you didn't feel up to going to the store," he said. "And I stopped to see Aunt Irene in town and told her you might not be able to visit for a few days. She assumed it was because of your sister. I didn't tell her about you being locked in the cellar or that somebody took Ina's journal. I thought it would upset her."

"Thank you, Hunter that was kind of you."

They went into the kitchen and unloaded the groceries. He had purchased strawberries, coffee, cereal, milk, cookies, formula and a truly terrible bottle of bubbly wine, pink and sugary.

"All the major food groups, I see," she said, her voice veering between laughter and tears.

"I just thought maybe you could use something to eat," his voice trailed off. He seemed uncertain whether he had done the right thing.

"It's perfect," she said. "Truly, Hunter, it's just perfect. Would you get me a glass of that wine?"

"I brought you something else too," he said reaching under his arm for the package wrapped in brown paper and twine.

"What is it?" she asked as she untied the twine and opened the wrapping. Inside was a sheaf of old black and white photographs. She smiled as she flipped through them, seeing Ina and Frank as a young couple and Irene as a toddler. There were pictures of the barn being built and even one of the old log cabin, the original dwelling on the property. "These are just wonderful. Thank you."

"After we talked about you wanting art for the house, I mentioned the old photographs to my father. Aunt Irene gave them to him when she moved into the Nursing Home. I wondered perhaps if . . ." His voice trailed off.

"What?"

"I thought maybe you might like me to frame some of these. I'm a pretty fair carpenter. It's just an idea," he shrugged

"A fine one, Hunter. Thank you. I would love that."

THEY SAT DOWN ON THE COUCH with their wine glasses. Neither of them spoke for a bit. When Hunter began to talk, he didn't mention the incident with the basement, Aunt Irene or Claire's death. Instead, he spoke about the old days at the farm when he was a little boy.

"Lillian Morand, your mother's grandmother, was always kind to me, at a time when prejudice against Native Americans was very strong. She made what she called Ranger cookies and Kool-Aid when we did the threshing. She thought I had artistic talent and encouraged me to keep painting."

"Hunter, do you mind telling me why you aren't painting now? If you can't talk about it, that's okay."

"I really don't know," he said, frowning in confusion. "For some reason, my hand won't pick up the brush. And my heart just isn't in it. I think it has to do with being here at the farm. I always wanted to get more art training and eventually be able to sell my work. It was my dream, and my mother's too, but it's hard with Dad being alone here. He's getting older and needs me."

"What is your favorite thing to paint?"

"Portraits. I loved capturing the essence of a person in my brush strokes. Sometimes, when I was proud of my work, I felt I had caught the person's soul," Hunter's voice was slow and calm. She felt his voice was a bond between them that kept her anchored and safe.

"Perhaps you need a Muse," Amber said sleepily. Hunter put his arm around her and she leaned against him.

"Can you sleep now?" he asked when she yawned.

"I think so."

Hunter followed her upstairs. She heard him walk into Minna's room and check on the baby. When he walked back past Amber's door he leaned in to speak to her.

"I don't want you to be scared so I'll sleep on your couch tonight. I'll be here every night, as long as you need me."

I just might need you forever, Amber thought, before sleepily reaching for a page from Nate's translation of Ina's journal. With the original missing, the copy was all she had.

Summer, 1917

When he came to the door my father looked dismayed to see me standing in the moonlight. My mother reached for baby Irene who woke up and started to cry.

"My husband is going to desert from the Army. I'm coming back home."

"You made your choice when you married him," my father said. His old face was sad and deeply lined. He seemed to hesitate for a moment, but then opened the door fully to usher us inside

When the sun rose, my father left the house saying he was going to get Frank. When he came back, my husband was with him. Frank reached for my hand, but I pulled away.

"We have to leave here, Ina. The Germans are already at the borders of our country."

"No one is safe now." My father's voice was deep.

"What about you?" I asked, feeling terribly afraid for my parents.

"We have had our lives," my father said, but I saw tears glisten in his old eyes, matching mine. My mother cried when she kissed the baby good-bye. She pulled me aside and said a quiet blessing over our heads. "Try to stay close to God, my daughter. Tear some pages from your Journal and send me a letter if you can."

I walked outside to the edge of my parents' property and pulled two cottonwood saplings from the earth. Back in the house, I poured water over an old cloth and wrapped them tightly. Wherever we were going, I would plant the cottonwood trees in memory of my parents. I would surely never see them again. Goosebumps from fear raced across my shoulders.

Hating it, I crawled into my father's filthy vegetable cart with baby Irene. It smelled of manure. My father pulled a tarp over us. My soldier husband who had looked so smart in his blue uniform wore the clothes of a dirty peddler. Rage exploded in my throat, gagging me. I felt turned to stone as the donkey took us down the road and away from my country.

TWENTY

AMBER WOKE FEELING SOMEWHAT STRONGER, although she still couldn't stop her thoughts from returning again and again to her little sister's last hours. It just seemed so terribly wrong that Claire hadn't lived long enough to see baby Minna grow up. Parents should never die before their children; it was against Nature. God or the universe should have prevented her sister's death. Amber sighed deeply and regret washed her heart. After feeding and dressing the baby, she decided to drive into town. It had been tough to get the struggling baby into her car seat, but Amber was desperate to talk about her sister, and Aunt Irene remembered her as a child.

As she drove into the parking lot at the Nursing Home, an ambulance drove past her with lights flashing and sirens screaming. She grabbed Minna from her car seat and raced through the automatic doors into the reception area.

"Where's Aunt Irene? Was that her in the ambulance?" she asked Mrs. Worth, trying to catch her breath. The ambulance's siren gave her a chill of presentiment, a terrible fear that Aunt Irene's life was coming to an end.

"Slow down, Amber. Yes, Irene is in that ambulance that just left. I'm sorry," Mrs. Worth's voice was filled with compassion.

"What happened? Where were they taking her?" Amber wailed.

"St. Croix Falls," Mrs. Worth said, reaching for her hands. "Amber, she had a stroke. She might not live through the ambulance ride. There's no point in you going after her. They will let us know what happens."

Amber trembled all over, fearing that she had seen Aunt Irene for the last time. Her stomach lurched and she could feel a pulse beat fast in her throat.

"I don't care, I'm going to follow that ambulance."

"Just give yourself a few minutes, dear. You shouldn't drive until you are calmer. You can't risk the baby, she's precious cargo. Should I call Mr. Rochet for you? I understand you two are dating."

"That's not necessary, but you're right, Mrs. Worth. I'll just take a minute," Amber said taking a seat on a chair in the reception area and forcing her breathing to slow.

BACK IN THE PARKING LOT A bit later, Amber was buckling the baby in her car seat when Marc Rochet's sleek sports car drove in. He rolled down his window.

"Mrs. Worth called me. What happened?" he asked.

"Aunt Irene's being taken to the hospital in St. Croix Falls. I'm going after them. I don't know how long this will take, but I hope to be back at the farm this evening. Could you come over then, Marc? We need to talk."

"I'll come around eight," he said. He patted her hand that rested on the open window of his car. "Try not to worry, Amber. Miss Irene Morand is a tough old bird." He got out of his car and reached to take her into his arms, but Amber turned away, tears falling. She got in her car and drove off. She knew he was hurt and in her rear-view mirror saw him looking after her departing car. He was frowning.

She caught up with the ambulance ten minutes later following the sound of the siren. When the ambulance pulled into the Emergency Room lot of the hospital in St. Croix, she parked her car, picked Minna up and dashed toward the paramedics who were unloading a terribly small body on a gurney. Then she stopped, feeling a qualm, recognizing the meaning of the white sheet covering the patient's face.

"Is she . . .?" Amber asked, dreading the EMT's response.

"Are you a family member?"

"Yes, she's my Great Great Aunt," Amber said. "She hasn't any other living family. I am—I am the last."

"I'm sorry for your loss, Miss." He glanced at the patient identification. "Irene Morand stopped breathing on the way over here. We did everything we could to get her heart started again, to no avail. I have to get a doctor to pronounce her, but she hasn't had a pulse in over a half an hour."

The young attendant pulled the sheet down gently from Aunt Irene's face and Amber felt the hair lift on the nape of her neck. Her aunt's face was almost gray, nearly waxy. She started to shake uncontrollably. Someone took her arm. Another person lifted Minna from her. She couldn't hear a sound. It was as if someone had wrapped her in clouds of white cotton batting. Finally, a person's voice penetrated the separate space she inhabited, deep inside the sharp swirling fragments of grief.

"Are you able to make a decision at this time about who you want to pick up the body?" the EMT worker asked gently. "Sorry, to ask, but the hospital needs to know."

She managed to say that she would have the funeral home in Apple River Falls call the hospital. Forcing herself to walk back to her car, she loaded a protesting baby into her car seat and drove slowly out of the hospital parking lot, sobbing so hard that tears cascaded down her cheeks. Aunt Irene's still form and fixed face stayed in Amber's mind all the way to the farm. Driving into the long driveway and past the big red barn at the farm, her cell phone rang.

"Hi Dad," she said, not even trying to mask the discouragement in her voice.

"Honey, what is it? My God, has something else happened? Tell me."

"Aunt Irene just died. She had a stroke and was in an ambulance taking her to St. Croix. I was right behind the ambulance, but by the time we got to the hospital she was gone," Amber couldn't stop sobbing. She felt like the bottom had fallen out of her life. What was life worth without her sister, and now without Aunt Irene.

"My God. . . . First Claire and now Irene. Of course Irene's demise was expected, but . . ." Her father's voice broke. Neither of them was able to speak for a bit. "She was the last of the original Morand family," he said, sounding totally dejected.

"I know, Dad. She had become my favorite person at the farm, as she was yours."

"I'm sorry to add to your difficulties, Amber, but you will need to arrange a funeral for her. Irene Morand lived in that community all her life. A funeral is expected in a case like this."

"I have no idea how to do that, Dad," she said, feeling utterly miserable and wishing someone else could take over the funeral arrangements and leave her to grieve, but even as the thought crossed her mind Amber knew it wouldn't happen. She was always expected to be the grown-up, although at that moment she felt like a small broken child.

"You can leave the details, like the casket selection, to the funeral home in Apple River Falls, but don't have her cremated. Irene Morand was Orthodox and their funerals are open-casket. Go to the Lutheran church in Apple River Falls tomorrow. The family attended services there. The Pastor will help you. I'm sorry to put this on you, Honey. If I could drive, I'd come."

"I know you would. I'll have to manage," Amber said, taking a breath and straightening her shoulders. "Dad, if I decide I want to stay at the farm for a while after the summer ends, would you consider coming to stay with me? Just for an extended visit?"

"If you are thinking about staying there longer, you need to know that I can't afford to keep the farm as things stand. I've taken over the finances for the property in the last few years so I'm aware of the money situation. The farm has been losing money recently. Let's just wait and see what Aunt Irene decided to do with the farm in her will."

"She would have left the farm to you, wouldn't she?"

"I doubt it. I am not a Morand. You and Minna are her only living blood relatives. If you inherit the farm, do you know what will you do?"

"I have no idea, Dad, but I've decided to hold off for a while on selling the house. It's paid for and was my legacy from Mom. And, although it's probably silly, I still hope to find the icon Aunt Irene mentioned and the family treasure."

AMBER PLACED BABY MINNA IN HER PLAYPEN when she got into the house. Then remembering Claire as a little girl and Aunt Irene's final days, she cried for a long time, only regaining her composure much later. She dialed Cassidy at the gallery and told her about losing Claire and Aunt Irene. Her tears came again at Cassidy's warm voice. Toward the end of their conversation, hearing the sound of a car in the driveway, she said good-bye, wiped her eyes and glanced out the summer kitchen window. Her contractor Ryan Amhurst and Chris, his carpenter, had arrived. She opened the back door for them.

"Hi," she said, a bit weakly, as two men approached the house.

"Hi Amber, we are going to try to open that cabinet you found under the staircase. And I still need to install the light fixture in the summer kitchen." Ryan hesitated. "You look upset. Are you okay?" he asked.

"No," Amber said taking a shaky breath. "I'm not okay. I might never be okay again. My sister was killed in an auto accident a few days ago and Aunt Irene just died."

"My God. That's just awful! I'm so terribly sorry," Ryan said. He looked pale and shook his head in disbelief. "It doesn't seem possible that Irene Morand would ever pass away. She was such a fixture in this community. She was here my whole life. In fact my folks knew her *their* whole lives. I can't remember a time when her vital presence wasn't the backbone of the farming community. It's a shock. I'm really sorry about your sister, too. Do you want us to come back later?"

Amber shook her head saying, "No, I need to find the deed to the farm for the Framingham representative. It might be in that cabinet I found." She led them into the dining room and gestured to the antique cherry sideboard.

Chris had an enormous round brass ring in his hands that must have held a thousand keys. He knelt down and began trying keys patiently—one by one—as Amber and Ryan walked into the summer kitchen. Ryan unpacked the light fixtures (historically correct, of course) that would hang over the peninsula, pulled out his electrical kit, climbed up on a stool and started the installation.

Amber went into the living room to check on Minna. Just as Megan had predicted, the baby had pulled herself up to a standing position in her playpen. Cam was looking down on her.

"My goodness, Miss Minna, you can already stand up?" Amber picked up the baby and snuggled her. "You are just amazing." She breathed into Minna's neck and the baby chortled. Although still feeling immeasurably sad about Claire and Aunt Irene, Minna always lifted her spirits. It was impossible to completely succumb to grief around such a happy baby.

Remembering her earlier feelings that life wasn't worth living, she realized it was—Minna made her life worthwhile. She carried the baby out to the summer kitchen.

"How are you coming along, Ryan?"

"I'm done. Turn on the switch."

Amber did so and the lights came on. They cast a warm light on the grey streaked soapstone countertops, something that looked modern to her, but apparently had been used on kitchen counters a century ago.

"Now that's what I like to see," Ryan said. "Oh, I nearly forgot. Megan sent something for you. It's in the back of the truck. She went to another darn garage sale. Our house is full of bargains we don't need," he said and rolled his eyes. "Take a look."

Carrying the baby, she and Ryan walked outside into the hot stillness of the late summer afternoon. The contrast between the perfect day and the memory of Aunt Irene's body with a white sheet over her face and her beautiful broken sister, now gone forever, crushed her.

She struggled to speak normally saying, "Megan is so wonderful," she told him seeing a white crib in the back of his truck. "Little Minna needed a bigger bed. Tell her thank you and let me know how much I owe her, will you?"

Ryan waved his hand, "It's nothing. At the end of this project, I'll add an hour to my bill. I'll put the crib together for you."

They walked upstairs carrying the pieces of the crib. Ryan had it together in ten minutes. It looked wonderful and safe, but had no mattress. I'll buy one tomorrow on my trip to the Nursing Home, she thought, before realizing there was no need to go into town now. Like Claire, Aunt Irene was gone. Tears welled up in her eyes. She turned her face to the floor. Sadness owned her.

Ryan patted her on the back, saying, "I'm so sorry, Amber. You're going to be okay," he said, over and over again.

A bit later, she heard Chris' voice calling, "Ryan, Amber, I found the key and got the cabinet unlocked."

When they walked downstairs into to the dining room, Chris said, "I didn't open the doors. Thought you would want to do the honors." He smiled, taking the key off the ring. "Here's the key that worked. Can you get a copy of it made at the hardware store and give this one back?"

"Of course. Thank you, Chris."

Amber had to tug hard on the two small doors, but they sprang open to reveal a leather folder. She pulled it out carefully. Inside was the ancient Homesteader's Deed to the Morand farm. It was what she needed to sell the property to Framingham.

Should I? She asked herself. Aunt Irene wanted me to start the Morand Dairy again. The words hung in the air as if they had been written in black ink calligraphy, a visible challenge flung at her from Aunt Irene and the world beyond the grave.

AFTER DINNER AMBER GAVE MINNA her last bottle of the day. When the baby's eyes closed, she carried her up to the little cradle. Half an hour later, she heard the sound of Marc's car. She walked out through the summer kitchen door to meet him.

"Hi, come in."

"I brought a bottle of wine," Marc said. His voice was husky. He slid his arm around her waist. Amber pulled slightly away from his touch.

Her mind still rode with the tiny motionless woman who had died in the ambulance and visions of the auto accident that claimed her sister's life.

Marc uncorked the bottle and poured two glasses. They walked into the living room. It was a warm evening and he asked if he should open the living room windows. Amber nodded, not trusting herself to speak without crying. When Marc patted the seat beside him on the couch, Amber shook her head and sat at the far end. He looked confused and a bit hurt, but Amber didn't feel up to handling his feelings just then. Hers were too overwhelming.

"What happened when you went after the ambulance?" Marc asked, his eyes deep with concern.

"She's gone, Marc. My dear Aunt Irene has passed away. She never regained consciousness after leaving the nursing home." Amber felt the onset of a piercing headache. Marc moved closer, wrapped his arms around her and she collapsed against him, crying hard.

He held her, kissing the top of her head and murmuring, "It's okay, Sweetheart. You just cry as long as you need to."

When she regained some semblance of control and met his eyes, Marc bent his head to kiss her, but looking up at him through her tears she said, "This is the second tragedy for me. My sister, Claire, was killed in an automobile accident a few days ago."

"My God, Amber, that's just terrible. It must be completely overwhelming for you." Marc's eyes were wide open and he looked shaken. "Is there anything I can do to help?"

"I need to know if you will support me if I decide to fight Framingham for the farm." She felt the responsibility for her legacy wrap around her. "You know Aunt Irene wanted me to start the Dairy again."

"Of course. But is that the reason you wanted me to come out?" Marc reached for her hand. "I thought you wanted to see me."

"I did, but so much has happened recently that I need your help. Did the police tell you someone locked me in the basement and stole the old family journal that Nate translated? He called me, wanting to see the original. I wondered if he might be involved in the theft."

"The officer stopped by, but I can't believe it would have been Nate. I was out of the office, on my way to Minneapolis when it happened, so I'm not able to attest to his being in the office the entire time. We talked when I got back and he'd been in the bank all day."

"I need to know who inherits the farm. Do you know?"

"Mr. Allswede has Irene's will, I believe," Marc's voice was distant.

"It sounds to me like you need an appointment with him, not here and obviously not with me."

"I'm sorry, but if this comes to a legal battle, I don't want people to know about our relationship."

"Relationship?" he sounded dubious and raised one eyebrow. "You seem more interested in the farm than in me." When she didn't say anything, he said, "I'm going." He stood up and walked from the room.

"Marc, please don't be angry with me," she called, but the only response was the slamming of the summer kitchen door.

Amber looked around the room feeling wretched that Aunt Irene hadn't lived long enough to see everything she had done to the house. The old lady had been such a vivid presence, such a fierce determined person, it didn't seem possible she could be dead. Amber felt her spirit still residing at the farm. Claire's too, even though she hadn't been at the farm for very long. She buckled forward as grief waved across her, dark as steel blue shadows on winter snow.

UNABLE TO FALL ASLEEP THAT NIGHT, Amber picked up Nate's translation of Ina's journal, hoping things were going better for Ina than they were for her.

Summer, 1917

When I agreed to this marriage, I never thought it would be like this. We have been on the run for two weeks. Frank hardly talks to me. He is terrified that the soldiers are on our trail because he's a deserter. It's very cold, frost coats the fields in the mornings. We hide during the day, deep in the forest and travel only by night. I have to wait until Frank sleeps or hunts for food to scratch out these words.

I was looking for my journal in the bottom of the wagon when I found a package tied with rough brown twine. I was afraid to unwrap it. I kept remembering the shame that flashed across my husband's face when he said he planned to desert from the Army. Had Frank stolen something? If he was captured, I knew he would be shot by a firing squad. What would become of me and my baby then?

We came to a little river town late yesterday. I begged Frank to let us stay at an Inn. Finally, he agreed, but made me cover my hair when we walked us inside. I was able to bathe and wash the baby. Despite Frank's protests, I gave our clothes to a washerwoman. She brought them back the next morning clean and dry. The food was good. Frank ate like a starving beast.

Where are we going? How long will it take? Does the Army follow us? I fear Frank's answers and so I don't ask the questions that repeat again and again in my mind. Each evening, as the light fades and darkness approaches, Frank urges the donkey forward with a whip. I feel the creature's pain.

Setting aside the translation, Amber felt more despondent than she had ever felt in her life. She got out of bed and walked into Minna's room. She picked up the sleeping baby and carried her back to bed with her. Placing the palm of her hand on the baby's chest, feeling her heartbeat and gentle breathing, she experienced a bit of relief. Her life was about Minna now.

The dog waited patiently until his favorite humans fell asleep and then climbed very carefully into the bed and laid down next to the baby.

TWENTY-ONE

Amber drove slowly to the Lutheran Church the following morning. It was what her father had told her to do and she knew he was right. Although she dreaded planning a memorial service for Aunt Irene, a funeral marked the passage from life for everyone and helped family and friends say good-bye. Her mother's funeral had been terribly sad, but the service had helped her accept the finality of loss. She glanced into the back seat seeing Minna's eyes close as Cam snuggled against her, and managed a sad little smile.

The church was a traditional white clapboard structure with a tall spire that stood on the banks of Reservoir Lake where black-backed gulls were diving for fish. Amber lifted Minna out of the car seat, trying not to wake her. When she opened the door, Cam bounded out of the backseat and ran splashing into the lake, scattering a mother duck and her ducklings. Amber called him back, somewhat amazed when he minded, and tied his leash to a small tree in front of the sanctuary.

On the east side of the church was a small cemetery with a tippy wrought-iron fence and gate. Amber made her way quietly through the gravestones. It should have been a dismal walk, but to her surprise, she found the place lovely. The grass was long and moved in the summer wind, bending like waves across the flat gravestones. Clumps of wildflowers, white Queen Anne's lace and yellow Black Eyed Susans, lifted bright faces among the stones. She located the graves for the original two Morand brothers, Frank and Charles Morand. Charles had died in nineteen seventy, Frank in nineteen seventy-two. Their wives, Alene and Ina, were buried beside them. She reached down to touch Ina's flat memorial stone hoping her journal would be found someday. Then she searched for the grave of Irene's brothers, Paul and Charles Morand, and found them in the next row. There was an empty space where her Aunt Irene, the eldest of Ina's children, would now join her parents and brothers. The wind picked up and she looked out over the lake, seeing white-capped waves and thinking of Ina and Frank braving the Atlantic Ocean in search of a better life. A quiet sound brought her attention to a man entering the cemetery. He wore dark trousers, a black shirt and a flat white collar.

"Hello," he greeted Amber pleasantly, "I am Father Christianson. It's restful here, isn't it?"

"It is. I am Amber Bradshaw, Irene Morand's grandniece. I don't know if you were informed, but she passed away recently," She swallowed, forcing down her tears. "I want to arrange her funeral. We would like her buried near the rest of her family."

"Of course," he said calmly and gestured to the Morand graves and the one empty plot. "This is where she will be laid to rest. She was one of a kind, that little woman," he smiled. "I could never convert her to Lutheranism. She attended our church but found the simplicity of our ceremonies dismal. She asked me why I couldn't wear embroidered robes like the Orthodox priests her mother had described. She wanted us to sing the ancient chants and swing brass censers with frankincense during the services." He shook his head, smiling, remembering her.

Seeing the feisty strong-willed woman in her mind, Amber felt her eyes grow hot.

He continued saying, "I know that Miss Irene's parents baptized her in the Orthodox faith. Would you like me to see if Father Stamatakos would perform the service? He's an Orthodox priest. His church is in Minneapolis, but I could see if he's available. He's very busy, so I doubt we could have the funeral until next week."

"Thank you. That would be lovely. We will schedule the funeral when he can officiate. It will give me time to put Irene's obituary in the local paper. Please let me know the date he could conduct the service. We can discuss more details at that time."

Despite her words, it still didn't seem possible that Aunt Irene was gone. She felt if she went to the Nursing Home and opened the door to room 109, she would still see her sitting there, giving her one last test. In fact, Aunt Irene had already given her the final challenge, starting the Morand Dairy again.

When the Pastor departed, saying he needed to work on his sermon for Sunday, Amber walked into the silent church, laid her sleeping baby on a pew and knelt down. She whispered a prayer for the soul of Miss Irene Morand who fought so passionately for the Morand Dairy. She took a deep breath and whispered, "Aunt Irene, you embody the spirit of this community. I will always remember and honor you." She brushed away the wetness on her lashes.

Then she prayed a long time for her sister, remembering all the years they had spent together as children, close as two peas in a pod. When Amber broke into harsh sobs, Minna squirmed, smacked her lips and made the hand gesture for 'milk'. She wanted her bottle. It was time to go.

As they were leaving the church, Fr. Christiansen approached and asked Amber if she would like to join his congregation. Her parents had not been church-goers, except at Christmas and Easter, but Amber said if she stayed in Apple River Falls, she would consider joining.

"Would you like to have a baptism for the baby?" he asked

"Oh, yes, definitely I would," she said, surprising herself with the force of her feelings. "The baby is my niece. My sister, the baby's mother, died in an accident and I wonder if you would say a prayer for her at the end of our service for my aunt."

"Of course I will say a prayer for her. What was her name?"

"It was Claire, Claire Morand Bradshaw," Amber said, blinking back her tears. "I need to go now. I have an appointment with Aunt Irene's lawyer."

DRIVING INTO THE VILLAGE, Amber knocked on the door of the converted storefront that housed Mr. Allswede's office and asked if Cam could come in. The receptionist said he was welcome and she sat in the waiting room, holding baby Minna in her lap with Cam at her feet. Ten minutes later, Mr. Allswede came through the door and held out his hand to shake Amber's.

"You must be Amber Bradshaw," he said. "I just learned that your Aunt Irene passed away. I am so very sorry. Who's this little one?"

"My niece, Minna. She's my sister Claire's child. Claire was killed recently in a car accident." Amber swallowed and brushed away tears. "And this is disobedient fur ball is Camelot," she said, touching him with her toe.

"I'm so sorry for both your losses, Amber. You've had an awful lot to deal with recently. Come on in, all three of you. I want to tell you about Irene Morand's Last Will and Testament."

Amber took a deep breath knowing whatever she learned in the next few moments would be important for the rest of her life.

"Years ago the executor of a person's will gathered the entire group of beneficiaries together to hear the dispositions of the deceased. Nowadays, this is seldom done and isn't necessary. The modern way is to send all the beneficiaries a letter. However, I believe it is better to tell people in person. What I'm sharing with you today is the Last Will and Testament of Miss Irene Morand. Miss Irene revised her will only a week ago in my presence. She named only one beneficiary, Amber. She left her entire estate and all her property to you," Mr. Allswede beamed.

Amber's touched her parted lips with her fingers and swallowed.

"You already owned the house, as you know, but you now own the entire acreage, in addition to the barns and farming equipment. She also asked that I give you the key to her apartment above the carriage house. Here it is." Mr. Allswede held the key out.

"I'm stunned, Mr. Allswede," Amber said in a tear-choked voice.

"As you are now both an heiress and a landowner, you have some decisions to make. The most urgent is to decide what you want to do about the sale of the land to Framingham."

Amber took a deep breath. "I appreciate Aunt Irene's generosity more than you can possibly know, Mr. Allswede, but I need some time to think about this." She felt the muscles in her neck and upper back tensing up.

"There is a Codicil to the Will that includes some instructions about the farm. If you decide to keep it, and that was what Irene hoped, the sharecropping is to be managed by Mr. Curtis Lundgren who owns the neighboring farm. She made provision for payment to Mr. Lundgren to come out of the income from the crops. If you decide to re-establish the dairy, Irene wanted it managed by Mr. Freedman. However, she said that since Mr. Freedman is in his late 60's, he wouldn't be able to manage the dairy alone for long. She urged you to try to get his son Hunter's help. All the profit from both operations would go to you."

"Did Aunt Irene leave any other messages for me?"

"She left a hand-written note that I was to give you, if you decide to keep the farm. And one more thing, Irene's nurse found her hand-written notebook and brought it to me for you." He handed her the notebook.

"What do you think we should do about Framingham? Aunt Irene wanted me to re-start the Morand Dairy, but it would be a life-changing commitment."

"Would you like me to write and inform Framingham that you are the new owner of the property and we need two weeks to consider our options? It would give you a little time to decide."

"Yes, please do that."

"There's one other thing I wanted to say, Amber. It's your business, of course, but I'm hoping you will stay here and keep the farm. In the last decade, I have had the sad duty of handling the legalities of foreclosing on many small family farms. Agribusinesses have purchased most of the land around here and it's been a tragedy for families. Selling to companies like Framingham is like feeding a voracious cancer. Once they take one farm, other people give up and sell their farms. Even years later, people will come to me to see if there is a way they could buy back the family farm. The Morands were pioneers in the dairy business and were the standard-bearers here for a century. If you sell to Framingham, it will cause a cascade and many other farms will fall." He paused, looked at her intently.

Amber felt a lump in her throat but could only nod.

"My parents once owned a farm. Selling the property took away my father's will to live. He died just a month later. My mother is in her eighties now and a day doesn't go by when she doesn't call me in tears, remembering our farm and wishing we had never sold up. One last thing before you go, Amber. What are your plans for the baby?" He looked at her inquiringly.

"What do you mean?"

"About the legal issues, guardianship, for instance. Did your sister leave a will stating who she wanted to raise the baby in case of her death?"

"No. She didn't," she said, feeling a qualm.

"In that case, you can petition the court to adopt her yourself, give her up for adoption, or contact the child's father. I'm sure you realize that fathers always have legal rights to their children." Amber was silent. She remembered Minna's father's name on the birth certificate. At some future date, she knew she had a responsibility to find him. "If you want to keep the baby, it would be a huge responsibility. You are a young woman, Amber. I wonder if you are ready for the challenge of being a single parent."

As do I, Amber thought, looking down at Minna in her lap and feeling the weight of her decisions on the life of the little one.

AFTER TUCKING BABY MINNA INTO BED that night, Amber again reached for Nate's translation of Ina's journal.

Autumn, 1917

I woke up in the vegetable cart at dawn. I was alone except for little Irene who manages somehow to sleep peacefully, even in this dirty wagon. I sat up and looked around. I didn't see Frank. I suddenly feared he had abandoned us. I felt a violent rage in my chest as if my heart had been split in two. If he had run away, I would track him down and kill him.

Then I heard the lowing of cattle and the farmer's dog barking, bringing the cows into the barn for the morning milking. I crept from the wagon. Grabbing a dark blanket to cover my white nightgown, I ran, hiding behind trees and bushes, to the edge of the farmer's field. One cow was standing at the edge of the forest. She seemed trapped, bawling and unable to catch up with the rest. A dark shadow was hunched at her feet. When he stood up, I could see it was Frank. He had been milking her.

I started back for the wagon, praying God would forgive me for my murderous heart. By the time Frank returned, with warm milk for our baby, I pretended to be asleep. Irene gulped down the nourishment avidly, poor baby. She was starving but she hardly ever cries. I opened my eyes to see my husband's face. My breath came in ragged shreds. His beautiful smile shone white in the early light of dawn. He had thought of a way to feed our child. I was grateful for the milk and managed a watery smile in return.

TWENTY-TWO

A MBER WAS GIVING MINNA HER CEREAL when the phone rang the following morning. The baby kept grinning at the sight of the spoon, but when the spoon reached her mouth, she would shake her head, often making cereal fly—landing frequently on Camelot. He was getting good at licking most of it off. It's an awfully messy business, this parenting stuff, she thought. Tears pricked her eyes, thinking of all that Claire would miss in Minna's life and how profoundly she would always miss her sister. When the bowl of cereal was empty, Minna held her hands down for the dog and Camelot licked them clean. Not terribly sanitary, she thought, but babies and puppies always make me smile.

The phone rang. She glanced at the phone recognizing Mrs. Miller's number and pushed the call-back button.

"Hi, Mrs. Miller, I mean, Joanna."

"Hi Amber. I just can't stop thinking about your sister," Joanna said. "I spent a lot of time with her when she was in high school. She and my son were good friends and they often hung out in my kitchen doing homework. When I called and told him she was gone, he took it very hard. I don't think he has been that upset since his father died. I never realized how close they were. He said he was quitting the band and coming home."

"Dad said there was a Michigan map on the passenger seat of Claire's car. Was there any area circled? Anything that would tell us where she went?"

"All we know is that when the accident happened, she was in southern Michigan. Whatever she had to do after she left your father in the hospital, she had done it and was on her way back. Claire was keeping her promise. She was returning to you and the baby."

Amber felt tears sting her eyes. "That makes me feel better," she said, deeply moved.

"She left you a huge obligation in Minna, Amber. Do you know what you are going to do?"

"The attorney said there were several options for the baby other than me raising her. He said I could give her up for adoption, which I couldn't do, or contact the baby's father. Claire put his name on the birth certificate, but I didn't recognize the name and have no way to contact him. I also wondered whether Dad would like to have Minna live with him. If he had a nanny, do you think it would work? I thought Claire's baby might help him through his grief."

"I'm afraid your father wouldn't be up to an infant, Amber, even with a full-time nanny. He's in his sixties now and has just gone through one knee replacement and has to have the other knee done. I'm not your mom, Amber, but I have known you since you and Claire were little children. I'm sure you know that Officer O'Brien was transferred to another post and Mary O'Brien asked me to keep an eye on the two of you. She hated leaving you girls."

"I know," Amber said softly, remembering Mrs. O'Brien's kindness the day she told her about the blood she saw on her fingers as she lay in the grass beside the lake.

It was the evening of the day their father entered treatment for his alcoholism before she told Mrs. O'Brien about the blood between her legs. Mrs. O'Brien got them an appointment to see the doctor the next day. It was an excruciatingly embarrassing examination, but afterwards the doctor said, "It's only her period," and Mrs. O'Brien nodded, saying she would handle it from there.

"It's a bit early, but perfectly normal," Mrs. O'Brien said when they were driving back home. "The bleeding means you are a grown woman now. It means that you are old enough to get pregnant and become a mother. In my grandmother's day it was called 'the curse' because you often feel a bit blue and down before the bleeding starts. Nowadays girls call it their period. The bleeding happens once a month and lasts several days. We will go to the drug store and I'll get you some supplies."

Amber tried not to think of it as a curse, but every month when her period started, she knew it was her penance for the selfish decision she made that could have cost Claire her life.

It hadn't though, Amber reminded herself. Claire lived long enough to bring Minna into the world. She had a moment of feeling better. Her sister's death had been a dreadful loss, but had given her a second chance, a chance to do things right for Minna.

"In all those years, I never once heard you ask for anything for yourself," Joanna continued. "You got excellent grades in school, never smoked or drank, you didn't even *date* until Claire graduated from high school. You ask me what I think you should do about Minna. I think you owe it to yourself to spend some time figuring out what you want."

Amber took a deep breath. "Thank you, Joanna. It's hard for me to talk about even now, but I need to confess something. I don't know if Dad told you, but after Mom died, there was one spring day when I forgot to get Claire after school. Instead, I went to the little lake by our house and went swimming. Claire was only in Kindergarten and when I didn't show up, she started to walk home by herself and got lost. It was the middle of the night before we found her," Amber couldn't continue. Tears were streaming down her face.

"My goodness, Amber, how old were you, twelve? You were just a kid. If you still feel guilty about this, you need to stop. It was ages ago."

"But Claire broke her arm, she could have been abducted, she could have died!"

"Lots of kids break bones," Joanna said calmly. "My son broke his hand falling off his bike. And Claire wasn't kidnapped, she didn't die. In fact, I doubt she even remembers much about that night. Your father has the greater guilt—although he's now been sober for over a decade. I don't know if you know, but he joined AA after rehab and completed their twelve step program. He said the hardest step was making amends to you and Claire. Forgetting to pick up your sister after school was pretty small potatoes in comparison to that."

"Thank you," Amber said. She felt moved beyond tears.

"If you do decide to be Minna's mother, you must do it because it's right for you, not because you feel you owe it to Claire. You are clearly your own worst enemy, Girl. Promise me you will get past this." She paused. "Changing the subject, did you get the funeral set up for Aunt Irene?"

"I did. It's the day after tomorrow. I asked Pastor Christianson to say a prayer for Claire at the end of Aunt Irene's service."

"That's a lovely idea. Did it occur to you that people will expect a wake after the funeral?"

"They will? Coming to the house you mean? I have nothing to feed anyone. Are you sure about this?"

"Yes, I'm sure."

"I could really use some help," she said sighing.

"Now that's what I'm talking about! Asking for help is a good thing, practically unprecedented," Mrs. Miller said and Amber could almost see her smile. "I can't do much to help from nine hours away, but I'll get the name of the grocery store in Apple River Falls and order food from the deli. I'm sure they can deliver it to the farm. Can you get someone to come to the house and bring the food inside while you're at the funeral? Maybe your contractor's wife? Your dad tells me you two have become friends."

"That's a good idea. Thank you," Amber said. After saying good-bye, she glanced at herself in the mirror. Her hair was a mess, decorated with baby cereal. Joanna Miller told her to ask for help when she needed it. Picking up the phone, she dialed Megan's number.

"Hi Megan. My Aunt Irene's funeral is at ten tomorrow morning and Mrs. Miller, my father's girlfriend, is going to order food to be delivered here after the service. Could you get one of your baby-sitting minions to come to the house during the ceremony and set out the food? I was thinking about Lizzy."

"I'll see what I can do, Amber. Don't worry about it. We'll manage. Do you want to leave Minna with me when you go to the funeral? Might be easier."

"You are my hero, Megan Amherst," Amber told her and said good-bye. She walked out to the garden and picked a single blue gentian blossom. Blue had been Aunt Irene's favorite color. She would place the flower in her coffin and wear her boots to the funeral. She smiled at the memory of Aunt Irene's hoot of laughter about their unsuitability on the farm.

TWENTY-THREE

WHEN AMBER ARRIVED AT THE LUTHERAN CHURCH, Fr. Christianson introduced her to the Reverend Father Stamatakos. They had talked on the phone the previous week and made decisions about the type of service she thought appropriate. Amber thanked him for his help and gave him an envelope with the customary gratuity. The priest was garbed in heavily embroidered vestments. He wore a long red robe and over it a shorter red and gold cape. The cape came to his waist in front. In the back, the cape was longer, dipping in a graceful curve. Both garments had gold banding and intricate floral stitchery. He wore a high rounded hat. Two assistant clergymen had come with him to chant the hymns and disburse the incense in the air. It would be the kind of service Aunt Irene had always wanted.

"We commonly meet the family with the casket outside the church and escort the deceased into the nave together," Fr. Stamatakos told her. "Our tradition is to have an open casket during the funeral service to acknowledge the reality of death and allow time for the farewell kiss."

"What is the farewell kiss?"

"The casket is placed parallel to the rows of pews so the family may approach to pay their last respects. Family and close friends walk by the casket in silent prayer and kiss the deceased's forehead."

"I don't think my congregants will be comfortable kissing Irene's forehead," Pastor Christianson said, frowning. "It is not part of our service."

"It is the duty of the family," Fr. Stamatakos said. "But all others may decline."

Amber remembered kissing Aunt Irene's forehead at the nursing home when she was alive but felt a chill at the thought of touching her lips to Irene's face now. It would make her death feel irreversible, absolute.

"Since I am the last member of her family, does this fall to me?" Amber asked in a quavery voice.

"It does, child," Fr. Stamatakos said, "But if you wish, you may kiss the air above her face."

"Then I will do that. I brought Aunt Irene a blue flower and some four-leafed clovers. May I put them in the coffin beside her?"

"Of course. After everyone has walked by the deceased, I will conduct the service and the worshippers are encouraged to join in the singing of the hymns and responses. After the hymns, I will offer a brief homily on Christ's teachings on life, death and eternity."

"Do you usually talk about the life of the person who died?"

"Yes, I will incorporate important aspects of Irene Morand's life in my remarks. Father Christianson told me she came here as an infant with her parents from Romania, fleeing the Germans. The family rose to prominence due to their hard work at the Morand Dairy. I will mention her brothers, Paul and Charles, and pray that she will soon join them and her valiant parents."

"I would like to say a few things about Aunt Irene if I could?" Fr. Stamatakos nodded, saying he would invite others to speak about her as well.

"Could the organist play Amazing Grace at that point?" Amber asked. She knew the hymn was not used in Orthodox ceremonies, but had spoken with the organist who was prepared to play it, if Fr. Stamatakos thought it fitting.

"Since her husband and rest of the family attended the Lutheran Church that seems appropriate," he replied.

"I don't know if you knew, but Amazing Grace was written by Sabine Baring-Gould. He was Captain of a slave ship who brought African Americans to the U.S at the time of the Civil War. He later found God and wrote the music as repentance for the years he captained a slave ship," Fr. Christianson said.

"I didn't know that history. Thank you," Fr. Stamatakos said. "After the hymn, I will seal the body with oil and sand and close the casket. When Pastor Christianson and I escort the deceased out of the church to the cemetery, you should go to the front door to receive condolences. I understand we will be saying a prayer for your sister Claire at the end of the ceremony. I'm sorry for both your losses." Fr. Stamatakos' eyes were kind.

The organist began to play Raindrop Prelude by Chopin, a piece Amber asked her to play prior to the ceremony. The light harp notes brought Amber to tears.

When the funeral van drew up to the church, Irene Morand's casket was taken from the van and placed on a rolling steel cart. Fr. Stamatakos escorted the body inside to the sound of ancient Greek chanting. Amber walked despondently behind them, her head down.

"Take my arm," a man's voice said and she looked up to see Marc Rochet beside her. She smiled gratefully and they entered the sanctuary together. She wondered if they would be the only two people to attend the service, but as they walked down the aisle toward the pulpit she glanced right and left. Every pew was full. She recognized Mr. Allswede, Mrs. Worth, the receptionist at the Nursing Home, Emma, Aunt Irene's nurse, Ryan Amherst and several of his crew. Many of the clerks from Latimer's Lumber Yard were also in attendance. Her eyes watered, thinking of all these people who had set aside their own lives this day to bid farewell to Irene Morand. She looked for Hunter, but didn't see him.

When Fr. Stamatakos asked her to come forward to make her remarks, Amber was shaking. She tried to calm herself as she ascended the podium, wanting to deliver her final tribute without breaking down. She looked out at the congregation, cleared her throat, straightened her shoulders and began. "I had a Great Aunt Irene. Today we bid her farewell. All of you knew her well, but I never really knew her before I moved here. On the day I came to Apple River Falls, she called me a nincompoop for wearing high-heeled boots. She said, and I quote, 'the Twit won't last a week.'" Several people in the congregation smiled and someone chuckled. "I wore those boots again today in her honor. My Aunt Irene Morand, was one of a kind—brave, hard-working, smart and strong. I will never forget her tart comments and ability to get to the heart of the matter. For those of you who don't know, I also lost my sister in an accident a few days ago." She stopped speaking as tears threatened and cleared her throat. "As we say our final prayers today for my Aunt Irene, please also pray for my sister. Her name was Claire Morand Bradshaw. She was only twenty and the mother of a baby daughter." She glanced at all the sympathetic faces, forced herself not to cry and continued. "Claire was not religious, but I found a short poem by Mary Elizabeth Fry that fits how I feel about her." She opened the book of poetry and began to read.

"Do not stand at my grave and weep. I am not there. I do not sleep.
I am a thousand winds that blow. I am the diamond glints on snow.
I am the sunlight on ripened grain. I am the gentle autumn rain.
When you awaken in the morning's hush, I am the swift uplifting rush
of quiet birds in circled flight. I am the soft stars that shine at night.
Do not stand at my grave and cry; I am not there. I did not die."

"Despite only knowing me for a short time, Aunt Irene left the Morand farm to me. By changing her will, she has changed my life. Before we met, Aunt Irene arranged for the farm to be sold, but something made her think I might be able to continue her legacy. It was my Aunt's final wish that I keep the farm and re-establish the Morand Dairy. If that's what I decide to do, on the day the dairy opens I will have a Grand Opening Party, and I hope you will all come." Amber's eyelids felt hot and her chest ached. Her lips trembled. "When we bring the Morand cows into the barn for milking, Aunt Irene will see through my eyes that her legacy continues."

Amber turned away to hide her tears, re-adjusted her shawl and stepped down from the podium. She nearly stumbled and Marc came forward, put his arm around her waist, escorting her to the pew. Fr. Stamatakos asked if anyone else would like to say a few words. Several people came forward. They talked about how Irene kept the dairy running for close to fifty years after her brothers died. They talked about her delicious strawberry jam. They spoke of her quirky sense of humor and how dedicated to the cows and the dairy she was. One elderly woman said Irene told her she kept the Morand Dairy operational so long to honor her parents who had homesteaded the land. Then Pastor Christianson resumed his place at the pulpit.

"Let us pray," he said and Amber closed her eyes. "Today we say farewell to two women, Irene Morand, and Amber's sister, Claire Morand Bradshaw. Through prayer we ask God to have mercy on their souls and recognize our losses at their departure. We are comforted by knowing they are both in the hands of God now. Let us spend a few moments in silent prayer to honor both Irene and Claire."

When the organist began to play "Amazing Grace," Amber and Marc Rochet walked back down the aisle together to the front entrance to the church. Fr. Christianson joined them, introducing Amber to each person as they came by. She invited everyone to come out to the Morand farm after the service for the wake.

Driving alone through Apple River Falls on her way back to the farm, Amber was stunned to see the streets lined with people. Young boys had turned off their lawn mowers to stand on the sidewalks. Women ran out of their houses still wearing their aprons to join others standing by the road. Men and boys removed their hats. It was a final tribute to Aunt Irene and all the years the Morands had lived and worked in this town. She was moved beyond tears.

TWENTY-FOUR

Tʜᴇ ᴡʜᴏʟᴇ ʟᴇɴɢᴛʜ ᴏꜰ ᴛʜᴇ ᴅʀɪᴠᴇ from the barn to the house was filled with cars when Amber arrived back at the farm. She parked by the milking shed, just as Hunter walked outside with Cam.

"Hi Amber," he touched her shoulder gently.

"Why weren't you at the funeral, Hunter?" she asked, feeling confused and angry.

He swallowed and brushed his face with his hands. "I spent the time remembering all the times Miss Irene worked here. I can still see that fierce little woman prodding the cows and telling them to move along. But the truth is," he hesitated and looked down, "I was afraid I would break down. After my mother died, Aunt Irene took over raising me. Irene's passing brought back my mother's death. Now both of them are gone and I will miss those two fine women forever." His eyes filled with tears and he turned away abruptly.

Amber reached out and took Hunter's hand. "I'm sorry, Hunter. I should have realized how devastating this would be for you. Please come up to the house now and join us. Can you?" she asked and he nodded. She walked quickly up the drive, a bit unsteady in her high-heeled boots.

Sliding open the door to the summer kitchen, she walked into the dining room. More than thirty people were there, talking quietly. The table was piled high with food. Every single one of Lillian Morand's pink and silver dishes were displayed on an old Irish linen tablecloth. Someone had created a floral arrangement of pink peonies and white iris with fronds of silver Artemisia. The flowers matched the colors of the lovely old china. Megan and Lizzie were standing by the table.

"Megan, did you do all this? It looks so welcoming."

"No, it wasn't me. I just got here. Someone else set out all the food, the dishes and the chairs."

"Goodness, who was it?"

"It was me," Joanna Miller said. Amber whirled around in surprise as Joanna held out her arms and hugged her tightly.

"I can't believe you're here. Thank you so much," Amber said. "I'm sorry you missed the service for Aunt Irene and the prayers for Claire."

"Everyone has expressed their condolences about your Aunt Irene. Some of them remembered Claire too, and your visits as little girls."

"Have you met the baby yet?"

"I am smitten," Joanna said. "Totally smitten. Seeing the baby eased a lot of my grief about your sister. I gave Minna her bottle but with all the commotion, she was fading. I put her in her crib for a nap."

"There's someone here I'd like you to meet," Amber said. She had spotted Marc and waved him over. "Marc, this is our neighbor and my father's dear friend, Mrs. Joanna Miller."

"Mrs. Miller, it's a pleasure," he said. "I understand you knew Amber's sister. I'm very sorry for your loss." He caught Amber's eyes saying, "I'm sorry, Amber, but I have to leave. Something has come up about my assistant at the bank. He seems to be missing."

"Nate?" she asked, frowning. "I wondered why he wasn't at the church."

"He hasn't show up at work for over a week now and left no message. This is very atypical behavior. I wondered if he'd been in an accident, or was is ill. I am going over to his apartment to check on him."

As THE SUN WENT DOWN, people began to wander out on the lawn. Megan, Lizzie and Mrs. Miller had set out every lawn chair they could find or commandeer from neighboring farms. Conversation flowed between small groups of neighbors and friends. Hunter walked around the lawn with Cam by his side greeting everyone. He seemed to have regained control over his emotions and listened attentively to people sharing wonderful anecdotes of the original family and memories of Irene. Minna woke up and Amber heard her talking on the monitor. She got her up and carried her outside, making sure everyone met the baby. Many people remembered Amber's mother, Grace, visiting the farm and Amber and Claire as young children.

Later, Ryan and Megan walked from group to group, offering bowls of ice cream covered with fresh raspberries. Little Connery and the other children ran around shrieking and chasing each other. As the sun went down, fireflies began to appear and disappear, tiny lanterns blinking above the grass, dancing to unsung music. When a slim crescent moon rose in the purple sky, the fields turned to dusk. It was almost midnight by the time the last car left the driveway.

While Amber and Mrs. Miller cleaned up the kitchen, they talked briefly about the missing treasure as well as the icon Irene had written about in her notebook. Amber wondered if the icon had been lost or was still hidden somewhere in the house. They agreed to look for it together the following day. They didn't say much else, both filled with gratitude for the compassion of everyone who came to bid Irene and Claire farewell.

Walking upstairs to her bedroom, Amber washed her face, stripped off her clothes and climbed into the white spool bed. She pulled the quilt, soft with a century of washings, up to her chin. Listening to the wind brush the leaves of the cottonwood trees, Amber reached for Ina's journal, knowing her journey to America was beginning, just as Aunt Irene's had ended.

Autumn, 1917

Today I saw the Black Sea. It is endless. I cannot see the shore on the other side of the wide water. Seeing white-capped waves, I remembered my father teaching me about maps. He said if you had one, you would always know where you were going. There were some words on his oldest map in Greek that said, 'Beyond here, there be monsters.' Were there sea monsters in the Black Sea?

The wooden boat rides the waves up and down as if it were a cart. When it comes down between the waves, it slaps the water hard and makes a crashing noise. I have vomited several times over the side. I haven't been able to keep anything down since we left the inn on the edge of the Sea. I'm afraid I'm pregnant again, although I see men who throw up also. Perhaps it is only the sea and the endless waves that cause nausea.

Baby Irene has only gruel to eat. I asked the boat captain for food for her and where we were going. He speaks another language. I couldn't understand him, but he gave me some goat's milk for the baby.

There is one little cabin below decks. It has four beds, but they are small and stuffed with hay. Ten people must sleep in that room. The first night when Frank reached to pull me under him, I fought him off. At least among all these people, he couldn't force me. The one thing I would deny him was my body. I won't write again until we are off this wretched boat. I was an idiot to have married Frank.

WAKING UP THE MORNING AFTER THE FUNERAL Amber remembered Ina's journal entries about being pregnant and Irene's birth. She hadn't been ready to become a mother, but when she held baby Irene in her arms, she felt a stab of love so strong it made her weep. Listening to Minna's little morning noises coming from the next bedroom, Amber felt tears wet her eyes.

She got out of bed, walked into the bedroom and lifted the baby out of her crib. Holding Minna's little body, she felt the baby's heart beat against hers. At that moment, every last vestige of reluctance she felt about keeping the baby evaporated and her doubts poured out like water. This time she was ready. Minna Grace Morand would belong to her for life.

"I hereby vow, Minna, that you and I are going to be together always," Amber said looking deep into the baby's gray green eyes. Minna gave her a dimpled drooling chortle in return. Amber kissed her. Raising Minna would be her farewell gift to Claire. As Amber made the commitment, she was was surprised to feel sudden stab of joy accompanied by a profound emotional release. The guilt that had dogged her for so long was leaving. In loving Minna, she was forgiving herself.

After feeding the baby her breakfast, Amber and Joanna played with Minna who was crawling everywhere, mostly in pursuit of Cam. The beleaguered dog kept giving Amber despairing glances. At one point, the baby managed to climb on the dog's back, using his long fur. Cam made a low rumbling sound in his chest and Amber picked Minna up, holding her high in the air. The baby shrieked in glee.

"Oh dear, another one who is going to want to fly off the roof like Peter Pan," Mrs. Miller said and Amber smiled remembering Claire who had always wanted to grow wings. She had once fallen off the garage roof in her attempts to master flight.

"How long can you stay, Joanna?" Amber asked.

"I'm going to have to get on the road soon. I can't leave your Dad alone too long. He's really suffering from the loss of Claire and of course walking is difficult."

"Since we only have a short time together, let's search for the icon, shall we?"

"What exactly are we looking for?" Joanna asked.

"Icons are religious paintings, usually of Mary and baby Jesus, often painted on wood. They date back to the very early days of Christianity. Aunt Irene told me her mother, Ina, brought an icon from the old country to the farm. I am hoping it's in the attic."

THE SECOND-FLOOR ATTIC HAD A LIGHT FIXTURE on the ceiling with a single bulb. Amber pulled the string cord to switch it on. The attic was dusty and filled with cobwebs in the corners, but the window to the west brought light into the room and a view of the dairy barn. Under the window was a trunk with a rounded top. When Amber opened it, a faint scent of lavender pervaded the air. Inside lay a fragile embroidered wedding dress. She lifted it out carefully, seeing the tiny hand-stitching and beautiful embroidery Ina Morand had done for Irene's bridal gown.

"This is Aunt Irene's wedding gown," Amber told Joanna. "She was engaged to the great great grandfather of the Lundgren family. They still live just down the road. They never married because he died tragically, buried in a silo during threshing."

"Farm accidents happen all too often," Joanna said, a grave sadness clouding her face.

They gazed at the fragile dress with its long sleeves made of veiling and an intricate lace bodice. Careful not to damage it, Amber laid it gently back in the chest and covered it with tissue paper. Looking around the space, she saw a small chest of drawers that would be perfect for Minna's clothes and toys. The rest of the attic was dusty, with spider webs hanging from the ceiling joists, but completely empty.

Having coffee in the kitchen afterwards Amber said, "It's discouraging that we didn't find the Icon or the family treasure."

"Your father told me about the treasure. He thinks whatever money the old people brought here was probably spent on the land, homes and barns. He said you believe some of it still exists."

"I have doubts, of course, especially since Ryan has already torn off all the paneling and drywall in the house and found nothing, but my mother believed it was here and so I continue to look. It was her last request that I find the treasure."

"Have you cleaned out your Aunt Irene's apartment above the carriage house yet? Maybe she hid the icon there, or even the family treasure."

"I've started. But I certainly didn't find anything remotely like a treasure."

"Still, you have the translation of Ina's journal which is a treasure of another kind." Joanna smiled.

"It certainly is. I recently read the parts about Irene's birth and the profound love Ina felt for her immediately. It made me feel a bond with Ina, as if I have inherited her hopes and dreams," Amber said. "Ina's love for baby Irene was as strong as mine for baby Minna."

"The dreams of those old people are the reasons your mother never wanted to sell the farmhouse," Joanna said. "I just remembered something else your mother once told me. There's another attic in this house, above the summer kitchen. Maybe the icon is up there. You can check it out sometime, but I need to start getting my things together. Come with me, will you?" They went downstairs to the main floor bedroom and Amber sat on the bed while Joanna gathered her belongings.

"We should talk more about Minna, Amber. She's adorable, and you have no idea how amazingly easy a baby she is. How are you feeling by now about this responsibility?" Joanna looked inquisitively at Amber.

Amber took a deep breath. "You told me to take my time and I appreciated your advice, but I've made my decision. This morning when I got her out of bed, I knew. All my misgivings, all my mixed feelings about my mother leaving me too soon and having to raise my sister when I was very young myself vanished. I'm committed to Minna forever."

"I knew that would be your decision," Joanna smiled. "You never disappoint. Just promise me you will stop feeling all that old guilt, will you?"

"I will. In fact, I've already begun," she said and they smiled at each other.

When Joanna left the farm an hour later, Amber waved good-bye with a lump in her throat.

TWENTY-FIVE

A MBER HEARD THE SOUND OF A TRUCK pulling into her driveway that evening, just as she gave the baby a last spoonful of cereal. Lifting Minna out of her high chair, Amber walked into the summer kitchen and looked outside. The lettering on the side of the delivery truck read "Hillside Gallery." The art had arrived—it was a spirit-lifting surprise. She wondered who her boss at the gallery would have assigned to drive it all the way from Chicago to Apple River Falls. When Amber opened the screen door, she heard a familiar voice call, "Amber Bradshaw."

"Cassidy," Amber screamed ecstatically. Her best friend jumped from the truck and ran toward her, stopping when she saw the baby.

"I don't want to squish this little doll. Let me see her," she said and Amber with all the pride of young motherhood held the baby up for Cassidy's inspection. "She's just precious. I'm sorry for the loss of your sister, Amber. I remember Claire well, of course and I will miss her, too."

Cam dashed out of a clump of shrubs, coming to a sudden dusty stop at Cassidy's feet. He jumped up and down in joy as she knelt to greet him. "My goodness, Amber, he has grown so much," Cassidy said. "He was a quarter of this size when you got him. He still remembers me," she said, fondly.

"How did you manage to convince the boss to let you drive the art up here?"

"I practically had to promise him my first-born, but decided to promise this little one instead," Cassidy said wrinkling her nose and grinning. At Amber's shocked look, she said, "Just kidding. When I told him about the basement incident, he said I better come up here and check on you."

"I can't tell you how happy I am that you are here."

"You have had such an awful time lately. How are you holding up?" Cassidy asked.

"Much better now that you are here. You have no idea how much seeing you means to me. Let's put Minna down for the night and get the art out of the truck. I can hardly wait."

"I am dying to see everything you've done with the house," Cassidy said. "It looked like a picture postcard when I drove up. I love those climbing white roses and purple clematis on the porch columns."

After putting Minna to bed, the women walked through the washroom located between the upstairs bedrooms.

"This is my dream bathroom, Amber. I love the Carrera marble on the floor and the vanity with the sink. It looks like you made it from an old chest of drawers."

"Actually my contractor, Ryan, did. Come look at my bedroom."

"I remember the white spool bed from the photo you sent. And this quilt is heirloom quality. Is the whole place really yours?" Cassidy asked.

"Not just the house, I own the entire farm now. My Aunt Irene willed it to me."

"I'm sorry about her passing away, Amber. I know you had gotten very fond of her."

"I had, thank you. Her last wish was that I re-establish the Morand Dairy. The Morands had one here for nearly a hundred years. Once Aunt Irene got too old to manage the dairy, she decided to sell the farm, but after I appeared, she chose to give it to me instead."

"Well, the house is fabulous. You can keep this place as a summer home after you sell the farm and come back to Chicago." Noticing at the clouds on Amber's face Cassidy added, "Tell me you aren't actually thinking of living here full time, are you?"

"I'm having a hard time deciding what to do," Amber admitted.

"I can't imagine you really want to live your life way out here in the country. Don't you miss restaurants, art galleries, shopping?"

"Sometimes I do, but I guess I could drive to Minneapolis if I needed a dose of city life. Minneapolis is the closest big city to the farm since we're located just east of the border between Wisconsin and Minnesota. Other than the last three years living in the city, I've always lived out in the country. My parents' place is on five acres, you know."

"Yes, but your father doesn't live on a working farm, Amber."

"It's not as if there aren't amenities locally," Amber said, defensively.

"Apple River Falls has churches, good schools, a grocery store and a nice library. Minna already has a doctor here and I have made some good friends."

"What about restaurants, Amber? You don't even know how to cook."

"So far I'm having lots of frozen dinners and sandwiches, but with a small baby fine dining isn't an option anyway. And I've surprised myself with how often I feel at peace here."

"It's true that you were always the one who wanted to leave bars early when we went out clubbing. You never enjoyed the singles scene. Come to think of it, you even met Brock when he came into the gallery, not at a bar," Cassidy said with a thoughtful look on her face.

The girls unloaded the paintings from the van, carrying them into the living and dining rooms. Cassidy had brought hammers, hanging wires, grommets and a level. Amber grabbed a step stool. Together they hung all the pieces.

"Cassidy, you are a framing artist. They are straight-up awesome. The Paul Ransom piece is brilliant. I love the Audubon birds above that cherry sideboard in the dining room. I can't believe you found the Eugene Iverd. Wait. My goodness, is that the original?"

"I wondered when you would notice. Yes, I actually managed to acquire the original of the "Two Masters." I hope you aren't going to be mad at me, but I called your father. He said he would purchase it because of all you were going through, and when Kurt heard about you being locked in the basement by some psycho, he was happy to handle the negotiation with the former owners."

"My father is so generous. I'll call him later to tell her how pleased I am. Please thank Kurt for me too. I am absolutely thrilled." Amber hugged Cassidy. "Did you manage to get the other pieces and frame them for my puny art budget?"

"I went over a bit but don't worry, I took it out of the petty cash fund at the gallery."

"I hope you don't get in trouble for that, Cassidy."

"If I do, I guess I'll have to give Kurt a kiss," Cassidy giggled.

"Cassidy, you wouldn't!"

"Of course not, Noodlehead," she shook her head grinning. "I couldn't stop thinking on the drive up here about you being locked in the basement. Do the police have any suspects?"

"There were four sets of fingerprints on the trap door, mine, my contractor's, the carpenter's and one unknown. Since those fingerprints aren't in the database, the person who did it doesn't have a criminal record. Did you remember that Ina's journal was stolen?"

"Yes, has it reappeared?"

"No, it's still missing, but luckily I had it translated before the theft, so I can still read it. On another note, it's July 4th tomorrow and they are having fireworks in town. I've been so depressed by the loss of Claire and Aunt Irene that I wasn't going to go, but now that you're here, I want to take you to a real country Fourth of July celebration. Marc Rochet will probably be there. We've gone out a couple of times. I'd like you to meet him, just to see what you think. And Hunter might be there too."

"Is Hunter the guy you said you were attracted to?" Cassidy asked and Amber nodded. "I can't believe you've managed to find two men all the way up here, you lucky duck," Cassidy said and grinned.

"One of these days we are both going find Mr. Right," Amber said.

"Oh, I think you've know who it is already, you just need to put on your big girl panties and tell him his fate," Cassidy said, laughing.

"You always make me smile," Amber said, feeing deeply grateful for her dearest friend.

TWENTY-SIX

AMBER AND CASSIDY LEFT THE HOUSE AFTER DINNER. They carried the baby and had Camelot in tow. Amber wore a bright turquoise blouse with jeans. Cassidy wore black leggings, a purple blouse and silver jewelry. They stopped briefly at the barn and Amber introduced Cassidy to Hunter.

"That is one hot guy," Cassidy said as they drove off.

"I like him a lot, Cass, but I'm afraid it's all one way. I kissed him once but I could feel him pulling back. He hasn't asked me out or hugged me or anything since. And I'm never going to put myself into a one-sided relationship like I had with my old boyfriend, Brock, again."

"I'm surprised Hunter isn't more interested," Cassidy said thoughtfully.

"Maybe I'm not his type. I didn't think he was my type at first, but I was attracted to him right away."

"He's drawn to you too, Amber. I saw it in his eyes when he saw you. Why do you think he hasn't pursued a relationship?"

"I think it might have something to do with him never realizing his dreams of being an artist or maybe it's his father who keeps him here. Did you remember that it was Hunter who saved me from being locked in the basement? He slept on my couch every night for over a week in case I was frightened. Sometimes in the mornings I would come down to find little sketches he had done. He's good, Cassidy, really good. He went away to art school when he was seventeen, but until I saw his work I didn't realize how talented he is."

"Well, the man is downright gorgeous."

"He's just my best friend," Amber said and Cassidy glared at her. "Sorry. I meant to say Hunter is my best friend at the *farm*. You are my BFF."

"HI MEGAN," AMBER CALLED THROUGH THE SCREEN DOOR when they arrived at the Amherst household.

"Come on in," Megan called from the kitchen.

Connery dashed around the corner to see who was visiting.

"Slow down, kid," Ryan said as Amber and Cassidy walked into the room. He grabbed Connery by the back straps of his dungarees and picked him up. The little guy kicked his bare feet in the air and shrieked in glee.

"Ryan, this is my best friend Cassidy from Chicago," Amber said. They shook hands as Megan came into the room, wiping her hands on a dishtowel. "Megan, are you sure you guys aren't going to the festivities tonight? I don't want to keep you away."

"Connery is still too little. We took him last year and he cried every time the fireworks exploded. Next year maybe we can all go together and take both kids," Megan said as she took Minna from Amber.

Will I still be here a year from now? Amber wondered. She felt the decision coming closer, like the inevitable end to the long golden days of summer.

"Are you leaving Camelot here with us?" Ryan asked. "My son who can't pronounce the letter 'L' has been telling him to 'Why down,' instead of 'Lie down.' The dogs actually minds him pretty well."

"No, I'm taking the dog with me. Cam, come here." She practically had to drag him out of the room. His belly was almost on the ground. "On your feet, Soldier," Amber said, crossly and led him out of the house. It's one thing him preferring Minna to me, but having him mind Connery and even understanding his baby-talk, is just too much. "You are my dog, Camelot Bradshaw," she said firmly as she loaded him in the car.

THE FOURTH OF JULY PARADE WAS IN FULL SWING in Apple River Falls when Amber and Cassidy joined the onlookers. Several floats of high school girls in their cheerleading outfits and boys in football uniforms rode by. A convertible with a sign reading "Fourth of July King and Queen," drove down the street. Amber asked one of the bystanders why there would be royalty for the parade and learned that local tradition was for the high school prom king and queen to ride in the parade. The young queen wore a strapless lavender gown and long white gloves; she smiled and did the parade wave. Half a dozen kids on high-stepping horses followed. High school girls twirled their batons. The band played "America the Beautiful." It was a fine night, warm and still and Amber felt a swell of pride in the wonderful people of America's heartland.

Every merchant in town had put tables and chairs out on the sidewalks. Most store owners stood outside greeting their customers. Some had their dogs with them. Camelot swaggered by the local dogs, lordly and disdainful, unwilling to even exchange a sniff. He had clearly recovered from being separated from Minna and was enjoying himself tremendously. Amber and Cassidy stopped at the ice cream parlor and emerged with blue moon and cookie dough ice-cream cones. Afterwards, they walked to the park where a little carnival had been set up. The Ferris wheel was spinning slowly in the darkening air. Everyone was smiling and many residents greeted Amber and petted her dog.

"I can see why you like this place, Amber. Everyone is so friendly."

"Take a look over toward the high school, Cassidy. See that tall man with the slender blond girl? That's Marc Rochet, the guy I've been dating." Cassidy raised her eyebrows. "At least I hope we're still dating after I made the cops check to see if his assistant locked me in the cellar."

The two young women walked toward the school, catching up with the duo.

"Marc, hi. This is my friend Cassidy from Chicago."

"Nice to meet you, Cassidy. Hi, Amber," he greeted them, "This is my little sister, Daphne."

Daphne greeted both women, complimented Cassidy on her jewelry and petted Cam. Marc reached to pet the dog also, but he sidled away.

Amber turned toward Marc saying, "Can we talk for a moment?" They stepped away from Cassidy and Daphne who were chatting.

"I owe you an apology for the other night, Amber. It was a terrible time for you, with the losses of both your aunt and sister. I was being an ass and I'm very sorry. The cops had better get the bastard who locked you in the cellar," his voice was low with suppressed anger. "I hope having your friend here is helping. We should get seats on the grandstands. Daphne loves fireworks."

The four of them found places on the highest level of the risers. As they chatted, waiting for it to be dark enough to start the fireworks, people lit Chinese lanterns and lofted them into the air. There was hardly any wind and the paper lanterns rose almost straight up. They glowed like a hundred suns in the dark summer night.

"In Asian tradition, when a lighted lantern is released into the sky, it takes all your cares away. Maybe it will help you, Sweetheart," Marc said smiling gently at her.

The fireworks were an ambitious display for a small town and lasted longer than Amber thought they would. The display ended with a fabulous cracking fusillade. Everyone clapped and descended the grandstands. Amber saw Hunter and waved at him, but when he spotted Marc, he turned away.

Marc took Amber's hand and walked her out to her car. When she called the dog to get in the car, Marc reached for his collar and Cam made a low rumble in his chest.

"Goodness, Cam, what is the matter with you? I'm sorry, Marc." She brushed off her pet's irritability, but it wasn't the first time she had noticed the dog's reaction to Marc and it troubled her.

"When can I see you again?" Marc asked. "Daphne is here for a couple days, but what about the end of the week?"

"Cassidy will be with me a few days too. She and Daphne seem to be hitting it off, don't they? What about Saturday?"

"Saturday it is. I'll pick you up at seven for dinner."

"Perfect," Amber said.

As they drove out of the little town, Amber glanced at Cassidy. "Well, what did you think of him?"

"He's gorgeous and Daphne is a darling. How do you have all the luck, Amber Bradshaw? All the way tucked into this rural backwater and you have two cute guys! I haven't had a date since Matt and I broke up and he left the States for the Army." A regretful expression crossed her lovely features.

They drove past the Reservoir Lake and turned on Morand Road, heading to the farm. When they picked up the sleeping baby at Amherst's house, Megan said she'd been perfect as always. The moon rose, laying a silvery mist across the fields. Amber rolled down the car windows and felt the cool air against her face. Cassidy reclined her seat and closed her eyes.

"LET'S GO FEED THE CALVES," Amber announced at four o'clock the next day. She had told Cassidy about the calves in her barnyard and that she and Hunter fed them each day. It had become a nice late afternoon ritual, although it bothered Amber that they took the calves away from their mothers to boost the cow's milk production. And their fate was unknown. The lucky ones would be sold to other dairy farmers to become milk cows or kept at the farm, if Amber made the difficult choice to re-establish Irene's Dairy.

"Hi, Hunter," Amber said when they walked up.

"Hello," he said and touched Minna's curly head. His smile was beautiful in his dark face.

"According to Amber, you don't have a girlfriend. It that right?" Cassidy asked. "I'm available if you're interested." She opened her eyes wide and batted them flirtatiously.

"Can't afford a girlfriend," Hunter said. "I still live at home with my dad. It's a small place, not like Amber's. I'd like a family someday, but I understand it's considered bad form not to get a wife first." He grinned.

"I would imagine girls would be lined up to go out with you," Cassidy said.

"Where?" he said looking around.

"Cassidy, cut it out. You're embarrassing Hunter," Amber said as they walked back to the house. "And stop looking at me that way! I told you I'm not chasing a man who doesn't want me."

"I think you should give him another chance. He's attracted to you, Amber, I can tell. It's worth finding out why he doesn't seem to pick up on your cues. But if you aren't willing to stick your neck out, then you clearly don't deserve him and I'd be more than willing to take him off your hands," she said and grinned.

LATE THAT NIGHT, ANXIOUS TO READ the next installment in Ina's life, Amber reached for the journal.

Winter, 1918

I haven't written in my Journal since we crossed the Atlantic Ocean. When Frank said we were in America, I felt my spirits rise, thinking the dreadful trip would be over soon, but he said we had a long ways to go yet. The winds were bitterly cold. The waves were huge and choppy. I was driven below the deck while we travelled the interminable St. Lawrence Seaway that would take us to the endless Great Lakes.

At first, I had no idea how Frank paid for our passage, but then I got a sick feeling. My jewelry and my furniture paid for this. He sold it all, even my dog. He dragged her off for the knacker man who killed unwanted dogs and sold their patterned skins. Bile rose in my throat. What I had wanted for my life before I began this trip to America meant nothing now. I was a captive, and my baby could lose her life on this unending trip. A righteous anger burns inside me.

Amber laid back in her bed. She couldn't read any more.

TWENTY-SEVEN

A PLUME OF DUST FROM THE REAR WHEELS of the Hillside Gallery van rose in the air as Cassidy drove out of the driveway early the next morning. Watching her leave, Amber leaned down and petted Cam, knowing he would miss Cassidy too. When she walked back into the house, she could hear Minna babbling upstairs on the monitor, as she did every morning. She smiled and went upstairs to get the baby. Having Cassidy visit had blown away a good deal of the pain from Claire and Aunt Irene's deaths. It was still tough, but each day since she lost them, Amber felt herself growing stronger, surer of the next steps in her life.

Minna had taken her first bite of cereal when she heard a light tapping on the summer kitchen door. She was wearing only a sleep T-shirt and panties, so she peered around the door. It was Hunter.

"Is everything all right?" Amber asked. She stepped back and opened the door wider. He smelled fresh, as if he had just stepped out of the shower. His hair was still wet and his eyes darkened, seeing her in her short nightshirt. Maybe Cassidy was right, perhaps Hunter is attracted to me, she thought, feeling a rising bubble of happiness.

"I saw the Hillside Gallery van drive by our place earlier, so I knew Cassidy had left and you would be up. I stopped to see if you wanted to go with me to the Creamery."

"What is this Creamery place?"

"It's the cream processing plant. I thought you might want to see what happens to the milk when it leaves the farm. I'm taking the milk from the Lundgren's to the Creamery this morning."

Amber hesitated, "I'm not even dressed and I need to finish feeding the baby. How are you at feeding babies, Hunter? I have to warn you, she has a habit of shaking her head just as you put a bite in her mouth and it gets everywhere. Camelot parks himself under her high chair. I swear she deliberately drops food for him."

"I think I can manage," Hunter said and smiled his slow smile.

"Okay, if you want to finish up, I'll throw on some jeans."

"Sure thing," he said and followed her into the kitchen.

It would be good to go on a little field trip this morning, Amber thought. It would help distract her from all her losses and from missing Cassidy. She wished her best friend could have stayed longer. I've had to say too many farewells lately.

When she came back downstairs, she was dressed and had put her wet hair in a ponytail. Hunter was rinsing the last of the cereal out of the baby's bowl. To her dismay, Amber noticed that Hunter had been far more successful at keeping the baby clean than her own feeble attempts.

"I have something important to tell you, Hunter. In case you didn't pick up the news at the wake, Miss Irene left me the farm in her will."

"How wonderful, Amber. My dad will be so pleased."

What about you, Hunter? She wondered. Will you be pleased? She almost said the words aloud before she stopped herself.

"Ready to go?" he asked and she nodded. He grabbed the car seat and they walked out to his pick-up. He competently installed the car seat in the truck's back seat and clicked the baby in. As they drove down the road, Amber glanced in the side mirror. The bed of the truck held a half-dozen large tin milk cans with dented lids. Between them stood one elegant, albeit dusty, Afghan hound.

"Cam is in the back of your truck," she told Hunter.

He nodded. "I know. I seem to have a knack with old ladies, babies and dogs."

"Are you calling me old?" Amber hit him on the shoulder. "How old are you by the way?"

"Twenty-eight. I think I'll wait until Minna grows up and marry her. It will probably take another twenty years for me to have enough money to afford a family."

"For your information, I just turned twenty-seven," she told him and he chuckled. The little interchange relaxed them both and they chatted all the way to the Creamery, sharing stories about their lives before they met.

HUNTER PARKED THE TRUCK and they walked into a cement block building with a concrete floor. An enormous stainless-steel vat dominated the center of the room. A young man, wearing a large white apron and plastic gloves was standing on a raised platform looking down into the large metal cylinder.

"Hey, Hunter," he called. "Looks like you managed to get a family since you were here last. You're one fast worker."

"This is Amber Bradshaw. She owns the old Morand place. And this little cutie is Minna. Dad and I are trying to convince Amber to start the Morand Dairy up again."

Two other men in overalls came out of the back carrying coffee cups. They greeted Amber and the baby.

"I'm glad to meet you," the older man said. "I'm John Jennings, the manager here. This is Ray Lundgren, his brother owns the farm down the road from you, and this is our student assistant and resident smart-ass, Jackie Boyd."

"Did you come for a milk bath this morning?" Jackie asked in a teasing voice. "I can put you down in there for a swim. Probably best if you take *all* your clothes off first."

"Jesus, Jackie, knock it off," Mr. Jennings said, frowning. "Just ignore him, Miss Bradshaw, we all do. If you want to see the operation, you can walk up the stairs over there and stand on the platform."

"Go ahead, I'll hold Minna," Hunter said. The baby didn't even protest when Amber handed her to him. In fact, she looked positively smug.

When she got to the top of the steps, Amber gazed down into the milk in the vast steel container. An automatic skimming arm separated the cream from the milk as it slowly swirled below her. The milk was a beautiful ivory color, as if a million pearls had melted and become a shining liquid. She glanced at Hunter and Minna and waved. To her delight, Minna waved back. When she descended, Amber took the baby and walked with Mr. Jennings who explained the purpose of pasteurization and why the cream was skimmed from the raw milk.

"We have a little store here," he said. "The Creamery sells butter, cream and milk. The excess liquid from making butter is made into buttermilk. We sell that too. There is a good market for buttermilk and cheese now. If you start the Morand Dairy up again, and can get a herd going, we will buy all your milk."

They walked through the area containing the processing vat into a light-filled room with refrigerated containers. Everything was spacious and antiseptically clean. Glancing out the window, Amber saw Hunter in the parking lot. He was unloading the large milk cans from his truck.

Minna started to whimper, opening and closing her little fist, making the sign for milk, and Amber reached into the diaper bag to give her the long-delayed bottle. Half an hour later, Hunter had returned the empty milk cans to the truck bed. Cam was off chasing a critter, but came immediately to Hunter's whistle and jumped easily in the back of the truck.

On their return to the Farm, Amber said, "Thank you for taking us this morning. It was fascinating. What happens to the milk the Creamery doesn't sell here?"

"It depends on the grade, but it is mostly sold for animal feed. They sell some of it to a plant where they make powdered milk. I don't think I ever told you, but the milk we give the calves in their bottles is powdered milk from the Creamery."

"I thought the milk in the baby bottles was directly from the calves' mothers," Amber said.

"No. We let them nurse for a few days after birth, and they get mother's milk then because it has nutrients they need for optimal growth. Then we switch them to powdered milk. Have you decided what you are going to do about the farm, Amber?"

"Not yet. I need time to consider my options. If I don't stay, Aunt Irene's will specified that the property be held in trust for Miss Minna."

"So, on top of her astonishing beauty, Minna is an heiress? Quite the combination," Hunter grinned.

CARRYING THE BABY BACK INTO THE HOUSE, Amber compared her trip to the Creamery with Hunter to the evening she and Mark Rochet went to dinner. There was a marked contrast. Riding in Marc's expensive sports car, wearing her new dress, Amber had felt proud of her escort and her own appearance. This morning, wearing old jeans with wet hair in a ponytail and a baby in her lap, she felt something quite different. She thought hard, reaching to identify the sensation. It was . . . tranquility, she thought. This morning, I felt at peace.

Looking out the front window of the farmhouse that afternoon, Amber saw dark clouds billow and heard heat lightening crackle. The rain began slowly, just a gentle patter at first before the wind rose and the rain began in earnest. The winter wheat field across the country road turned blue through the veil of falling rain. She had always loved rainstorms and felt a release deep inside when they began, like the feeling she got from a perfectly executed painting, or a man's appreciative smile.

A bit later, she heard baby noises and walked upstairs to get Minna up from her nap. When she walked into the bedroom, Cam was facing the crib with his tongue hanging out. Minna wrinkled up her face in fierce concentration. Then she poked her tongue out. Amber picked up the baby and stuck her own tongue out at the little one. Looking almost cross-eyed in determination, Minna stuck her tongue out in return. Amber could not stop chuckling.

Carrying Minna, Amber walked down to the summer kitchen to load more wet clothes from Aunt Irene's apartment into the dryer. She had been doing laundry ever since Cassidy left, getting her Aunt's clothes ready for donating to charity. The load banged loudly as it twirled around inside the drum. She set the baby down in her seat and pulled out items one by one, trying to figure out what was causing the noise. There was one long white sock with a knot in it. Something hard was stuffed in the toe.

Amber's heart started beating faster. Her fingers trembled as she struggled to untie the knot in the wet sock. Once the knot came open, she tipped the sock over and a heavy key fell ringing to the counter. The key had a round open circle at one end and a series of square cuts at the other. There was a number etched into it. Her father had a similar key. It was the key to their safe deposit box. Amber was pretty sure she knew now where the family treasure was. She dialed her dad's phone.

"Hi, Amber. How are you this afternoon?

"I'm coming along. How are you doing?"

"Better. Mrs. Miller had been helping me with my exercises and I'm going to PT every day."

"That's good. Keep it up. I called because I found a safety deposit key among Aunt Irene's things. If there really is a family treasure, my guess is it's in her safe deposit box at the bank. I'm going to head into town soon and see if I'm right."

"Are you still hoping to keep the farm in the family, Amber? I'm not sure we can afford it, even if there is a treasure to be found. I'm sorry, but I can't see how it's going to work."

"We need to talk more after I made my decision," Amber said and bid him good-bye.

MR. ALLSWEDE CALLED AT DINNER TIME. He had heard back from Mr. McMillan, the rep from Framingham. They were still determined to push her into selling the farm.

"Can Framingham actually take the farm now that it's mine?" Amber asked.

"They can't force you to sell, but they know you aren't from the area and are young. They will continue to pressure you to let them have it. Apparently, they are prepared to raise their offer and to play legal hardball."

"My father doesn't think we can afford to keep it," Amber said, feeling discouraged.

"You take all the time you need," Mr. Allswede said.

After Minna went down for the night, Amber sat down with her tablet to calculate the cost of keeping the farm. She would need all of Aunt Irene's savings just to clean and insulate the barn and equip it with the self-milking system. After that, there wouldn't be anything left to purchase a new herd or operate the farm until it turned a profit. Selling some of the farm's land would give her enough money to buy the cows she would need, but if she sold the land, and Framingham even got a toehold in the area, they would move to acquire more farms, like the hungry metastatic cancer Mr. Allswede had described.

THE FOLLOWING MORNING the Framingham representative called. He wanted to meet with her again about their offer to purchase the farm. She had lain awake most of the night thinking about what to do. She got up, dressed and drove her fussy teething small one to Megan. Then she took the twisting two-track to the Freedman's small-holding. At her knock, Mr. Freedman opened the door and told her to come in.

"Can I show you some numbers I've been working on?" she asked, holding out her tablet. "I'm trying to figure out if I can keep the farm."

"Come in and sit down, Amber. Let me take a look," Mr. Freedman said.

"Do you think if I had Irene's Dairy up and running again that the farm would make a profit? It's critical if I'm going stay."

"It would be close, Amber, but you can't just feed dairy cattle on pasture all year in northern Wisconsin. It's too cold here. You have to feed the cows in the barns in winter and for that you will need grain and silage. You also have to have to heat the barns once the temperature falls below freezing. Fuel oil is pretty expensive for a big uninsulated space. We supplement the cow's diets with grain as well as dried hay. They need salt and selenium also."

"I could buy salt and selenium, I suppose. Would we make enough money selling the milk to support me and Minna?"

"Nothing is guaranteed in farming, Amber," his expression was serious. "The price for milk has stayed the same for decades, penalizing dairy farmers. It's not a life that will make anyone rich. There are always years with poor yields or drought. Cattle require veterinarian care and medicines when they are ill. You have to have the services of a trained person to handle the breeding. You need a vet when the calves are born. There's a lot more to running a dairy than you might think." He looked at her intently. "Running a farm is hard work, probably too hard for you. At least, all by yourself. I am prepared to help, and I hope you end up keeping the farm, but a dairy is a big job."

Amber took a shaky breath before saying, "Working on this problem last night, I got to thinking about the impact of my decision on you and Hunter. Your work on the Morand farm is your major source of income, isn't it. If I sell, what would you do?"

"Do more work for Lundgren's I assume, but that's not your problem," Mr. Freedman said and patted Amber on her back.

Driving to Apple River Falls, Amber called Mr. Allswede.

"Allswede," he answered the phone.

"Hi, it's Amber. I'm on my way to meet the Framingham rep about the land. I'm thinking of offering them a few hundred acres on the west side of the property. It would give me enough capital to cover the cost of acquiring a herd, starting the dairy up again and running the farm until it could turn a profit."

There was a long pause before Mr. Allswede said, "That's how this begins, Amber. If you even open the door a crack, they will move in. Lundgren's property at the end of the road is their next target."

"I'm really struggling with the decision. My dad is not in favor of keeping the farm. He says it's a losing proposition money-wise."

"Let me look at the numbers with you, please. Maybe together we can figure out how to keep the farm, if not profitable at least breaking even."

Amber was quiet for a long time, before saying, "Okay. I'll cancel my meeting with Framingham . . . and I'll drop off the income statements."

Late that night, listening to the wind in the cottonwood trees, Amber sat down to read another excerpt from Ina's journal.

Ina Morand Journal Entry
Winter, 1918

Last night Frank handed me a package wrapped with paper and tied with rough twine. I remembered it from the vegetable cart, the day I was too frightened he had stolen it to see what it contained.

"Open it, please." He smiled pensively at me.

My hands trembled.

"What is it? Did you get me some paper to write on?"

"No. This is to keep you close to God."

I was shaking so hard, I couldn't open the wrapping. He gently untied the twine and pulled the brown paper away. It was an icon, the most spiritual I had ever seen. A master artist had engraved an image of the Virgin Mary and her child on a sheet of what looked like gold leaf pressed onto a wooden panel. My heart pounded. I feared Frank had stolen it, but could not keep myself from grabbing it out of his hands.

"Where did you get this, Frank? Did you steal it, tell me."

"I took it for you, Ina.

"If you stole it, it doesn't belong to me. I can't keep it."

But even as I said the words, I clutched it tightly in my hands. I had never wanted anything more than the lovely contemplative face of the mother of God.

"That icon is still somewhere here in this house. I just have to find it," Amber whispered as she looked out the window at the cottonwood trees beneath the star-studded night sky.

TWENTY-EIGHT

Amber woke the next morning remembering the attic above the summer kitchen. She felt a surge of excitement, got out of bed and walked downstairs. Looking up at the wooden ceiling of the room, she saw that it had been made from strips of hardwood. In the middle of the ceiling there was what looked to be the outline of a pull-down hatch. Sometime in the past someone had nailed it shut. She felt a quiver of excitement. She called Hunter and asked him if he could come over to help her get into the attic. He said he'd be over in about an hour.

Standing on a ladder in the summer kitchen with a claw hammer, Hunter started prying the antique nails that sealed the hatch out, one by one. They had been in place so long, each one screeched as he pulled it out. Finally, he wrenched the little door open. He came down the ladder and smiled, "Ladies first," he said. Amber climbed to the top and Hunter boosted her up through the hatch. He climbed up after her.

The tiny attic was mostly empty, except for some old books and magazines in one corner and a steamer trunk. It was dusty and Hunter sneezed. In the area by the window someone had hung a floor to ceiling curtain creating a small alcove. Amber pulled the curtain to one side, releasing a cloud of dust and saw a standing easel on a braided rug. She and Hunter tiptoed around it, fearful of toppling the old wooden support.

The sun was at just the right angle. The beam hit the icon like a spotlight. The ancient object on the easel had unmistakable power. Neither of them spoke or moved, caught in its spell. It was a raised etching done in gold, about six inches wide and nine inches tall. The centerpiece was a representation of the Virgin Mary and the baby Jesus. The frame was made of an old copper-colored metal that the artist had hammered into a pattern. Inside the frame, a second square bordered the central image. The interior frame was made of wood with raised insignias, miniature golden representations of Mary's face.

Mary was seated with Jesus in her lap. Her halo was also made of gold, and around her halo was a raised decorative rim, as if she wore a turban. Her features had been so carefully detailed, Amber could feel her devotion to her child even now possibly thousands of years after it had been created. Baby Jesus' face was tiny, nearly lost within his large halo. The carving was so masterful, the fabric appeared to move, to cradle the mother and child.

"I'm afraid to touch it," Amber whispered.

"Me too."

They stood a while longer, studying the icon carefully and appreciating the artist's supreme skill. Whoever the long-dead artist was, he was clearly a master of his craft.

"This icon has clearly survived for hundreds of years, but it should really be protected. The attic heats up to boiling in the summer and goes down to freezing in the winter," Hunter said.

"I know. Eventually the heat and cold would cause damage. It's too precious to take that risk."

"Do you have any idea of what you will do with it?"

"Not yet, but I will always keep the rest of Ina's sacred space untouched, exactly as she left it. I bet she made that beautiful braided rug on the floor. Up there I had a strong sense of her presence."

THEY CLIMBED DOWN FROM THE ATTIC, carrying the precious artwork as if it were made of snowflakes—so fragile the touch of a hand could melt it.

"Thank you, my friend," Amber whispered. They looked at each other intently. Hunter bent his head as if to kiss her.

"I can't do this," he said suddenly and lifted his face from hers. Amber took a deep breath, sadness washing over her.

What held him back, she wondered. Cassidy would tell me to ask him, but what if she is wrong. Perhaps he isn't attracted to me after all and I don't think I could take knowing that.

SEVERAL DAYS LATER, AMBER NOTICED that the wheat across the road from the farmhouse had turned a burnished yellow gold. The glowing color signaled to the farm families that it was time to begin threshing. The timing was critical. If the autumn rains started before the grain was harvested, much of it would be ruined and winter would see shortages of feed for the cattle.

When Amber discussed the upcoming harvest with Mr. Freedman, she learned that Hunter and his father had always done the threshing for Aunt Irene. The money they earned supported the two of them for most of the following year. However, Hunter had recently visited his doctor who told him he couldn't run the threshing machine this year. He had asthma and the dusty air would only make it worse. Amber said she would take his place.

"It's harder than you might think," Mr. Freedman said. "Maybe wearing a mask, Hunter could still get it done. That's what he's done in other years."

"No. I'll do it. Aunt Irene would expect me to," Amber said, stubbornly.

That afternoon Hunter tapped on her door. "I am going to teach you how to run the thresher," he said, "much to my father's dismay. Are you sure you want to do this?"

"Definitely, do I need to change my clothes?" Amber was wearing jean shorts and had tied her shirt in a knot at her waist.

"What you're wearing is okay for today. Once the actual threshing starts you will want more coverage, jeans and a long-sleeved shirt. The grain and stalks are sharp and can cut skin."

"Okay, I can hear Minna waking up. I'll get her, and we can make a start."

They carried the baby's playpen down by the barn and installed it under a huge oak tree. Cam ran around it in circles before settling near the baby. An enormous piece of farm equipment with a long neck like a swan was parked near the silos.

"That's the threshing machine," Hunter told her. "They delivered it this morning. We rent it each year. It cuts the wheat and separates the grain from the straw and makes the straw into bales. We pitchfork the bales onto flat wagons and drive them to the barn. Then the bales are carried up the ladder to the haymow. As long as the weather holds, it will take us two or three days to cut the wheat, another day to blow the grain up into the granary and to load the straw bales into the barn."

For over an hour Hunter tried to teach her to drive the enormous John Deere combine with limited success. Amber was frustrated by how hard it was. She could start the engine, but whenever she tried to shift into drive from neutral, the machine sputtered and died. The gears made loud grinding noises.

"Stop, stop," Hunter said every time the engine died. "Turn off the key for a moment. Okay, now start again. Don't fully release the clutch until the combine starts to move," he said, starting to laugh at her hopelessness. They were both laughing hard by the time she finally got it.

"I'm going to drive it down the road," Amber called out, grinning, raising her arms high in triumph.

After driving the combine to the crossroads and back, she returned the vehicle to the barn and turned off the key. Her momentary euphoria was gone. If she stayed on the farm, this was going to be her life: planting, threshing, harvesting. Was raising Minna and running a dairy farm her destiny?

When she walked into the house, Hunter was giving Minna her bottle.

"What happens next?" Amber asked, taking a deep breath.

"Tomorrow, we cut the wheat," Hunter said. He was coughing. She noticed his normal ruddy complexion was pale.

"How many acres do we have in wheat?" she asked.

"Two hundred," he said and Amber felt overwhelmed. "We will all work twelve hours a day for the next few days. You need to see if Megan will keep Minna."

"Hold on a second there, mister," Amber said. "The deal was that I would run the threshing machine and you would learn to change diapers. What about that?"

"Already did it," he told her, a twitch of self-satisfaction in his face.

"Something tells me you got the better of this deal," Amber said, amused.

AS SHE WAS GETTING INTO BED THAT NIGHT, the phone rang. It was her father.

"Hi, Dad."

"We have a surprise for you, honey. We are coming to the farm for a visit."

"When you say we you mean you and Joanna?"

"Yes. I think it will raise both our spirits to see you and the baby. And we need to talk about whether you're keeping the farm."

"When can you get here?" she asked, feeling excited about seeing both of them.

"Middle of next week, just wanted you to have some notice. I can't wait to see you and the little one."

"It will be good to see you too. Bye, Dad," She glanced at the journal translation on her bedside table, wondering how attached Ina had been to the farm, once their long trip was over. Given her resentment about Frank ripping her from her homeland, was Ina ever happy here? Would I be happy if I stayed?

Ina Morand Journal
Winter, 1918

It was snowing hard by the time we reached the raw frontier city of Chicago. When I walked off the boat, my legs trembled. Even on dry land, I felt the water surge beneath me. I staggered like a drunk.

We stayed in a boarding house in this city that seemed enormous to me. It was the first place we had been since we left the old country where I was able to sleep comfortably. The baby had milk to drink. My milk had dried up weeks before. The food tasted delicious. I begged Frank to find work in the town. I needed people around me and dreaded the dark forests, but he said that he and his brother purchased a farm in a place called Wisconsin.

"Is it good dark soil at least?" I asked.

No, it seems my idiot husband has bought a farm with an enormous hill that is useless for growing crops. My rage sleeps beside me. Frank never asked if he could use my jewelry and my furniture to buy a dirt farm. I remembered bitterly the day I saw him haul my dog from the yard. I knew her patterned skin was desirable to furriers. He never asked me if he could sell my dog and I would never have agreed.

Two days later, Charles and Alene burst through the door in our Chicago boardinghouse. Frank was euphoric that his brother had made it out alive. The men talked about the farm and how far away it was. Their cheerfulness only fanned the flames of my bitter heart. If I knew how, I would have cursed them both.

Alene and Charles are staying in this city until spring. I'd always thought my husband's brother wasn't very smart, but now I see he is brighter than my useless husband. They are spending the winter in this warm boarding house while we travel north in winter to Wisconsin. When Alene told me she was staying, I hated my sister-in-law's bragging, smirking little mouth. I could have killed Frank for continuing this trip of fools. My need for revenge rises whenever Frank reaches to touch me and I always pull away.

Last night Alene showed me six golden coins. Her expression was serious, intense. "It is enough money to buy your freedom," she said. "If you take this, you could get yourself a room and a job in this town as a seamstress. It's yours if you will let me raise your baby. I don't think I will ever have a child of my own." She sounded wistful, her eyes moist.

"Where did you get the gold?" I asked her. I felt a shiver cross my shoulders. What crimes had our husbands committed? Alene didn't answer, just tipped the coins into my open palm. Oh, I was tempted. We were on land again. I could find work in this town and live on my own for the first time in my life. I slowly began to hand the baby to Alene, but Irene cried and held on to my fingers tight with her tiny hands. I couldn't do it. I dropped the coins ringing to the floor. Somehow I will live through this and keep my baby safe.

TWENTY-NINE

R YAN ARRIVED AT SEVEN THE FIRST MORNING of threshing to take baby Minna to their house. As soon as they left, Amber walked down to the barn, surprised to see several pickup trucks and men in Wrangler bib-overalls milling around. The Freedmans had brought a large coffee urn and Hunter was passing out cups of coffee from the pull-down gate on the back of their truck.

"Who are these guys, Hunter?" Amber whispered. "You know I can't afford to pay them."

"They own the nearby farms and have come to volunteer their help," he said. At her stunned expression he said, "These men are our neighbors. They want you to succeed, to keep the farm. After they work for you, they go back to their own farms and cut their wheat at night. Until the wheat is in the barns, we all work around the clock."

"Are you sure I shouldn't at least *offer* to pay them something?" Amber asked. Hunter frowned.

"No. They would be offended. All you can do is thank them. Everyone, this is Amber Bradshaw. Amber, this is Jasper Ray, Chad Lundgren and George Boyd." Hunter continued, introducing her to all the men.

Amber shook hands, thanked them gratefully and climbed into the cab of the combine. It was so early the metal seat was ice cold. She had trouble getting the machine into gear and lagged behind the others. When she entered the golden wheatfield, some of the larger rigs were already driving from one end to the other, spaced out like enormous lawn mowers. With their vast rotating blades on the front, threshing machines could cut a swath of grain twenty-five feet wide. The stalks fell like grass, leaving nothing behind but golden stubble. This day is all bright blue skies, puffy clouds and showers of golden grain, Amber thought, profoundly moved by the beauty of the farm country.

Hunter and his father drove tractors pulling hay wagons behind the threshing machines. The pitchforks caught the light as they forked the bales onto the flat wagons. At noon, Amber heard a whistle. The combines and tractors came to a halt and the men walked back to the barn. Amber switched off her key and ran to join them. Megan was standing by the silos, holding a tray of sandwiches and pink Kool-Aid.

"Couldn't you find juice or soda?" Amber asked.

"Kool-Aid is traditional. Aunt Irene always called it bug juice. At three o'clock, I'll bring Ranger cookies. According to Ryan, they were your great grandmother, Lillian's favorites."

"Who is watching Minna and Connery?"

"Cam is," Megan covered her mouth with her hand, stifling her laughter.

"Megan, you didn't leave the babies alone with the dog did you?"

"Of course not, Silly. My mom is there too, but she says the dog does a pretty good job all by himself."

By the middle of the afternoon, Amber was so stiff she could hardly get down from the cab of the threshing machine. Her legs were trembling and she remembered Mr. Freedman telling her running a farm was hard work. She had no idea it would be this hard, and it was just the first day. Trudging up to the farmhouse at dinner time, Amber noticed that the leaves on the cottonwood trees had turned the color of burnished brass. Summer was coming to an end. Decisions loomed like thunderheads.

AMBER WAS GETTING OUT OF THE SHOWER around eight o'clock when she heard the phone ring. She was too tired to get it and just listened to the message.

"Amber, it's Marc. I need to talk to you right away. It's urgent. Please call me."

Almost too tired to stand up, Amber managed to pull on her long T-shirt nightgown and walk downstairs to the kitchen. She dialed his number.

"Marc, it's me."

"Amber, I have to see you. Did you hear the news?"

"No I didn't, I was threshing all day. Why?"

"Can I come out?"

"Marc, I can hardly stand up. There are more days like this before the grain is in the silos."

"This can't wait," he said and hung up before she could protest again. She sighed with weariness but unlocked the back door and flipped on the back porch lights. The house seemed empty without baby Minna and Cam. Megan insisted the baby had to stay with them until threshing was over and her disloyal dog utterly refused to leave the baby.

"But I want her to come back home at night," Amber said. "I miss her."

"You don't know what you are up against, Amber. Your arms will shake so bad, you might not be able to lift her. Leave Minna with me," Megan said.

AMBER WAS SITTING AT THE KITCHEN TABLE when Marc burst through the back screen door fifteen minutes later.

"God, I'm sorry," he said. His face was devastated. He went down on one knee by her bare feet. "Forgive me, Amber. Please forgive me. I should have known."

Amber put a hand on his shoulder. She had no idea what he was talking about. "Come sit here, Marc," she said.

"It turns out you were right to suspect Nate," Marc said, looking sick. "It was Nate who trapped you in the basement and took the Morand journal. I was listening to the news on the radio around six o'clock. The newscaster said a rare Romanian journal from the period between 1916 and 1918 had recently been discovered. The book had profound historical significance—including a list of objects sent by the Romanian government to Moscow to avoid their seizure by the Germans during the First World War That's when I knew Nate had stolen Ina Morand's journal. He talked to me often about some valuables his family had which were sent to Moscow." His face was dark with shame.

"What are you saying?" she asked, struggling to understand.

"Nate never came back to work after the journal was taken. About two weeks later, I got an e-mail from him apologizing for leaving without giving me any notice. I called and basically badgered him for over an hour until he confessed to taking Ina's journal. He's turned himself in to the authorities."

"Nate was the one who locked me in the basement? How could he! He knew you and I were seeing each other."

"You have no idea how terrible I feel about this, Amber," Marc took a deep breath. "As to why he stole Ina's journal, apparently books were often used to conceal lists of treasures that were smuggled out of countries. Nate wanted the original journal to see if there was a list tucked into the book's spine and there was. It was an inventory of the paintings, jewelry and religious icons taken by the government from its citizens so they wouldn't be stolen by the Germans. Nate believed some of those things belonged to his family. The list is what he was after."

"He could have just *asked* me to look for the list. I would have helped him. When he locked me in the basement, he put Minna at risk too. She fell off the bed and bumped her head! She could have died."

"You're right, Amber. What he did was completely unjustified. He said about an hour after he locked you in the cellar, he came to his senses and drove back to the farm. It was four o'clock by then and he saw Hunter walk into the house. He watched a while and when he saw the two of you together, he knew you were okay."

"And Minna, what about her? He risked her life," Amber's rage at Nate's behavior rose inside her like acid.

"He didn't know about the baby. I didn't mention her and when he was at the house, Minna was apparently upstairs sleeping. He will be prosecuted for the theft and for endangering your life and Minna's." Marc kissed her gently on the forehead. "I'm just so glad you and the baby are okay. Perhaps you will be able to use the list to prove ownership of your family's treasures."

At that moment, all the pieces of the puzzle clicked together for Amber. Frank and his brother had been guards on the Romanian treasure train. She had read about the Romanian government sending their most valuable artifacts to Russia before the German invasion. The icon and the gold must have been stolen from the train. The headlong flight from Romania to the U.S. was taken to save Frank and his brother from a deserter's firing squad.

"Did Nate think he could claim his heritage if it was authenticated?"

"Apparently so. Did you get the doctor to check Minna?"

"I did. She's fine. It was just a little bump on her head."

"How do you want to proceed in this matter?" Marc asked. "It's up to you."

Amber was quiet for a moment, thinking about how she should handle this. She wanted to do the right thing, ethically and morally. She spoke slowly, feeling her way. "My family have been stewards of the Morand journal for a century, but Ina's journal really belongs to the Romanian people. I will write a letter to the Romanian government, detailing the provenance of the journal and gifting it to the country. It would be wonderful if the journal led to the recovery of any families' treasures, including Nate's. Provided the journal is handed in to the authorities in Romania, I don't intend to file charges against him."

"Amber, you are an angel. Are you sure that's what you want?" Marc hesitated and then said, "In my mind, Nate deserves punishment for what he did. And I should have been supervising him more closely." Marc flushed.

"All I want is for Ina's journal to go back to the old country. Having Nate stand trial wouldn't accomplish that. I don't blame you for any of this."

Marc rubbed his forehead with his hand. "Amber, is there any wine?"

"Yes, in the fridge. Get me a glass too, will you?"

Marc pulled the bottle from the fridge, opened it and poured two glasses. Handing one to Amber he said, "Come here, Sweetheart." He sat at the table and pulled her on to his lap. He put his arm around her shoulders and Amber felt herself relax against him.

"You are exhausted. I'm going to put you to bed." Marc picked her up and carried her to the bedroom on the main floor. He went back for the wine and sat on the bed beside her.

She reached out her arms for him. "Hold me, Marc," she said. "Just hold me."

Marc set the wine glasses down. "Let me stay, Amber, please," he whispered. He loosened his tie and started to unbutton his shirt. He sat down on the bed and removed his shoes. He leaned toward her and kissed her. When he started to unbuckle his belt though, Amber knew she had to stop him.

"I'm not ready, Marc," she said. "I'm sorry, but it's too soon."

Marc nodded slowly, disappointment flooding his handsome features. "I will sleep on the couch then," he said. "Call me you change your mind."

"I won't, Marc," Amber told him gently and reached for Ina's Journal.

Ina's Journal
Summer, 1918

Last night Frank told me the story of how he came by the icon. He said it happened early on a pale gray summer morning in 1917 when the treasure train arrived in the Russian city of Moscow. Frank and his brother were guards for a last dangerous attempt to protect our heritage from the

German invasion. On board the train were beautiful court jewels, thousands of paintings, ancient manuscripts and 14th century icons. Armed Russian guards in black uniforms guarded the treasures as they were unloaded. It took all day for the soldiers to carry the treasures into a beautiful Orthodox church with an onion dome that rose into the morning sky.

Returning to the train after carrying the last packages to the church, Frank almost stepped on a small brown paper package. It has fallen from the train and lay forgotten in the dust. High-ranking Army soldiers were ordering everyone to get on board. Frank hesitated but then picked up the package. When he untied the string, he was stunned to see an icon. Knowing it would either become the property of the Russian state or be destroyed in the war, he decided to keep it as a gift—for me.

Frank's brother had not helped unload the treasures. Instead he hid in a closet and waited until the car with the gold was unguarded. He carefully counted out only the amount his and Frank's father had deposited in the national bank. Afterward, he climbed up on the roof of the train. Once the train started back to Romania, he climbed back down, his pockets bulging with their inheritance.

"We used the gold for our passage and to buy the farms," Frank told me. "But the icon would have been destroyed or lost forever and I saved it for you."

I said I wished I could give him something equal in value.

"You already have," he said and picked up baby Irene.

THIRTY

AMBER WAS LOOKING OUT HER BEDROOM WINDOW watching Marc's car pull out of the driveway the next morning when she heard Hunter's voice calling from the summer kitchen. She dashed downstairs feeling guilty.

"Good morning, Hunter. I'm ready."

Unspeaking, he walked out of the house.

"Hang on a minute." Amber hurried to catch up with him.

He turned around sharply and grabbed her by her shoulders. "Was Marc Rochet here all night?" he asked, his eyes fierce as a bird of prey.

"He was," she whispered, "but we didn't . . ."

He dropped his hands from her shoulders and turned away without another word.

Amber followed, walking several paces behind him. Neither of them spoke.

By noon Amber could hardly walk. Hunter had assigned her to carry the bales of straw up the ladder into the haymow. The bales were heavy and scratchy. She could only carry one at a time. Her shoulders ached. When Megan came with the Kool-Aid and cookies for the mid-day break and saw Amber's face, she asked her what was wrong.

"Nothing," she said. "It's just harder than I thought it would be."

"Ask Hunter if you can be in the grain wagon. It's an easier job. When the grain comes out of the chute all you have to do it level it off so it doesn't spill out on the ground."

"I hate to ask him for anything right now," Amber said, her voice low and quiet.

"Why? You've kept your end of the bargain by running the thresher," Megan said.

"I let Marc Rochet stay here last night."

"Does Hunter know?"

"He saw Marc's car leaving this morning . . . but Megan I didn't sleep with him."

"But Hunter doesn't know that and he will think you are a couple now. I heard a rumor from a friend of mine who works at the bank that Marc is a finalist to be president of a larger bank in Minneapolis. He isn't going to stay around here, Amber." Seeing her stunned face, Megan said, "Didn't he tell you?"

"No. He didn't." Amber said, feeling disappointed in him for keeping that information from her.

Hunter met her eyes only once that day, and his glance was grave and disappointed.

THE NEXT MORNING SHE WAS UP BY SIX. The sun was coming up. She looked at herself in the mirror, seeing her dark curly hair a mass of tangles. She pulled a brush through her hair, combing pieces of straw from her curls and tied a bandana around her neck. Walking to the barn, Amber saw an enormous pile of straw bales that remained to be stowed in the haymow. She lifted one onto her shoulder, wincing in pain. She climbed the ladder into the warm hay-scented space and added her bale to the golden staircase of straw. Climbing down the ladder, she saw Mr. Freedman drive in. He was alone in the car.

"Good morning," she called.

"Good morning, Amber."

"Isn't Hunter coming today?" she asked.

"Wasn't feeling up to it," Hunter's father said and Amber's heart sank.

The rest of the men began arriving. Amber got the coffee dispenser out of the Freedman's truck and filled their mugs. The dew burned off the wheat stubble in the golden fields. It rose in the air like the tendrils of steam from their coffee cups. One of the men started the tractor to retrieve some straw bales that were still in the now-stubbled field. Two others headed for the haymow, carrying bales as they climbed.

"What should I do today?" she asked Mr. Freedman.

Hunter's father gestured to the ladder standing beside the barn and she lifted a straw bale on her agonized shoulders. Reaching the haymow she dropped the bale and groaned, rubbing the back of her neck.

"Do you want to do something else?" Mr. Boyd, one of the farmers who was stacking bales in the haymow, asked.

"Anything," she told him, gratefully.

"Are you willing to work in the silo? The grain has to be blown into the silo from the grain wagon. I have to warn you, they can be deathtraps when grain cascades out of control. It can asphyxiate or crush victims. If you aren't willing, I can ask someone else."

"I'll do it," Amber said, squaring her shoulders. But looking toward the top of the silo, she shivered, remembering Aunt Irene's fiancé dying in just such a cylinder, buried alive in the cruel beads of golden grain.

"Sure you're up to it?" Mr. Boyd asked and Amber nodded.

Swallowing her fears, she climbed down the ladder to the ground. Together they entered the silo from a door at the bottom level. The interior was dark and smelled of fermentation. She felt her anxiety rise and her breathing quickened.

"You need to level the grain when it shoots out of the neck of the combine," he told her handing her a wide rake. "Start 'er up," he yelled to the men running the machine and a roar like a hurricane filled the silo.

Amber was drenched instantly in grains of wheat as it blew in like a waterfall of golden hail. It piled up so fast it was horrifying. The space was very dark and she struggled to breathe. She quickly pulled the kerchief up around her mouth and nose. Coughing and choking, Amber pushed the grain flat with her rake. They worked fast, climbing up the mounds of slippery grain as they piled higher and higher. Once she fell and the grain buried her almost instantly up to her waist. She screamed, flailing around desperately for something to grab on to.

Mr. Boyd yanked her from the grain yelling, "Keep your feet moving. You can get buried in this stuff. Farmers suffocate every year."

Amber shivered knowing it was how the Lundgren boy Aunt Irene planned to marry had died. The interior of the silo got hotter and hotter. Sweat ran down her face and trickled between her breasts. A tiny kernel of grain flew in one eye. She stopped moving for a moment, trying to dislodge it, but the surface was flowing and she fell again. She struggled to her feet, feeling she was scrambling for her footing on a surface of a thousand moving marbles. When the combine stopped and they heard the whistle for the mid-morning break, Amber dropped her rake.

"You can't do that," Mr. Boyd told her, sharply. "It will disappear. We have to flatten out all this grain before the thresher starts up again."

They barely got the grain flat when she heard the machine roar into life and the thick fall of grain poured down atop them again. By afternoon, Amber finally got her footing and sheer determination forced her on. When the day ended, she and Mr. Freeman were the only people left. She helped him feed the calves.

"Most of these are going to slaughter next week," he said.

"I wanted to keep them for Irene's Dairy," Amber said miserably, brushing straw off her arms and legs. She petted each calf, feeling a deep sense of shame. Then she sat down on the ground and pulled her boots and socks off. There was even grain between her toes. She leaned back against the barn closing her eyes as the sun went down.

"This work is too hard for you," Mr. Freedman said. For once, Amber was too tired to argue.

She trudged slowly up to the house and called Ryan to ask if he would bring Minna and Cam home. She was sitting at the kitchen table when he arrived with the baby and the dog. Minna got a big grin on her face when she saw Amber.

"I have missed you guys so much," Amber said, reaching for her. "Thanks a lot, Ryan. Please help yourself to the iced tea in the fridge. I'm too weary to stand. How are you are coming on Irene's apartment?" It was the last job she had asked him to do. The renovation of the main house was already complete.

"I took all her old furniture to the dump. God knows I hated to do it, but it was falling apart from wood rot."

"You couldn't save anything?"

"Only Aunt Irene's little rocking chair. I'm almost finished sanding the hickory on her floors. The last thing to do before your folks arrive, is to rip off the exterior staircase from the carriage house and build a new one."

They said good-bye and Amber gave Minna her bottle. Still shaking from muscle spasms, she managed to put the baby to bed. She was going to call it a night, but heard her phone ring and a man's voice leaving a message. She listened.

"Amber, it's Marc. I should have told you before, but I wasn't sure it would work out. I am one of three finalists for a presidency of a bank in the Twin Cities. I love Minneapolis, it's a beautiful clean city. Maybe when you get a break from the farm, we could take a couple of days to relax and explore the town. I'll call again soon. I already miss you." His voice was so warm, her heart caught in her throat.

Maybe Minneapolis wouldn't be so bad, she thought. It was only about an hour from the farm. If she ended up with Marc, she and Minna could spend weekends and even summers at the farm. Maybe Mr. Freedman was right when he said running a farm was too hard for a woman alone. Aunt Irene had done it for a long time, but in the end even she gave up. And it was ridiculous to envision Marc Rochet as a farmer.

Amber opened Ina's journal, hoping to read at least one short episode before she couldn't keep her eyes open any longer.

Lake Superior, America
Spring, 1918

Although it is early spring, ice still covers the Great Lake and the ice screams in pain as our boat plunges into the dark waters. Ice even coats the deck of the little fishing boat we boarded, as we began the final leg of the trip. I was terrified that baby Irene would fall from my arms. I held her so tightly she cried. When we finally landed at a tiny settlement on Lake Superior and I stepped carefully through icy pebbles onto the rocky shore I saw what I thought was a vision. A white Orthodox church with two spires stood among the bottle green pines. I ran with baby Irene into the sanctuary and barred the door so Frank could not follow us into God's house.

An hour later, I heard tapping and opened the door to see Frank's serious face, he was standing beside a priest.

"I brought Fr. Allekos to baptize the baby," my husband said.

I felt as if a heavy hand had been lifted from me. If baby Irene died now, at least she would be in the arms of God. I opened the door and the priest came inside. Frank followed him. The priest carried a large golden vessel filled with water. I was reluctant to put my poor child into cold water.

"Don't worry, little Mother," the priest told me. "I warmed the water. Please remove her clothing."

I liked him for his ability to discern my fears.

Praying the words for her soul, he lowered her into the water three times. She coughed when he raised her out of the water, but didn't cry. Like her father, my baby is a stoic. The priest made the sign of the cross in the air above her small body.

There is a part of the ceremony spoken in Greek by the priest and a chorus of responses, usually sung by the choir. I looked at my husband and haltingly he began to sing the responses. The priest nodded in satisfaction. He placed his hands on my daughter's head, which symbolizes the taking of possession of the baby in the name of the Holy Trinity. The priest blew three times in the form of the Cross to drive away any evil spirits, blessing her each time saying, "In the name of the Father and of the Son and of the Holy Spirit. Amen."

After the baptism, the priest handed Irene to my husband and said he wanted to speak with me alone. When Frank left, the priest looked at me intently.

"Your husband says you will not sleep with him in the marriage bed."

I was furious with Frank for telling the priest the private matters of our marriage.

"He is a good man, my child, you must try to forgive him for bringing you here. I will pray for you." His eyes were dark with compassion. His kindness brought me shame.

Throughout my life, I have tried to draw myself closer to God. That day I prayed for the strength to give away my resentment of Frank. Bringing the priest to baptize our child—it was a loving thing my husband had done. I took a long deep breath and felt a little bitterness leave my heart.

THIRTY-ONE

T HE NEXT MORNING AMBER WAS UP BEFORE MINNA WOKE. Going downstairs to the kitchen, she flipped on the coffee maker, relieved that threshing was over. She mixed up Minna's cereal and made her bottle. She glanced at the calendar on the wall. It was the nearly the end of August. It was time to make decisions, about the dairy and about Marc.

Gazing around the completed kitchen, seeing light shining on the soapstone countertops and a vase of bright pink cosmos on the tin-topped table, she knew, despite her father's reservations, the house would stay in the family. It is time I make these decisions for myself, without always thinking about what my father wants, she thought.

After feeding the baby and giving her a bath, Amber took the little one out to the front yard. She spread a blanket on the grass and lay down beside her. The tyke had grown so much, Claire had missed so much. She remembered playing badminton with Claire when they were small children. They hadn't a court or even a net, just batted the white birdie back and forth in the long summer twilight. The baby started fussing. Amber picked her up and took her inside. When the phone rang, she was cuddling Minna with a blanket.

"Hello, Amber, it's Allswede here. I've figured it out. In the last five years, Irene Morand had cut her herd of dairy cattle down to just a half dozen cows. That's why the income had fallen off so dramatically. That's simply too small a herd to generate enough income to cover the costs of a farm the size of yours, although it was all Irene could handle by herself. All you have to do is buy more cattle, and if they are good milkers, you can keep the farm intact. You'll start making enough to run the farm and support yourself almost immediately. I'm not saying you will get rich, but you can save the farm." He sounded absolutely overjoyed.

Amber thanked him for his work and said good-bye, feeling a flush of pleasure. It was going to be possible. Now all I have to do is find the family treasure and I'll be able to buy the herd. It isn't going to be easy to tell Dad, she thought. But I have to choose my own path in life and to my surprise it seems to have led me to this farm.

A breeze came in through an open window and she suddenly felt Aunt Irene's presence the day Amber told her not to die before she could bring her out to the farm. She had a sudden sense of Ina standing nearby too, looking at her expectantly. It was as if both women were awaiting her decision. Amber looked around the house, imagining Ina caring for baby Irene in the old log cabin and Frank building the summer kitchen. In her mind, the decades spun past and she saw her mother as a young woman spending summers at the farm and bringing her and Claire for visits as children. She saw Aunt Irene living alone in the carriage house, prodding the cows into the barn for milking.

Her ancestors were waiting. It was time for her to pick up the torch. Staying at the farm, keeping the farm, would mean being a part of something bigger than herself. The art business had drawn her eye, but the farm had captured her heart. She would not be the one to break a chain of lineage a century long. It wouldn't be an easy life, but it was the life she was choosing.

She looked out the kitchen window at the big red barn and experienced a sudden joyful sensation of having been set free—free the regimented world of nine-to-five employment, from friends who expected her to enjoy smoky clubs and flirting with strangers, free from the world of mainstream urban life and from the years she had devoted to her father and her sister. Her father had Joanna now. It was time to commit to keeping the farm. Commitment is what transforms promises into reality, she thought. This is the place I'm meant to be.

AFTER LEAVING MINNA WITH MEGAN THE NEXT MORNING, Amber drove to Apple River Falls. She stopped briefly in Mr. Allswede's office to tell him her decision.

"I'm keeping the farm, Mr. Allswede, so I'm ready to read Aunt Irene's note. You said she had left one for me. When I was cleaning out Aunt Irene's apartment above the carriage house, I found a safety deposit box key. It's possible there's something in it that would help me buy the cows I'm going to need."

"I'll tell my mother what you've decided," Mr. Allswede said, looking deeply moved. "She'll be so pleased. She knew Irene Morand and respected how long she was able to keep the dairy going. Let me get that note for you." He took it from his desk, handed it to her and she opened the small envelope seeing Aunt Irene's old spidery handwriting.

Dear Amber,

Since you're reading this, I know you are staying. I knew you would do the right thing. Please return the icon to the church where I was baptized. It's on Lake Superior. Ina's Journal should go back to the old country but I leave to you the choice of what to do with the family treasure. Yes, it exists. It's been a blessing, having you come into my old life. Throw away those pricey boots, girl. They don't fit your new life. In case you didn't get it, I loved you right from the start. Don't ever forget, the real treasures are you and the baby.

Aunt Irene.

Amber felt tears on her face, remembering the independent old woman who went her own way right up to the end. Irene Morand had been a blessing in her life too.

SHE DROVE TO THE BANK WITH HER FINGERS CROSSED, hoping to find that the key in Aunt Irene's knotted sock opened a safety deposit box.

"I'm delighted to see you," Marc said when she arrived. He was impeccably dressed as usual in a pale gray suit, a white shirt and beautifully patterned tie. Looking at the key, he said, "It's definitely for a safety deposit box. We have three hundred boxes here."

Marc took another set of keys from his pocket and called his new assistant, Nora. She was a serious-looking girl dressed in a navy suit. "Will you get me the key for this box and pull the paperwork on the owner, please?"

When Nora returned, she handed Marc the key and the paperwork.

"Yes, I was right. The original owner was Frank Morand. He was Irene's father, your great great grandfather. He passed away in 1953. His sons, Paul and Charles, paid to rent the box until they died, and Miss Irene paid the box rental religiously since. The box obviously contains something they all valued highly."

The three of them walked to the vault door. It was circular, made of metal and was about ten feet in diameter and over two feet thick. Marc inserted his key and Amber could hear the tumblers move. Then Nora used her key and Marc pulled the enormous steel handle to the left. The thick circular door swung open soundlessly.

Marc checked the number on Amber's key and they walked deeper into a secondary room. Its walls had been made of hundreds of numbered silver boxes. In the center of the room was a marble-topped table. A bright halogen light from the ceiling fell on its surface. Marc located the box matching the number on Amber's key, pulled the box out and set it on the table, unopened.

"How does this work, Marc?" Amber asked.

"Opening a box takes two keys. The owner has one and the bank keeps one."

Amber took a deep breath as one by one both the bank key and hers inserted easily.

"I'm going to leave you now. It's protocol that the owner of the box is unaccompanied by bank officials while examining the contents."

Alone in the quiet room, Amber lifted the lid of the safe deposit box. A folded document and a small wooden box lay inside. She carefully unfolded the ancient document. It was the Last Will and Testament of Frank Victor Morand. She read it briefly, seeing the farm willed to Paul and Charles Morand and a subsequent document transferring ownership to Irene Morand. A shiver passed through her body as she raised the lid to the wooden box. She couldn't wait to see the golden coins. Then her heart sank, for inside the box was only a small leather bag. Sliding her finger down inside it, she pulled out . . . another key. She sighed. Aunt Irene was still testing her, there was once more secret to ferret out. Picking up the paperwork and the leather bag, Amber walked out of the conference room and into Marc's office.

"Were you pleased with what you found?" Marc asked.

"Partly. What I found was Frank Morand's Will and a little leather bag containing a key. I have no idea what it will open. Aunt Irene is no doubt chuckling up in heaven right now. She's thrown down the gauntlet again."

WHEN AMBER PULLED IN TO THE FARMHOUSE DRIVEWAY, she saw Hunter and a crew of men cleaning the interior of the barn. She had agreed they could use Irene's money to get it cleaned and insulated. The high pressure hoses were removing almost a hundred years of straw, manure and grime off old timbers. Hunter looked up briefly, but continued working.

"Mr. Freedman, can I see you a minute?" Amber yelled over the noise of the pressurized water. He walked out and stood beside her. When he smiled the sun lit his narrow features. "I want you to know that I'm staying. Irene's Dairy is going to be a reality. Have you decided whether you will manage the dairy for me?"

"Thank you, Amber. Yes, I have decided. I will be the manager for Irene's Dairy."

"Thank you so much," Amber said and hugged him.

"My son will help clean the barn, blow in the insulation and put in the new equipment, but he is troubled, Amber. I think he is considering leaving here—probably in the next few days. Without him here, running the Dairy alone could be too much for me."

Amber felt as if a cold shower had drenched her. "Do you think I could convince him to stay?" her voice was despairing

"*Maagizha*," he said and shrugged his shoulder.

Amber thought the word meant perhaps in the Ojibwa language. She had learned a few words from Hunter.

"*Miigwech, Mr. Freedman*," Amber said and a ghost of a smile lit the man's dark features.

"*Giga-wabamin Menawah*, Amber," he replied.

Amber smiled at him. "I know *miigwech* means thank you, but did you just say good-bye?"

"In the Ojibwa culture there is no word for good-bye. Once a person enters your life, they join your circle and will always be a part of you. What I said means, I will see you again."

"And so you will," Amber said, loving the beautiful concept. "Pease don't let Hunter leave before I have a chance to say good-bye, will you?" He nodded. She reached for his hand and squeezed it, but turned away quickly, not wanting him to see the tears that welled in her eyes.

AFTER MINNA WENT DOWN FOR THE NIGHT, Amber poured herself a glass of lemonade and reached for Ina's journal. The couple were close to arriving at the farm.

Wisconsin, America
Spring, 1918
    We took a flat river barge down the St. Croix River. The barge was

unstable and it had only a canvas sheet and four poles as a shelter. I sat on icy wet boards, clutching my baby to my breast and grinding my teeth. Resentment had returned to my heart with a vengeance.

When we reached the small town of St. Croix Falls, I watched as Frank bought a wagon and two muscular workhorses. Golden coins flashed in his hand as he passed them to the other man. They must have been stolen. How else would Frank have that kind of money? We loaded everything we brought with us on the wagon. It was so little, some blankets, clothes and cooking pots. Frank said we were only fifteen miles from the farm. His eyes sparkled, but I turned away. I wouldn't meet his glance.

There was no road to follow, only two ruts between walls of high frozen grasses. Winter seems to last forever in this country and although it is March, the trail led through woods, lakes and ponds coated in ice and snow. Twice we had to drive the horses across frozen rivers. When late afternoon sunshine hit the trees their last leaves twisted in the wind, forlorn. Like me.

When we arrived at our destination in a spitting freezing rain, there was only a deserted two-room log cabin, squat and dark. The door had rope hinges. Inside, the only furniture was a bed with no mattress and a kitchen table with a tin top. The wind wheeled in through cracks in the chinking and despite all the hazards of the trip, I had never felt so miserable.

My furniture and my jewelry were sold without my permission. My little dog was sacrificed and this desolation was what my husband bought? I ground my teeth to keep from biting him.

THIRTY-TWO

"**D**AD, I AM SO HAPPY YOU AND JOANNA ARE HERE," Amber said as they drove in a few days later. She had been preparing for their arrival all day, dusting, cleaning, putting fresh sheets on beds and picking flowers for arrangements on tables and nightstands. Her father was getting out of the car with some difficulty, using a cane.

"This must be Claire's little one. Hello, Pumpkin," he said and smiled.

"Let me have that adorable baby," Mrs. Miller said as she got out of the car and held out her hands for Minna.

"It's so good to see you both." Amber said. She swallowed with tears in her eyes.

"It's wonderful to see you too." Her father stopped walking for a moment, short of breath. "Seeing Claire and hearing about the baby really lifted my spirits. The night she came to the hospital your sister said she needed me to be part of her baby's life—since Minna's father apparently isn't in the picture. I was honored by her request." He looked deeply moved.

"I'm happy she did that," Amber said and kissed his cheek. "I know you still miss her terribly as do I. She is always on my mind." She cleared her throat, trying to stop herself from crying. "Let's go inside."

"I love what you've done with the summer kitchen, Amber," Joanna said as they opened the old screen door. "I came up here once with your mother years ago. She said it was her favorite room as a kid."

"Come into the main kitchen and sit down. You've had such a long drive. Let me get you a glass of wine, Joanna. Dad, I'll get your ginger ale."

"You are an angel," Joanna said as Amber poured.

"We wanted to ask you something, Honey. There was a news story on the radio about a World War I journal from Romania that could lead to the return of artwork stolen by the Russians. They said the ownership of the journal was being investigated. Do you think it could be Ina's journal?" her father asked.

"It was. This is what happened. I've been dating Marc Rochet, the president of the bank in Apple River Falls. He had an assistant, Nate, whose family came from Romania. Nate could read Romanian and translated Ina's journal for me. He was the person who stole it."

"Why did he want it?" her father asked frowning.

"Nate's family came from the same area of Romania as the Morands and he learned that lists of stolen treasures were often secreted in the spines of books. He hoped to find documentation that could prove ownership of his family's lost treasures. Nate's now in the custody of the authorities, although he will be released soon, because I have decided not to press charges."

"Why not?" her father asked. "I think you should consider it."

"Aunt Irene wanted the journal returned to the old country and I can do that now, so I don't see the point of punishing Nate. But, but let's not spoil our first evening together with this. I'll make a salad and put the casserole in the oven. My contractor's wife, Megan, made it for us."

The casserole sent its delicious aroma into the room and everyone started to relax. After dinner and more wine, Mrs. Miller asked, "Where do you want us to sleep tonight? I'm sorry to be fading, but I am exhausted."

"Irene's apartment in the carriage house is yours for the duration. It has all new furniture and a king-sized bed."

After washing up the dishes, they walked outside. The sun was setting. The sky was a mix of mauve and gold. A soft breeze lifted her hair as Amber led her father up the solid new staircase into the once-private domain of Miss Irene Morand. Joanna carried the baby.

"Come look at the screened-in porch, Joanna," Amber said. "If Dad snores tonight, you can sleep on Aunt Irene's daybed out here. The breeze is luxurious."

"This is perfect," Dad told her. "It will be nice and quiet. Just smell the blossoms on that mock orange shrub."

"It's such a blessing to have you here," Amber told him, her eyes welling.

She kissed them both good night and walked back to the house, carrying Minna on her hip. The baby was already asleep, warm and solid against her.

MARC CALLED THE NEXT MORNING to see if he could stop by in the afternoon.

"My father and Mrs. Miller are here visiting," Amber told him, wondering if he would beg off.

"I would like to meet your father," he said and she felt pleased.

Marc drove up around five and Amber walked out to his car to greet him. It was starting to cloud over. The lawn was browning and the grass looked thirsty. Sufficient rain made a tremendous difference to the crops. In Chicago she had only thought about the weather in terms of her own comfort. Here the land and its needs held hegemony over everything.

When Amber brought Marc inside and introduced him to her father, he was his most charming self.

"Mr. Bradshaw, I am pleased to meet you," Marc said. "I can see your daughter resembles you."

"Poor thing," Dad said and grinned. "Too bad she didn't look more like her beautiful mother."

"Dad!" Amber said, frowning in vexation, but she couldn't help grinning.

"I remember you from Irene's wake, Mrs. Miller. You look wonderful." Marc kissed her on both cheeks in the European fashion.

"How continental of you, Marc," Joanna said. Amber could tell she liked him.

"Come sit in the living room. I'll get us some drinks and appetizers." Amber left for the kitchen. Marc followed her.

"I'll give you a hand," he said.

As Amber was reaching for crackers, grapes, celery stalks and cheese, she heard the sounds of Minna waking up from the baby monitor. "I better get her out of bed."

"I'll do it," Marc said. He smiled at her look of surprise.

"Don't forget to change her diaper. They are in the dresser." Marc nodded and in just a few minutes, she could hear him talking to Minna upstairs on the baby monitor.

"Any problems," Amber asked, raising her eyebrows innocently when he returned carrying the baby. "She's pretty wiggly."

"Not a one," he said and she warmed to his willingness to change the baby dressed in his elegant suit. Amber carried the snacks, beverages and Minna's bottle into the living room. Marc carried the baby. They chatted about the weather, her father's recent experience with knee surgery and their trip. Minna made the hungry sign with her little hand and Marc said, "What does she want?"

"She's hungry. Do you want to give her a bottle?" Amber asked, pleased he was trying to decipher Minna's wishes.

"Yes, I'd like to," he answered, startling Joanna who raised her eyebrows glancing at Marc's suit.

When Minna finished her bottle, Marc sat her up in his lap. She grabbed for his silk tie and pulled it into her mouth to chew on. He just looked down and smiled. Even after Amber took the baby, Marc didn't get up to wash the spot off his tie. The whole time Camelot stood in the corner, his eyes fixed on Minna.

"Camelot Bradshaw, you stop that," Amber said and he backed down. "Sorry. He's very protective of Minna."

"Mr. Bradshaw, could I could borrow your daughter for the evening?" Marc asked with an impish grin.

"While we babysit?" Joanna smiled at Amber. "Gosh, I think we could manage an evening." Giving Amber a quick glance, she said, "Really, Honey it will be fine."

"It will be our privilege," her father said gruffly.

"Okay. If you are sure. Should I change?" Amber asked Marc and he nodded. "Snap! You have already seen my only dress," she said. "Oh well, guess I'll have to wear it anyway."

When Amber came downstairs in her black dress, heels and jewelry, Marc stood up and whistled.

"You are gorgeous," he said, whispering in her ear.

"Joanna, there is plenty of left-over casserole in the fridge for you and dad for dinner. Minna has cereal at dinnertime. Her rice cereal is in the cupboard beside the sink. You can give her a final bottle at around seven-thirty. They're all made up and in the fridge. She needs a bath and her pink jammies are in the top drawer of her dresser. Please put her into bed at eight. If you put the dog in the room with her, she doesn't fuss."

"Such an organized young mother you are. You don't need to worry about us, Amber," Joanna said, smiling.

OPENING THE BACK DOOR TO THE OUTSIDE, Amber felt a light misty rain on her face. They ran to the car, laughing. Marc drove them to a gray granite building on the river near the city of Eau Claire. It had been a grist mill once and the old wheel still jutted out over the water, turning slowly in the tumbling current. The host led them toward the back of the building where Marc had reserved a private room with French doors that opened to a lawn sloping down to the riverbank. The doors were slightly ajar and the rain came down softly making circles in the water. The air smelled clean and cool.

Marc held out his hand for Amber's and leaned across the table to kiss her. The waiter came in and turned abruptly, apologizing for interrupting them. Amber laughed at his embarrassment.

"Don't worry about it," Marc told him. "If this evening goes the way I hope it will, I plan to have many more opportunities to kiss this beautiful woman."

"You're one lucky guy," the waiter said and Amber felt herself blush.

After dinner, Marc pulled a small box from his pocket. The breeze from the open French door tousled his hair as he said, "Amber Bradshaw, I am hopelessly in love with you. I cannot stop thinking about you. Every night I spend away from you lasts forever. I want an exclusive relationship and I'd like us to live together."

Amber felt her cheeks flare with warmth. She leaned forward and cupped his face in her hands. They kissed for a long time, her cloud of dark wavy hair making a veil around them.

"I hope your kiss means you feel the same way about me. I bought you a gift that shows how much you mean to me." He opened a black velvet jeweler's box. Inside was a stunning pair of earrings, made of semi-precious amber ovals encircled with tiny yellow diamonds. "The amber stones represent you, of course, and the circlets of diamonds are my pledge to give you a diamond ring one day."

"The earrings are exquisite. How did you know, Marc?" she whispered. "I have always loved yellow diamonds."

"I will confess to a bit of help," he grinned. "I consulted with Cassidy in Chicago. I drove down to the city day before yesterday, and she went with me to pick them out. Put them on, will you? I want to see how they look on you."

Amber stood up and walked to the women's rest room. Standing in front of the mirror, she took the earrings from the jeweler's box and put them on. She turned her head to the left and right, seeing the diamonds catch the light. She absolutely loved them, but at the same time knew she wasn't ready to move to the next stage in their relationship.

When she rejoined Mark in the dining room, he stood up to help her into her chair. Was that kiss your answer, Amber?" he asked. "Can we move in together?"

"I am sorry, Marc but I need more time to think about this," Amber said and started to remove her earrings, but he stopped her with a gesture.

"Please keep them, Amber. Regardless of your decision, I bought them for you. You never have to give them back. And, if you agree to marry me someday, I want you to know that I want to adopt Minna and be her father."

Tears formed in Amber's eyes as she looked at his passionate face.

"I am honored by your gift, Marc. I promise I will give you my decision soon."

"I will count the hours," he said, smiling.

Amber lifted her eyes to the window. Outside, the pattering of summer rain was barely audible. Mist rose from the river, bathing the fields in moisture.

"It's going to be good sleeping tonight," she said quietly.

"How I wish I could hold you in my arms and we could listen to the rain together," Marc said and his intense desire for her wrapped around her like a blanket. "But I won't ask that of you. I'm sure you wouldn't be comfortable making love to me with your father there. But I love you so much, I can't wait for us to be together," Marc smiled.

THIRTY-THREE

<hr>

Driving back to the farm, Amber asked Marc about something that had bothered her since their first date.

"Marc, I'm troubled about why you seem to be in such a hurry to move our relationship to the point of moving in together. We really don't know each other that well and we haven't even slept together yet."

"Not for my lack of trying," Marc said and grinned.

Amber rolled her eyes good-naturedly.

"Actually, I've respected you holding me off. I want you to be as sure as I am. But there is another reason for wanting a commitment so soon." He hesitated before continuing, as if weighing his words. There was a sudden grim twist to his mouth.

"I should have shared this with you before. I'm sorry I didn't," he exhaled deeply. "When I was in my early twenties, I fell in love. Her name was Chantelle. She was tall and willowy." He paused. "We dated for four years before I asked her to marry me. I was thrilled when she said yes." He tried to smile, but it faded quickly. There was no pleasure in his eyes.

Amber waited silently. The interior of the car seemed too hot, too dense to contain Marc's feelings and the story she already sensed had a tragic outcome.

Marc glanced at her and then focused his eyes to the road again. "We got married a year later, on a sunny June morning. She wore her grandmother's wedding gown with flowers in her hair," Amber saw his eyes shine with tears. "We didn't have the money for a honeymoon and so delayed our trip for a year. She wanted to hike the mountains in Mexico. I would have gone anywhere she wanted." He cleared his throat and pulled the car over into a small roadside park. They sat in the car as he continued the story. "When we left on our trip, Chantelle was already pregnant with our first child, a baby girl."

"What happened?" Amber asked, dreading his answer.

"Chantelle got up early one morning to go for a run. I stayed in the villa we rented. I was going to make us breakfast. She was in a hurry and I didn't," he cleared his throat trying to dampen his emotion. "I didn't even . . . take the time to kiss her good-bye." There was an unnatural stillness to his body.

Amber waited in silence as the air darkened around them.

"Chantelle was bitten by a feral dog. She barely mentioned it until a week later. By then she was having spasms and a fever. The dog was rabid. They gave her the treatment, but she died. Despite everyone's efforts, I lost her. I lost them both."

Marc put his face into his hands and his shoulders shook with silent sobs. Amber leaned across the seats and put her arms around him. She could find no words of comfort for his devastating loss. The pain was too brutally raw. The drive back to the farmhouse was long and silent.

When Marc drove into the driveway at the farm, Amber said, "I am so terribly sorry, Marc. I don't want you to have to put on a front for Dad and I would rather go inside by myself." A brief look of regret crossed his face.

She looked at him then, wondering if she and Minna mere replacements—substitutes for his lost family.

"I'm leaving the country in a few days, Amber," Marc said. "Now that the investigation about the provenance of Ina's journal is settled, and you agreed to give it to the people of Romania, the authorities are going to release it to the Romanian government. They have approved my request to be present for the ceremony."

Amber frowned, feeling confusion and anger. "I should be the person to take Ina's journal to Romania."

"I'm sorry, Amber," he said, looking surprised at her reaction. "I wanted to do this for you. And Minna is too young for the vaccinations required for international travel."

"I would have figured out how to go, Marc," Amber said, glaring at him. She was deeply disappointed he had proceeded without asking her.

"I'm sorry. You're right, of course, but it's too late now to get passports and approval. I already have appointments with government officials. I wanted to do this for you, to be your agent in transmitting the journal to the people of Romania."

Amber's chest tightened. She was upset by his decision, but in the wake of the devastating story about his wife, she told herself to let it go. "I'm disappointed, Marc, but since it appears settled, at least returning Ina's journal to Romania was what Aunt Irene wanted."

"I'll be gone for almost two weeks. When I get back, I'll come out to the farm. I want you to know how much I love you, Amber Bradshaw."

She didn't answer, still upset by Marc's presumptiveness and walked inside alone. The door to the summer kitchen squeaked as it snapped shut behind her. Both her father and Joanna had fallen asleep on the couch, but Joanna woke at her touch. Putting a finger to her lips, they walked into the kitchen.

"How was your evening?" Joanna asked.

"Memorable," Amber whispered. Pulling her hair back she said, "Marc gave me these earrings. He wants us to move in together and said he plans to propose."

"How exciting! Congratulations, Amber. Marc is quite a catch. He seems good with Minna, too."

"He offered to adopt her, if I agree to marry him, but I didn't give him an answer. I need more time."

"Why are you hesitating?"

"I found out tonight that Marc was married before. His wife died on a trip about a year after they married."

"How awful," Joanna said, frowning. "That's just terrible. Poor, poor man."

"When I asked him why he was in such a hurry to get married he told me the story. His wife was pregnant when she died. It all makes sense to me now, his rush to move our relationship to a more permanent footing, his wanting to adopt Minna. He wants what he lost."

"And here you are. You and Minna, a ready-made family," Joanna said thoughtfully.

"I truly believe he loves me," Amber said, "For him, it was clearly love at first sight. I care a lot for him too, but I don't know if I'm in love with him. I've known him such a short time. And Cam doesn't like Marc," Amber said, frowning. "I couldn't figure it out until now. His wife died from a rabid dog bite."

"Cam can probably sense his fear," Joanna said.

"I won't give Cam up."

"Certainly you aren't going to let your dog make your decision, are you?"

"No, but there's another problem."

"Ah yes, the Hunter problem," Joanna's eyes twinkled. "I met him at Aunt Irene's wake you will recall. I could tell then you liked him. Years ago, when I was a young woman, I had a choice between my husband and another suitor. It was a hard decision. I hated hurting the other man, but it was the right one. If you had a choice between the two of them and chose Hunter, would you become a country mouse?" Joanna tipped her head to one side, smiling.

"What are you talking about?"

"It's an old children's book about a mouse that has a choice between living in the city and living in the country. She chooses the country."

They were both quiet for a moment before Joanna continued.

"On the other hand, if you chose Marc, I bet he could get a position in Chicago and you would be close to your father and me. You have a lot to think about and it's late." She patted Amber's arm.

BEFORE SHE FELL ASLEEP TO THE SOFT SLOUGH of the wind whispering in the cottonwood trees, Amber thought about Marc's gift and his request to move in together. Despite her hesitations, she knew he was sincere in his feelings for her. The man was gorgeous, intelligent and successful. His offer to adopt Minna touched her deeply. If she married Marc, he would want to have another baby. She would have a sibling for Minna. And I'd like another baby someday, too, she realized.

But did he truly love her, or was she just a replacement for Chantelle and their unborn child? Despite caring for him, she knew she hadn't fallen in love. Her feelings for Hunter stood in the way. She sighed, feeling a wave of regret that Hunter didn't seem to return her feelings. Could she learn to love Marc in time? She thought of Ina and Frank and wondered if Ina would ever learn to love her husband? She reached for the journal.

Ina Morand Journal Entry
Apple River Falls, Wisconsin
Spring, 1918
We had been at the farm for over a month before the weather finally broke and there was a thaw. I took the two cottonwood saplings out of the cloth they had been wrapped in so long. I managed to keep them wet all this time and hoped they would still take root. Digging in the dirt was a

struggle, but I estimated how tall they would be when they were grown and placed them far apart. Maybe when the weather warms, their white fluffy seeds will sail across this land to my homeland and my parents. I had sent several letters, but had never heard back from them.

Frank decided to take the horses and wagon to buy flour, sugar and more supplies at the closest railroad depot. I had a funny premonition watching him load the wagon and almost asked him not to go, but we were out of everything.

I learned later when he reached the Rail Depot, a small dog ran out barking. The team bolted. The reins were pulled from his grasp. Frank tried to grab the reins by walking down the wagon's tongue as the horses raced down the street. He lost his balance and fell beneath the horses' crushing feet. Three men pulled him from beneath the wrecked wagon. They found a doctor who came with them when they brought him home. The men laid Frank down on the tin- topped kitchen table.

"His leg can't be fixed," the doctor told me. His old face was wrinkled like a walnut and he reeked of alcohol. "Give him some whiskey and hold him down. I have to amputate." He pulled out a saw and told the men to hold Frank until he passed out.

When Frank screamed, I fainted. When I came to, my husband had one leg. If Frank died, what would become of us? Then I felt a burn of guilt that I had only been thinking of myself.

How were we ever going to farm this land now? I remembered threshing time on my parent's farm, when the whole village came to help. Women carried food to the men and cool drinks. When the grain was in the barns, there was a festive celebration. But there was no community here, only a one-legged man, a woman and a baby.

Forcing myself, I bathed Frank's stump and dressed it with cloth. Slowly, the wound began to close. The doctor came a month later and fitted Frank with a peg leg. It was painfully embarrassing to see how hard he worked to master the wooden post. Sometimes, I felt a twinge of compassion for Frank, but I never let him know. He had taken my life. God had only taken his leg.

THIRTY-FOUR

The next morning Amber woke having dreamed about the horrible accident that claimed Frank Morand's leg. Even after his leg was amputated, Ina hadn't been able to forgive her husband and find peace. Amber felt disappointed in Ina for holding on to her resentment for so long. Her own anger with her mother for making her responsible for her sister, as well as her guilt about Claire had seemingly vanished. Committing to Minna and the farm, in addition to Joanna's kind words and support, had allowed her to forgive herself.

She got out of bed, pulled off her nightgown and looked at herself in the mirror. The hard work on the farm had tightened her whole body. She hadn't needed a gym at all. She picked up the exquisite amber and diamond earrings from her dresser. Although they were ridiculously inappropriate for her jeans-and-T-shirt outfit, she couldn't resist putting them on. Her mobile phone rang as she finished getting dressed. It was Cassidy.

"Hi, Amber. What's been happening?"

"Hi Cass, I was going to call you today. I've decided," she took a quick breath, "I'm not coming back to Hillside Gallery. I'm sorry to tell you so late in the day."

"My friend, I saw the writing on the wall a long time ago. I knew you weren't returning. Kurt already hired your replacement. I still think you're a nutcase to want to live on a farm. Hey, do you remember me telling you about the Viviane Gallery in Minneapolis? I applied for an assistant director's position and I got it! So, now about those earrings?"

"You have impeccable taste my friend, but I didn't give Marc an answer about us moving in together. I told him I needed more time."

"When Marc came to Chicago to pick out the earrings, I told him I didn't think you were ready, but he's so deeply in love, he didn't hear a word I said."

"I felt terrible telling him I wasn't sure, but I'm not."

"If he gives you more time, will you say yes?" Cassie asked.

"I don't know," Amber said and sighed. "I really don't know. Living here has helped me deal with the grief I still had about my mother's death and my failures with Claire. I'm more confident in my decisions now." She paused before saying, "Do you want to stay here until you find an apartment in Minneapolis? It's only about an hour's drive to the Twin Cities, and you know I would love to have you."

"I'll be up at the end of the week. We can talk more then. Love you, girlfriend."

When Amber walked downstairs carrying Minna, her father was in the kitchen making coffee. "Hi Dad. Nice morning, isn't it?"

"Certainly is. Good morning, Honey. Get yourself a cup of coffee and I will give Minna her bottle." Amber smiled at her father looking tenderly at the baby.

"Joanna told me you have made the commitment to raise Minna."

"Yes, I'm at peace with that decision and I want you in Minna's life too," Amber said quietly and hugged him. "Later today I want you to meet Hunter."

"So Joanna told me. Sounds to me like you have a big decision to make," he said

She took a deep breath. "I care a lot for Marc, but there's something about Hunter I'm strongly drawn to," she stopped. "I don't know if I can talk about being interested in two men with my own father," she wrinkled her nose and grinned.

"Sounds like I better meet this Hunter guy," he said gruffly. They drank their coffee in companionable silence.

"I've made another important decision, Dad. I wanted to tell you first. I'm going to keep the farm as well as this house. I'm going to live here."

"You and I have discussed this, Amber. I see how much you love this place, but the taxes, insurance and upkeep on the old place and running a farm long distance are high. The farm used to be self-supporting, but when I took over financial guardianship, I discovered that the farm was losing money."

"My attorney, Mr. Allswede, discovered the reason the income had fallen off so drastically. Aunt Irene could only handle half a dozen milk cows by the end. It takes at least fifty cows to make a farm this size profitable."

"That makes sense. Aunt Irene's pride stood in the way of her telling us, I presume."

"Did I tell you Aunt Irene left me a note saying there really is a family treasure? If I can find it, I will have enough money to buy the new herd of cows and put the farm in the black," she paused and smiled at him.

"But you haven't found it yet?"

"No, but I will. I'm sure you remember the day I found a key to the Morand's safe deposit box? Inside the box there was a little leather pouch with a second key in it. No doubt it's another one of Aunt Irene's little mysteries. However, since I already found Ina's journal and the icon, I'm sure I can solve this mystery too. I am determined not to need any help at all from you, Dad."

"Well done, Honey. I'm proud of you. This summer on the farm, enduring the losses of Claire and Aunt Irene has changed you. You've grown up and I'm proud of you." He looked at her smiling.

"I've made another decision too, I'm going to re-start Irene's Dairy. I gave a lot of thought to simply growing hay and grain. It would have been much easier, but starting the dairy again was Aunt Irene's last wish. And you know how I feel about honoring last wishes." She smiled.

"I do indeed," he said.

"Hunter's father has agreed to manage Irene's Dairy and Mr. Lundgren from down the road will manage the planting and threshing."

"I suspect all this has an impact on whether you say yes or no to Marc Rochet." Her dad's eyes twinkled.

"I suspect you are right, old man," Amber grinned and hugged him.

AT FOUR O'CLOCK THAT AFTERNOON, Amber took her father and Joanna Miller down to the barn to see the calves and meet Hunter. As soon as the dog saw Hunter, he raced to him and stood up on his hind legs, putting his front paws on either side of Hunter's neck. They were almost the same height. Hunter rubbed his hands along the dog's ribs. Her father walked over to introduce himself to Hunter as Amber turned to Mrs. Miller.

"Did Dad tell you that I'm committed to staying here at the farm, Joanna? He still has reservations, I know, but I'm determined to save it without his help."

"He did tell me, and I'm glad. You fit here. Don't worry, Honey, if it's the right thing for you, he'll adjust to the idea."

"I'm going to re-start Irene's Dairy, too. I feel a duty to the dreams of Aunt Irene and her parents, to all those who came to this place before me," she said.

"Your mother told me she kept the house all these years for the same reasons."

"Are you okay watching Minna? I need a little time with Hunter." At her nod, Amber handed the baby to Joanna who smiled as she took the little one in her arms.

"Come walk with me, Hunter," she said, holding out her hand to him. It was time to find out what he truly felt for her.

THEY AMBLED BEYOND THE BARNYARD and along pasture fences to the foot of the big hill. Amber gazed up through a field of Queen Anne's lace so tall it reached up to her thighs. Patches of purple knapweed clung to life in the stony soil below the floating lacey foliage of the taller flowers. Here and there a patch of yellow coreopsis raised their cheerful faces. Climbing to the top, as the wind blew her hair back from her face, Amber experienced a moment of profound peace. At the summit, there was a cluster of large gray boulders backed by tall oaks. She and Hunter sat side by side on the largest stones, warm from the heat of the summer sun. Looking down at the farm, it resembled a toy farm set for a child. She could see her calves milling around in the barnyard.

"We need to talk about our feelings for each other," Amber told him and he nodded, looking intently at her. "Down there I see my heart's true land, but your father says you are thinking of leaving."

"Below us, I see my history—but I also see a trap."

"A trap?" Amber said. She swallowed. Her heart felt crushed.

"After my mother died, I needed to be here for Dad. I've stayed far longer than I ever intended."

She tucked a piece of hair around her ear. The yellow diamond earrings caught the light and Hunter leaned forward and swept her hair back with his hands.

"Where did these come from?" he asked.

"A gift from Marc. He wants to move in with me, but I haven't given him an answer," Amber said, feeling a lurch in her stomach.

"But you haven't told him no, have you?" Hunter asked in a resigned tone of voice. He looked off into the distance.

"Do you remember the day we went to the Creamery, Hunter?" She asked. He nodded. "It seemed to me then that we were already a family, you, me, Minna and Cam. Was I wrong?"

"No, you were right," he said, but his voice filled with pain. "I felt it too, but I always planned to leave this place. Do you remember the day I said I couldn't kiss you?"

"Of course. Tell me why?"

"My mother always believed in my talent. She found out about a school for First Nations kids with artistic ability. They gave me a full scholarship when I was seventeen. Toward the end of my second year, my father called. My mother was dying. It was time to come home. I went home that day. I have not left the farm or painted anything since." He stopped talking for a moment. And then added, "I was holding her hand the day my mother passed away. I've stopped myself from leaving here a thousand times because of Dad."

"I never realized before how similar our histories are, Hunter. When my mother died, she asked me to look after my father and my sister," Amber said. "I put my life on hold for years while Claire grew up. In fact, I only came to the farm this summer as part of my promise to my mom."

"When you arrived, I saw a door swing open to my future. With you and Minna here, Dad would have a family again. That's why I can't kiss you, can't make love to you. It's not that I don't want to," he said, and his eyes were full of longing.

"What are we going to do about our feelings, Hunter?" she asked softly, looking deep into his eyes. She leaned in close and took in his scent, so earthy and clean.

"I am torn, Amber," he said. "I need to find out if I can still paint. I think my confidence would come back if I weren't here, in the place where my Mother died, but when I look at you, when I touch you . . ." his voice trailed off. "Before you arrived, I was drowning. On the day we met, I saw dry land."

She reached for him and they kissed for a long time. She could feel him giving himself fully to her and love filled her heart. Her soul opened like a flower. When the kiss ended, she said, "Hunter, you know I used to work at an art gallery in Chicago. I've seen your sketches from when you stayed with me after I was locked in the cellar. You are enormously talented. I believe I could get some of your work exhibited and sold."

"Don't you see, Amber? Don't you know?" Hunter's brow was furrowed. His voice was harsh. "I have to keep my word to my mother to keep painting and I can't paint here. There's something else, too. I need to be as successful as Rochet, to stand beside him on equal ground. If you chose me, I wouldn't want you to regret your decision someday down the line."

"Oh, Hunter, I wouldn't. I want to be the place you come ashore."

Hunter sighed. "Not yet, Amber. Maybe never. And you need to decide about Rochet without me here."

Amber struggled to control her tears and forced herself to be the grown-up her father said she was, to honor Hunter's needs. "It's taken me a long time to know my own direction in life. How can I ask you to stay here when you are not ready? I will wait for you, Hunter, but not forever," her voice was serious. "And promise me you won't return unless you are going to stay and be with me."

"You have my word," he said. He kissed her once more, leaving her weak in the knees. At that moment, she almost couldn't let him go. But he stood up, smiled at her and walked down the hill. Tears formed in her eyes watching Hunter's tall slimness departing. She remembered the night he came to the farmhouse after rescuing her from the cellar, the terrible wine and strawberries he brought and all the things they talked about—the old people at the farm and his memories of Lillian Morand. His was the only voice she could hear above the terrible roar of fear she felt. How have I let myself be swept into a relationship with Marc, when all along it has been Hunter?

She realized then she wouldn't marry Marc but would make her way in life alone if necessary and maybe someday, when Hunter had achieved the success he sought, he would return. She lay back against the rock and felt the sun warm her body. If I can't have the man I love, I have Minna and the farm. Just like Ina had baby Irene and the farm, she thought. But then she remembered—Ina hadn't run the farm alone. She had Frank.

LATE THAT EVENING, AMBER STOOD at the foot of the cottonwood trees with a carefully wrapped package in her arms. Mr. Freedman called and told her his son was leaving, but that he would stop to say good-bye. Hunter parked his truck by the calf pen, walked up the driveway and joined her by the big trees. She started to cry.

"Shush," he said quietly. "I just came to say good-bye."

"I have something I want you to take with you," she managed, handing him the package.

"What is it?" His expression was unreadable in the soft moonlight.

"It's the icon. In Ina's journal, she wrote about a double-spired Orthodox church on the shores of Lake Superior. Aunt Irene was baptized there. In her final letter, she asked that the icon be given to that church. I just hope it still exists. If it does and you can find it, I would like the priest there to decide where the icon should reside permanently."

"I will make sure that happens. Tonight I think I'm crazy to leave you, Amber, to leave this place," he said, his expression was filled with regret.

She took a deep breath. "It took me months to know what I wanted. I understand you needing the same thing, the time to know beyond hesitation where you belong. Ever since I learned you would be leaving, I struggled to resign myself to your absence. Then I realized I was looking at your dreams in the wrong way. Supporting your desire to be an artist is my definition of love."

"I know you won't wait forever," Hunter said. "Can I kiss you good-bye?"

"Always," Amber replied and held out her arms to him.

He kissed her with such tender passion, she could not hold back her tears. He put his hands on her shoulders and for a moment she was lost in the warm darkness of his eyes.

"Good-bye, Amber," he said and walked down the dusty driveway in the moonlit darkness.

"Hunter?" She called after him.

He turned around.

"Don't forget me."

"Never," he said as he got in the truck and pulled out of the driveway. The wind cooled her face. The stars hung in the trees like paper cut-outs.

SHE WALKED INTO THE HOUSE IN silent tears, sat down on the love seat and opened Ina's journal.

The Farm, Wisconsin

Spring, 1918

I haven't written in my Journal since the night the doctor cut off Frank's leg. The snow is melting now and the wolves no longer howl at night. I see them at dusk creeping past our house, moving shadows among the trees. They are getting fatter, eating rabbits and deer weakened by the winter snows. Frank can't hunt yet. We are thin as sticks, but he has promised when summer comes, he will build us a better house.

Alene and Charles arrived at our wretched farm a week ago. I was embarrassed at how it looks. Our little cabin was not even as big as my parents' home in the old country. Alene loves Charles and wants nothing more than to give him a child. Sometimes when she holds Irene, I remember that awful night in Chicago when I almost gave her away. I cannot forgive her for offering to buy my baby when I was at my most desperate. When I see baby Irene's face, I'm glad I resisted and kept her. She is the one good thing Frank has given me.

Summer, 1918

It's high summer and despite Frank's promise to build me a decent house, the men have started building a barn! I am outraged. I'm supposed to live in this pigsty of a log cabin, but Frank is building a barn? For what? We don't have any livestock. Not even chickens. I swore to Frank that if we didn't have a house by autumn, the baby and I would move into the useless barn.

Today Frank borrowed a plow and two mules to break up the prairie and create fields. I tied Irene to my back and Alene and I pulled rocks from the earth to make a stacked-stone wall around the field. Dust was everywhere and I was filled with fury. Later that night, I pressed Frank to answer my questions.

"Will we grow vegetables here, Frank?"

"No, we will plant hay and wheat."

"We can't eat hay and wheat, Frank. You shoot rabbits and deer, but Irene needs vegetables. I need chickens for eggs. I am taking a corner of the field for a vegetable garden."

The men were too busy to help us, so the next day Alene and I walked for miles to our closest neighbors. I gave the woman one of our golden lei, a coin I stole from my husband's pocket.

"What am I going to do with this?" The farmwife asked me. "I can't spend it in this country."

"Take it. It's gold," her husband said gruffly. She nodded and gave us seed, three hens and a rooster.

When the fields were planted, I reminded my husband of his promise to build me a real house.

"Where will we live if I tear down this cabin?"

"Build the house around the log cabin. Then you can take it down."

It took all summer, but our house was larger than any in my village. It even had an attic. Now I had a place to put the icon. Now I had a place to pray.

THIRTY-FIVE

AMBER WAS PLANNING TO DRIVE into Apple River Falls and apply for a loan to purchase the cows she needed, when she saw Ryan's truck pulling in behind the house. He hadn't been around much in recent days and she was happy to see him.

"What brings you here this morning, Ryan?" she asked, walking out to meet him.

"Megan told me last night you found a little key in your Aunt's safety deposit box. If it's an antique key, I might be able to tell you what it's for."

"Come on in. I should have thought to ask you since you're our resident expert in antiques around here." They walked into the house together and Amber offered Ryan some coffee. She pulled the key out of her wallet and set it on the kitchen island. "It's not decorative at all, that's why it didn't occur to me to ask you. It's just a plain simple silver key. I doubt you will know what it's for."

"Ah, but there you would be wrong, Miss Amber Bradshaw, I do know what it's for," he raised his face to hers grinning. "Do you remember when we argued about the side-by-side refrigerator freezer you wanted?"

"Of course. You wanted me to have a refrigerator with no freezer! I won that battle as I recall. By the way, Ryan, you still haven't electrified the burners on the stovetop," she narrowed her eyes, but felt amused. By now she knew it was unlikely he would ever connect them to power. She had even grown to enjoy lighting the kindling beneath the burners. Drat the man, she thought. He's converted me.

"To continue," Ryan said, "In the old days refrigerators didn't have freezer compartments. Later they had these tiny freezer sections, only big enough for a pound of meat and an ice cube tray. Even up to the late 1950's, people rented freezer space in town. They would drive in to town every few days to get frozen meat and vegetables," Ryan's grin was practically ear-to-ear.

"Are you telling me that this key—the one I've spent hours trying to determine what it opens—is the key to an old freezer unit in town?"

"I believe it is, but the problem is that the town freezer closed long ago. The shop has been converted to a specialty butcher's shop. It's where hunters bring deer in the fall to be dressed. You can still rent units there for storing venison."

"But Aunt Irene wasn't a hunter. She probably relinquished that cubby decades ago," Amber said, shaking her head in despair.

"Oh I doubt it. Would the Aunt Irene we all knew have left a key in her father's safety deposit box that opened nothing at all? And didn't she pay the rent on the safety deposit box all the decades since her brothers died?"

"Ryan, you are a wonder," Amber said. "I was about to apply for a loan to buy more cows for the farm, but clearly I need to visit the town freezer first." She felt a sudden welling of excitement. She was getting close, she could feel it. The treasure was almost within her grasp.

THAT EVENING WHEN AMBER REACHED FOR INA'S JOURNAL, she saw there were only two pages left. She would miss Ina's story when it was over.

Ina Morand Journal
Summer, 1918

Today twelve black and white spotted cows walked down the dusty two-track road to our farm. Frank and Charles kept them in line with whips and crooks. As the cattle walked into the barn, I named each one. There was one who looked at me sweetly with her big eyes and long eyelashes. I named her Iona. I told Frank her name and he smiled.

"Cows have to be milked every morning and night, Ina. Would you do the evening milking? By evening, my leg aches badly."

I agreed. He would do the morning milking and bring milk up to the house for Irene to drink. He had even made a miniature dairy can out of tin for our daughter's milk.

That evening I sat on the milking stool, taking in the sweet and nutty smell of cows and their feed. The floor was scattered with dusty bits of straw that caught the light. I leaned against the cow's flanks and breathed in her milky scent as I pulled on the engorged teats. It was peaceful, sitting by the cows, with the scent of fresh milk in the air. A feral cat slunk into the barn. Her nipples were enlarged. She had kittens somewhere. I squirted a bit of milk in her direction. By the time I finished milking, the cat would sit near me and I could squirt the milk directly into her open mouth.

"What will we do with all this milk, Frank?" I asked him.

"There is a Creamery in town. They will pay me well for it."

"So you used the gold to buy these cows. It doesn't feel right, Frank. I never met your father and only have your word that the golden lei came from him."

"I have never lied to you, my wife, and I give you my promise that what I've told you is true. I have asked God for forgiveness for taking the icon, but I will have good milk for our child." His whole self was a stubborn statue as he said these words. "And the money to buy this farm, build this barn and our houses, to buy these cows—it was my legacy from my father."

Irene needed the milk. Frank was right. He had been right about so many things, even about coming to this land. It was time to give the past away.

AFTER LOADING MINNA INTO HER CAR SEAT and Cam into the backseat the next morning, Amber drove into Apple River Falls. It took a bit of driving around, but she eventually found the Wild Animal &Venison Butchery. It was located at the rear of the grocery store, opening on to the parking lot. She managed to keep a struggling Cam in the car with one hand, while lifting Minna out with the other, and walked toward the building with the baby riding on her hip.

"Can I help you, Miss?" a young man wearing a long white apron asked as she approached the counter.

"I hope so. I understand there is a part of your store with lockers where people used to keep frozen meat before refrigerators got so big. I have a key I'd like to try on one of those lockers," Amber said.

The young man whose name tag read "Lennie" looked doubtful. "I have only worked here a few months, but we've been doing a lot of construction recently. Most of the old lockers have been pulled out. In fact, I saw some by the big dumpster yesterday." At her sudden pained expression, he added, "Maybe I better get one of the older guys to help you."

Amber waited, feeling herself tremble. She had reached the tipping point. If the old locker was still here, and the treasure was inside, she would have kept all her promises to her mother. If it had been discarded, she had no other trails to walk down. She found herself crossing her fingers. Several minutes passed before an older man with white hair came out from the rear of the butchery.

"I understand you are looking for one of the old lockers," he said. "You got here just in time. We've been ripping them out to make space for a large cold-storage room. Lennie said you have a key?"

Amber dropped it into the man's hand wordlessly.

"Not sure I can even read the number," he said and her heart fell. He studied the key closely before saying, "Write down these numbers, Len. Z18MOR. There's more, but that's enough to start with. We were supposed to track down the people who rented these lockers. I couldn't find anyone for this set of numbers, but I don't want to get into trouble giving it to you. Where did you come by the key?"

"I'm Irene Morand's grandniece, Amber. This key was part of her estate that I inherited. She passed away recently."

"I have a list of names I need to check. Lennie, can you grab the paperwork?"

When the young man returned and handed him the list, he said, "Morand you said? Right. I see it here. Sorry, but I just had to check before letting you have the contents. The oldest lockers were ripped out day before yesterday and already hauled to the dump. I think this was one of them but maybe it's still here. Come out with me to the parking lot."

Amber's knees were shaking. She had a hard time even following the old guy across the parking area to the large dumpster, afraid she would pass out and drop the baby.

"You're going to have to climb down in there, Len," the older man said, gesturing to the dumpster. The young guy frowned and started to protest before the man said, "Just do it, Son." Len climbed reluctantly into the bin, swearing furiously under his breath, and Amber could hear him moving things around. "Can't see it," he said and Amber swallowed, biting her lip.

"Look again," the old man ordered. She could hear Len grousing inside the dumpster and then amazingly, he said, "This might be it." She saw his head pop up. He was holding a large metal box in his hands. She closed her eyes in relief, feeling a tightening connection to Aunt Irene.

The older guy gave Lennie a hand up out of the container and once he was standing on the parking lot, he put the box down on the asphalt. "Do you want to try the key?" he asked.

"Could you try?" she asked, her fingers were wet with sweat.

Len fussed with the key, trying and failing to get it open before the old guy grimaced and said, "Just give it to me."

For one heart-stopping moment, she thought it wasn't going to open. Perhaps it was the wrong key, or the wrong locker. Maybe Irene's locker had already gone to the dump. She felt short of breath. But then the door on the box swung open and the older man said, "There's a little quilted bag in here." He held picked it up and held it out, "Is this what you wanted, Miss?"

"I think so," Amber said, holding out her hand and feeling a sudden swell of relief as the heavy little bag was placed in her hand. "Thank you. Thank you both."

"Like I said, you were just in time," the old guy said. "Hope there's something in there worth Len having to dumpster dive," he laughed and punched the young guy in the shoulder playfully. "You stink, Buddy. Go inside and get washed up."

Turning back toward her car, with the heavy cloth bag clutched tightly in her hand, Amber felt a profound sense of being in the right place. The treasure her mother had promised had existed and she had it in her hands. "I did it Aunt Irene. I solved the mystery," she whispered and felt the old lady smile.

Cam was sitting in the driver's seat when she reached the car. She shoved him into the back, clicked the baby into her car seat and sat there trying to slow her breathing. The quilted bag had a drawstring that had been tied in a knot. Her hands were trembling and she wondered if she should drive back to the farm before untying the string, but knew she wouldn't. Using her fingernails, she worked and tugged at the knot. When it finally gave and she reached inside, she felt a static shock and then a sense of cosmic correctness. Opening the drawstring fully, she looked down and saw what seemed to be a hundred golden coins.

The day of the cattle auction, Amber woke at dawn feeling excited. The air was cool as well-water when she dropped Minna off with Megan and drove to the Freedman's place.

"I understand you found the fabled Morand treasure," Mr. Freedman said when he came out to greet her. "Ryan told me."

"I did indeed. I never would have found it except for him. The first step was finding Aunt Irene's safe deposit key. When I went to the bank and opened her box, I found a little leather bag. Inside was this simple silver key. I was practically tearing my hair out trying to figure out what it opened, before Ryan told me it was for a freezer unit that Irene rented in town. It had been years since Aunt Irene had been inside that shop, but she kept paying the rent. I got there just in time. The locker had been ripped out and was in their dumpster. Inside the locker was a little cloth bag containing 100 golden Romanian lei. It was a thrill when I reached in and touched a stack of golden coins that had been there for almost a hundred years. With the family treasure, I can buy all the cows we need to start the dairy. I already exchanged the Romanian money for American dollars."

"I believe Aunt Irene would be very proud of you today," Mr. Freedman said, smiling.

THEY ARRIVED AT THE CATTLE AUCTION and walked across a dirt parking lot to the auction barns. Cattle in pens were milling around mooing, the sound was tremendous.

"We are looking for cows with large udders and less muscle than beef cattle," Mr. Freedman told her. They walked from pen to pen looking carefully at the stock.

"Have these cattle all been bred?" Mr. Freedman asked an attendant.

"Yep. They all took and are pregnant," the man assured Mr. Freedman.

"We are buying all pregnant cows?" Amber asked, amused by the thought.

"To maintain peak milk production cows are bred every year. Cow pregnancies last nine months and then we allow them two to three months rest before they are bred again. A year from now when we breed the herd, we will need to have an artificial insemination technician come to the farm. And we have to buy high quality semen."

Amber started to laugh. The idea of buying semen struck her as hilarious. Hearing her giggle, Mr. Freedman frowned. Apparently, this was serious business.

By the end of the day, Mr. Freedman had successfully bid on all the black and white Holsteins he wanted and went to pay the auctioneer for their livestock. Men began separating the Morand cattle from the rest and driving them into holding pens. Amber stood by the fencing, petting every cow that got close enough for her to reach. By the time they walked back to the car, she had spent all the remaining money from the treasure Frank Morand brought to this country, but she had kept her promise to her mother and Aunt Irene. Pride rose in her chest.

THREE TRUCKS HAULING ANIMAL TRAILERS arrived at the farm the next morning and backed up to the barnyard gate. Mr. Freedman had created a temporary fenced run leading from the back of the trucks into the barnyard. When the cows entered the run, Amber could feel how terrified they were. They bumped into each other, frantically, mooing. Once in the yard, they quieted. Mr. Freedman had cleaned out the muck in the barnyard and covered it with sawdust. The cement watering trough sparkled when light hit the water.

Later that day, the Lundgren boys were returning the half-dozen cattle Aunt Irene had placed with them when she entered the Nursing Home. In their distinctive swaying gait, the cows would walk down the same road the original Morand cattle walked. To her immense satisfaction, Amber was going to be able to keep the calves she and Hunter had fed all summer.

"Do we start milking today?" she asked Mr. Freedman once the drivers left.

"I'll milk them tonight and again tomorrow morning around seven. Do you want to come to the barn to see how the system works?"

"I wouldn't miss it for the world." Amber told him. "I know you have reservations about running the dairy alone. Well, you aren't going to have to. I'm going to be with you every step of the way."

CASSIDY CALLED AT DINNERTIME.

"Hi, Cass. How's the new job going?"

"It's good. Lots to learn. This is a higher level gallery than Hillside and I like the clients. Some of them actually know constitutes quality art work," she said wryly. "I got your text. So Marc is going to be there Friday?"

Amber took a deep breath. "He is. I'm going to give him my decision then. I can't marry him, Cass."

"You know what I think. Hunter never said he loved you, didn't promise to return and Marc is gorgeous, rich and mad about you. Plus, he wants to adopt Minna! No contest."

"Cass, the cows got here today," Amber said in a quiet voice. There was silence at the other end.

"You've gone ahead with the dairy then?" Cassidy's voice sounded resigned.

"When the cows walked into the barn, I named each one. I'm staying at the farm and I need to tell Marc good-bye."

Cassidy was quiet for a moment before she said, "I think you're one crazy fruitcake, but I guess I had better be there Friday."

"Please come my friend, I'm going to need you."

"I'll come, but what if Hunter doesn't come back? What if he falls for some other girl while he's gone?"

"I will always love him, Cass. And no matter what he decides, this place is my solid ground."

THE NEXT DAY AMBER POSTED A NOTICE in the Apple River paper inviting anyone who had ever bought milk from the Morand Dairy to come to a Grand Opening event. She stopped by the nursing home to offer a personal invitation to Emma and Mrs. Worth, feeling a wave of sadness. She couldn't ask if someone else now lived in room 109. It would have been too painful.

She walked to Mr. Allswede's office and invited him and his mother to come. She rented a huge white tent, tables and chairs, dishes and silverware. Megan had offered to make hamburgers, hot dogs and potato salad.

The day of the Grand Opening dawned bright and cool. Amber and Megan dashed back and forth between the kitchen and the tent. Ryan set the chairs around tables and tapped a keg of beer. At the last minute, Amber remembered her boots. She dragged them from the back of a closet, dusted them off and put them on. They were tight and felt funny on her feet. How she wished Aunt Irene had lived to see this event. She felt her eyes tighten and blinked away her tears. For a few moments, she was lost in memory.

Around three that afternoon, people began to arrive. Some Amber had never met hugged her and thanked her for re-opening the Morand Diary. Many of the attendees were very old, but they wore the happy smiles of childhood. Mr. Freedman took farmers into the barn to show them the new self-milking equipment. Kids ran madly around, jumping in piles of autumn leaves. One woman asked if she could see what Amber had done to the house and by the time they were ready for the tour, there were a dozen excited women. Everyone was very complimentary and Amber felt a loosening inside. Muscles she had held tight for a long time relaxed. She was one of them now, part of the community of fine hardworking farm families.

When everyone got seated for the meal, Amber stood at one end of the tent with Minna in her arms beside Mr. Freedman.

"Welcome, everyone," she said. "For anyone I haven't met, I'm Amber Morand Bradshaw and this is Mr. Ned Freedman, the manager of Irene's Dairy. Without his help, none of this would have been possible."

"Hey, Ned, how come Hunter's not here?" a man called out.

"He's in Minneapolis," he answered and nodded for Amber to speak. She stopped a moment and took a deep breath, trying to regain her self-possession.

"When Aunt Irene asked me to re-open Irene's Dairy, I had no idea how much work would be involved." She shook her head. "The day of her funeral, as those of you who were there will remember, I promised to be her eyes and ears the day we opened. I said my eyes would be filled with tears of joy on that day, and so they are," she said. "I also promised I would wear my high-heeled boots. I'll never forget Aunt Irene calling me a Nincompoop and a Twit for wearing them on a farm. She was right. When we light the bonfire later, I will consign my high-heeled boots to the flames. Does anyone have something they would like to say? Any questions?"

"I do," a little red headed girl said, "Is there going to be ice cream?"

"Honey, there's going to be ice cream, a chocolate fountain, strawberries, raspberries and even candy sprinkles." The crowd cheered and the little girl beamed.

Amber and Megan walked around the tables with food, Ryan filled empty glasses and Mr. Freedman answered a hundred questions. Afterward, the noise quieted, as it always does when people have been well fed. Megan started the soft ice cream machine and kids shrieked and formed a line. People brought their chairs to sit around the bonfire after dinner.

The last of the cars left quietly around eleven. The moon rose as Amber and Megan walked up to the farmhouse.

"It was such a good party, wasn't it, Megan?"

"It was terrific, Amber."

The two hugged each other and Ryan hit the horn in the pick-up. "Let's go Megan," he yelled in exasperation. She grinned, shook her head and walked out to join her husband.

Looking at the old red barn, Amber felt a rise of pleasure in her heart. The farm community had welcomed her. It wasn't surprising really, she was the owner of the Morand Dairy after all. Just the latest in a century of Morand ancestors. By her commitment, the hundred year old chain connecting the Morands to the land remained unbroken.

THIRTY-SIX

MARC CALLED AMBER FROM NEW YORK two days later. He was brimming with excitement about his trip.

"Amber, you can't believe what a beautiful city Bucharest is. It is the center of Romanian culture and art. In the period between the two World Wars, the city was nicknamed 'Little Paris'. Although the buildings in the historic city center were heavily damaged by the war, some survived and many others have been rebuilt. In recent years, the city has been experiencing an economic boom."

"It sounds lovely, but don't keep me waiting. Were you able to give the Morand journal to a museum? "Amber asked.

"Yes, it went to the Museum of the Romanian Peasant. Part of the museum was designed to show a peasant home as it would have been at the time your ancestors immigrated to the States. Visitors climb a short staircase to a platform where they can look through a pane of glass into an attic bedroom. Inside they will see a bed, a table and a lamp."

"Where will the journal be?"

"It will be placed on the bedside table."

"It sounds perfect. Did you meet any representatives of the Romanian government?"

"I actually met the Prime Minister. He is going to have a metal plate made with Frank and Ina's names engraved on it and your name as donor. He is also going to have every page of Ina's journal inscribed in Romanian and English on plaques mounted on the wall adjacent to each step on the staircase. Anyone who comes to the Museum will be able to read Ina's words."

"Did you take pictures?"

"Dozens. I can't wait to get to the farm and see you. I get into Minneapolis late tomorrow and I'll be with you Friday night."

"It will be good to see you, Marc," Amber said, glancing at the velvet box on her dressing table with the earrings inside. She could not delay telling him her decision any longer.

MARC DROVE IN AT EIGHT O'CLOCK. Cassidy had arrived an hour earlier. When he came into the house, he grabbed Amber and twirled her around in a circle, kissing her. When he stopped and looked up he saw Cassidy holding Minna in her lap. He looked a bit surprised, but recovered graciously.

"Hello, Cassidy," he said and kissed her on both cheeks, French style. "How is my little sweetheart?" He patted Minna on the head.

"Hi, Marc. We're dying to hear all about your trip," Cassidy said.

"It was the trip of a lifetime," Marc replied sitting down on the couch. He smiled at Amber as she handed him a glass of wine. "The Romanian people are so wonderfully alive. There is none of the jockeying for power that exists in our society. They care deeply for each other and profoundly regret the loss of their heritage."

"I understand the Russian government never returned the jewels, paintings, manuscripts or the gold that came from the Romanians," Amber said.

"A few paintings and an icon or two were found and returned to their original owners, but none of the gold came back. The gold on that train was valued at $1.25 billion. The Army had made a list of the valuables on the train. Nate's great grandmother told him that such lists were often placed in the spines of books. That's why he wanted Ina's journal. Although his legal status is still unclear, he's made a formal claim for his family's heritage."

"Could the list really help get the objects returned to their owners?" Cassidy asked.

"It's been a hundred years. War is war and many treasured and sacred objects disappear or are destroyed during armed conflict. The Romanian government intends to continue suing for their heritage, but they know it's unlikely."

"Then what good was the list?" Cassidy asked.

"The jewelry has probably been melted down and re-fashioned, the golden lei has been long spent, but some paintings and icons might still re-surface. The European Art Squad is searching for them. They never give up."

Marc sat back, sipping his wine and smiling. "Tell me what has been happening here at the farm?"

"The dairy cows have arrived," Cassidy said, lifting an eyebrow. She hesitated and Marc looked at her, waiting for her to continue. "Amber has named them," she said.

"You're keeping your promise to Irene then, Amber." Marc said. He took a deep, somewhat shaky breath, obviously striving for calm. "But since you have Hunter and his father to run things here, you can keep the house and let them run the business, can't you?" His expression was intent. His eyes were sharp as blades.

"Come with me, Marc," Amber said. She stood up and took his hand. "I want to show you Irene's Dairy."

They walked down the dusty driveway to the barn together. Amber showed Marc the spotless facility, the cows in the barnyard and the new self-milking system. She pointed out each cow and told him their names. She petted the littlest one she had named Iona, to honor the name Ina had given her favorite cow a century ago.

"Amber," Marc said, taking her hand. "What are you telling me? You know I want to marry you. I want you with me in Minneapolis or wherever my career takes us. I love you, Amber Bradshaw," the pain in his eyes was intense.

"I know," Amber said. Her voice was low and filled with compassion. "I'm sorry, Marc. You have no idea how much it hurts me to say this, but I can't marry you," she said. Her chest felt crushed, knowing the pain she was causing him.

"It is over then?" he asked. She nodded. "You know I would do anything to have you in my life." Pain was raw in Marc's voice.

"I can't leave here, Marc. The farm is my legacy, my inheritance."

"I'm not asking you to do that!" he said, frustrated. "You can keep the farm. We can come for vacations, weekends, but I want you in my house and in my bed." His eyes were dark, filled with a powerful longing.

"I have promises to keep, Marc. A promise I made to Aunt Irene and to myself. I hate saying this, but I . . ." she hesitated. "I don't love you enough to make it work. I wanted to. I have tried so hard. You deserve someone who loves you as much as you love me."

"Is it because of Hunter?" his voice sounded devastated.

"Hunter left here over a month ago. But I've decided this is where I belong. I want to run this dairy. I want to raise Minna here."

"Are you trying to spare me with this? I know Hunter is part of your decision. He fits here and I don't," his face darkened with pain.

"He does, and I care deeply for him, but he doesn't know if he wants this life . . . or me."

"If he doesn't come back, then he's even more of an idiot than I thought he was," Marc said, scuffing the toe of his polished shoe into the dust.

Slowly, Amber removed the little jewel box containing the amber and diamond earrings from her pocket and held it out to Marc.

"I told you when I gave you the earrings that you could keep them," Marc said, his voice was raw. "I bought them for you."

"I know," Amber's voice was low. "But I don't feel I should. It's a tie between us that's been severed." She held her hand out, the jewel box resting on her palm.

Marc took it tentatively and slipped it into his pocket. "If you won't keep it, I will return it to the jeweler. I will use the money to make a contribution to an orphanage I toured in Romania. I'll make the donation in Minna's name." He looked down, blinking away tears and swallowing hard. "You know I had hoped to become her father."

"I know," she said, in tears. "Good bye, Marc." She stood on her tiptoes and kissed his cheek.

Marc walked quickly up the driveway toward the house. He didn't go inside and Amber heard his car start up and drive away.

She stood beside the pasture fence for a long time, imagining the separate farmsteads like oases in sea of grain. She envisioned women turning on house lamps, the smell of dinner cooking, the sounds of conversation and music on the radios reaching out to the darkening autumnal fields. The countryside seemed as remote as an ocean. The winding gravel roads between the trees were bordered with golden asparagus fern, the fields pale with stubble and broken stems. She brushed away her tears, straightened her shoulders and walked back to the house. The wind had died and the leaves on the cottonwood trees were completely still.

THIRTY-SEVEN

Afew days later the wind turned cold and an early freezing rain came down hard outlining the branches of trees and shrubs in glistening coats of crystalline ice. As he was walking to the barn that afternoon, Mr. Freedman fell and hurt his wrist. When he told Amber about the fall, he brushed it off saying he was fine. All he needed to do was to tape it up. She told him he was an idiot and took him to the doctor. The wrist was broken. He needed surgery.

"He can't return to work for three to four weeks and it might take longer," the orthopedist told her. "We're keeping him in the hospital overnight. He's not a young man, you know. He told me what he's been doing for you and how the accident happened. If possible, I suggest you get some additional help."

Driving back to the farm from the hospital, Amber knew she faced a moral dilemma. She could call Hunter. If he knew about his father's injury, he would certainly return and perhaps she could convince him to stay, but would he resent her? Would he feel pressured and then leave again?

She called Cassidy's phone from the car.

"The Viviane Gallery," it was Cassidy's professional voice.

"Cassidy, I need some advice. Have you got a minute?"

"Let me go back into the stock room," she said. Moments later, she returned to the call. "I have something to tell you before you tell me what you called about. I saw Hunter yesterday. He came into the Gallery to tell me about the icon. He took it to the Orthodox Church on Lake Superior. Amazingly, the old place still existed. The priest there contacted the Patriarch of Bucharest. That's the title for the head of the Eastern Orthodox Church. The Patriarch asked that the icon be given to the Minneapolis Institute of Arts. Hunter wanted you to know that the MIA is a top-ranked museum and he was pleased it has free admission. He said it was important that anyone who wanted to see the icon could do so. The Museum will list you, Aunt Irene and Ina Morand as the donors."

"Did he ask about me?" Amber asked, knowing Cassidy heard the pain in her voice.

"No, Amber, I'm sorry, we didn't discuss you. What did you want to talk to me about?"

"Mr. Freedman broke his wrist. He can't go back to work for a month or so. The doctor suggested I get some additional help. I'm trying to decide whether to call Hunter and tell him. I know it would make him come home. What do you think?"

"I think you should do what the doctor suggested. Hire somebody to help Mr. Freedman," Cassidy said. "Maybe one of the Lundgren boys down the road would pitch in. Having talked to Hunter recently, I believe he will come back eventually, but it has to be his choice, Amber."

"I appreciate your advice, Cassidy, and while I won't tell him about his father's broken arm, I think the time has come to end this stalemate with Hunter."

"I wondered when you would get the guts. Do you want his phone number?"

"Yes," she said. Squaring her shoulders, and taking a deep breath, Amber dialed the phone number Cassidy gave her.

"Hello." It was his lovely deep voice.

"Hi Hunter, it's Amber. Cassidy told me about the icon and the museum. Thank you for doing that," her voice trailed off.

"I was glad to do it, Amber," Hunter said. "I wanted you to know that I'm painting. I could never figure out why I was blocked from painting at the farm until I got here and then I remembered. My mother wanted me to complete my art school program. She told me on the last day of her life, but I had forgotten until just recently."

"Have you gone back to school then," Amber asked feeling utterly depressed. If he went back to school he would never return to her.

"I contacted the program and although it's been six years, they said I could apply to Art Instruction Inc. in Minneapolis and if accepted, they would transfer the credits I earned and with just another year or so would grant my degree. I've already applied for admission."

"That's good," she said, trying desperately to sound happy. "But I spend every day missing you. You need to decide between me and art school, Hunter, and it needs to be soon. I love you and I know you love me, even though you've never said it. I told you before, I won't wait forever." Her voice trailed off.

He didn't respond and Amber hung up the phone wondering bitterly why his determination to succeed as an artist was more important than the love of a good woman. You could have Marc in a heartbeat if you gave Hunter up, the voice in her head said, but it would be wrong. It was Hunter she loved.

LATE THAT NIGHT TRYING TO DISTRACT HERSELF from Hunter's decision, she reached for Ina's journal. There were only a few pages left.

Ina Morand Journal
Fall, 1918
Two nights ago Frank called me to come down to the small shed he keeps the milk cans in. He had been going down there after I finished milking every evening for months. I thought he was avoiding me but he asked me not to enter the shed and I had done so. I hurried down the path carrying Irene on my hip. She slumped against me, sleepily. The shed was dim until he lit the oil lantern. Golden brown curls of wood from hand-planned logs had fallen to the floor.

He gestured and I saw his work, a walnut dining table and four chairs. The wood glowed. I ran my hands over it. I could feel the tree it came from and how it stood in heat, rain and snow for so many years. My furniture had returned. Tears surprised my eyes.

"Look in the back corner," he told me.

He had made a spool bed. The wood was nearly white and every spool was perfectly turned. On the bed there was a mattress, stuffed with wool and covered with a blue and white ticking. Frank said Alene had made the mattress for the two of us. I stood beside the bed, thinking of sleeping in it, listening to the wind in the cottonwood trees. I touched it, feeling it give softly to my palm. Frank was a man of few words. The furniture was his mute apology, a plea for my forgiveness for selling my dowry to pay for our passage to Wisconsin.

"This bed will last a hundred years, Ina. Someday Irene's children will sleep here," he said softly. He took my elbow and led me deeper into the barn to see a cradle he had made for Irene.

"She is getting too big to sleep with you any longer. I should be sleeping with you in this bed," he told me and I colored. His love for our child touched my heart and when he draped his arm across my shoulders, for the first time since we left my homeland, I did not shrug it away.

"We could make another baby in this bed, my wife."

My cheeks flamed. I remembered the priest saying I had to forgive Frank. But I wasn't ready, I would not ask him to join me, not even in the bed he had made for the two of us. Not yet. Before that day arrived, Frank owed me an act of contrition for selling my little spotted dog.

THIRTY-EIGHT

The Lundgren's sons were happy to help out with Irene's Dairy. Mr. Freedman's wrist was healing and he worked alongside the boys, supervising them and doing what he could with his splinted wrist. Freed from day-to-day responsibility for the livestock, Amber resumed her life as Minna's mother.

Thinking back to the day her mother died, Amber felt as if she had been on a raft in a wild rocking river for many years. All the steps she had taken, the promises she had kept, felt like huge boulders she had navigated, dangerous rapids she had successfully passed beyond. There was nothing ahead for her now but satin smooth water and a pine-scented forest on either side of the tumbling Apple River.

She didn't understand why, but since the day she and Hunter had talked on the phone, her anguished yearning for him had slowly dissipated. She no longer felt like half a person who needed Hunter to complete her. He had left to pursue his dream, and she was living hers. Relinquishing the possibility of him returning had been a critical step. Until then, she had been living on tenterhooks, hoping daily to see his face. Now she found herself in a place of indolent peace. Every time she fed the baby, bathed or patted her back as she fell asleep, she felt blessed. The gentle hands of a sovereign serenity were all around her.

In December a freezing rainstorm entered the high plains and blazed across the state, leaving coats of ice on the trees and roads. Amber kept a fire going in the fireplace and the coffeepot on. She listened to the weather forecast on the radio. Thousands of cars were being pulled from ditches. She thought of Hunter, painting in his dark minimal apartment, and although she told herself it had been his choice, her heart still ached, not for herself any longer but for what he was losing.

That day Minna was particularly trying. She stood by the front door crying to go outside for hours. It was far too slick to carry her down to the barn to see the cows, which was where she wanted to go. Amber was relieved when it was time to finally put the tyke to bed. Around eleven that night, Amber heard a cautious tap on the summer kitchen door. Thinking it was Mr. Freedman and worried he might have fallen and re-injured his wrist, she switched on the light and threw the door open saying, "Come in, for goodness sakes. You know you don't have to knock."

But it wasn't Mr. Freedman. It was Hunter—standing in the freezing rain, dark-eyed and very wet. Behind him, the muscular cottonwood trees wrestled with the north wind. The ice-coated branches of the trees burned with a cold light and the frozen moon rose, casting a blue radiance on the snow-covered ground.

"What do you want?" she demanded, fiercely. "What the hell, after all this time, when I had given up seeing you here again do you want, Hunter Freedman?" She covered her mouth with her hand then, to stop her voice. He stood unmoving in the freezing sleet, stricken into immobility by her anger, like a small shamed son.

"Can I come in?" he asked.

"Hunter Freedman, you are the most stupid, inconsiderate, selfish and thoroughly irritating man I have ever met!" she said. "How dare you come now, without any warning, when I've finally achieved peace without you and . . ." Her voice trailed off. She bit her lower lip realizing it was trembling. She glanced up at Hunter who seemed to be quashing a little smile. He reached for her hand. Then he pushed the door open and stepped inside. He pulled her toward him powerfully.

"I want what I've always wanted," he said.

"Have you made your choice then? I'm not letting you in if you aren't sure."

"I have, Amber. I choose you."

Icy cold and wet, Amber took him into her arms. When they broke apart, he lifted her left hand, looking at her ring finger.

"I ended it with Marc months ago," she said. "I haven't seen him since."

"I have something to tell you, but I have to get out of these wet clothes first." He was shuddering from the cold.

Amber led him by the hand into the house and to the bathroom. She started filling the claw foot tub, adding bath oil that filled the space with the scent of lilacs. Hunter unzipped his jacket and pulled it off. Amber unbuttoned his shirt. Slowly Hunter began removing his boots, T-shirt and pants.

Neither of them said a word. Cam whined outside the bathroom door. Amber let the dog in and he leaped up, standing tall against Hunter's bare chest. She looked at them standing there, chest to chest, her man and her dog, feeling a painful sweet tightness in her throat.

When Hunter stepped into the tub, Amber took his wet clothes out to the summer kitchen and started the washing machine. She grabbed two large white bath towels. Walking into the living room, she switched on the player piano. The beginning notes of Pachelbel's Cannon in D filled the air, the sounds haunting and evocative. The music had always sounded to her like heartbeats, like a perfect accompaniment to making love.

When she returned to the bathroom, Hunter's long beautiful body was lying relaxed in the warm water. She walked over to the bathroom window. The motion light by the back door came on, triggered by the movement of the trees. The cottonwoods Ina had planted a century ago were molten silver. Amber picked up a large porcelain pitcher and filled it with warm water from the sink.

"You could have called me," she said, quietly. When he didn't answer, she added, "Or written, or something. How could you expect I would be waiting for you when you got here tonight? And what about school? The last time we talked you said you were going to finish art school." She was breathing hard—feeling her frustration rise. Why had he come now, when she finally felt she could live without him?

"I needed to have something to bring to you besides myself, Amber. You draw me like the moon draws the tides. If I we had been alone even for a few minutes, I would have come back without ever knowing if I had any talent."

"Damn it, Hunter. I could have told you that."

"But I wouldn't have believed you," he said and smiled, just a little. "Cassidy called me today to say that several of my paintings have already sold. They are asking for more of my work."

Amber felt tears sting her eyes as she said, "Then the promise you made to your mother has been kept, Hunter."

"Yes," he said, sounding pleased and smiling. "I know. That's why I could return. As far as school goes, I am going to be able to finish the last courses in my program on-line." He smiled and closed his eyes.

"If you ever leave me again, I won't take you back," she whispered.

His eyes opened and met hers. "There won't be a next time."

"Ever?" she whispered.

"Never. You are the one great love of my life, Amber," he said and the corner on one side of his mouth turned up.

Hearing his words, Amber remembered Ina who had married Frank and given birth to his child but still couldn't forgive him, until the day he declared his love. Hunter's words melted her heart.

"Lean back," she said, softly and slowly poured the water from the pitcher over Hunter's head. She knelt beside the tub and began washing his long dark hair. He settled lower in the warm water. They didn't talk, but the muscles in Hunter's face eased. As Amber massaged the shampoo into his hair, he gave a peaceful sigh. Amber refilled the pitcher and rinsed his hair clean. She walked over to the medicine cabinet and took out her razor. Her every movement was measured then, like a dancer in slow motion. She let her desire for him build slowly, deep inside her body.

Using her lemon soap she spread white froth gently over his upper lip, chin and cheeks.

"I'll do it," Hunter said, reaching for the razor.

"No," Amber whispered, "I will." With soft even strokes, she shaved his cheeks. She ran the razor gently over his upper lip. He started to say something, but she put a finger to his lips, leaned forward and kissed him. When he was clean-shaven, she took a steaming washcloth and washed every trace of soap from his face.

He stood up and stepped from the tub. He used a towel on his hair while she dried his body all over with the other towel, rubbing him from his shoulders to his toes, like one would for a small child. His copper-colored skin glowed from the hot water. He could have been a statue, she thought. He was that perfect.

"I don't have any other clothes," he whispered.

"You won't need any," she said, and they met each other's eyes smiling.

"Have you decided to stay permanently at the farm, Amber?" He asked.

"I will be here forever," she told him, certainty strong in her face. "I will end my days here. As I told you the day we went to the hill, this place is my solid ground."

"I am blind with need for you," he said and his eyes narrowed with desire. Amber wrapped her arms around his neck. He lifted her up until their faces were close together and kissed her. He lifted one of her legs in a dancer's lift. She wrapped both legs around his long hard body.

Later, they walked upstairs. The moonlight came through the window at the top of the stairs, splashing their bodies. The dog walked behind them, his fur as white as the downy seeds from the cottonwood trees. At the top of the stairs, Cam turned and walked into Minna's room. He lay down by her crib. Hunter followed the dog and Amber watched him pat Minna's back as she turned away and slipped into the white spool bed.

When he walked into the bedroom, he asked, "Is this the bed Frank Morand made?"

"It is," she said and pulled the covers back for him to get in. Hunter clicked on the bedside lamp.

"Turn off the light," she whispered.

"Not a chance," he said and grinned. He laid down beside her and pulled her to him.

WHEN THE SUN SLANTED INTO THE DARK ROOM the next morning, Hunter woke her with a kiss.

"So, how was Marc Rochet as a lover," he asked, a tiny note of calm amusement in his voice.

"I never found out," Amber said.

"What do you mean, you never found out. He spent the night with you during threshing."

"On the couch," Amber said. "We never made love, Hunter, but I don't think he would have been as good as you are."

"You don't think?" he asked, raising himself up on an elbow.

"I'm not completely sure," she said smiling. "I will probably have to make love with you several thousand more times to be completely certain."

Hunter began to laugh, low and quiet. "Good," he said. "Good."

THIRTY-NINE

Two days later Amber heard Hunter's truck drive in behind
the house as she was walking downstairs to start her day. They had
discussed whether he should move in with her at the farm, but he wanted to see how his father was doing before he moved in. His broken wrist
had still been giving him some trouble. And Hunter felt he owed it to his
father to reassure him that he had come home for good.

"Good Morning, Hunter," Amber whispered as she ushered him into
the house. "Minna's still sleeping. Want coffee?"

He nodded and they sat together companionably at the kitchen island. They chatted a while about the dairy and a painting Hunter was
working on. He had refused to tell her anything more about it except
that the painting was going well and it was almost finished. She got up
and went over to the stove.

Setting down his coffee cup, Hunter asked, "So, do you think you
would like to be married in the Lutheran church?"

Amber's back was to him and she stopped stirring the cream-of-
wheat she was making. Turning around, she opened her mouth to say
something and then thought better of it, feeling spots of color rise on her
cheeks. Finally she said, "Would you be asking me to marry you, Hunter
Freedman?"

"Yes," he said quietly.

"No," she said. She bit her lower lip to keep from smiling.

"What do you mean, no? You won't marry me? I thought it was a
foregone conclusion. Isn't it?" Hunter frowned in confusion.

"A foregone conclusion? Hardly. What I mean, the one great love of my life, is that asking a girl where she wants to be married is a pretty poor excuse for an actual proposal of marriage."

"I see. Well then, I believe I will start over," Hunter said with a grin. He stood and walked out of the kitchen and she could hear him opening the door of his pick-up. When he came back into the house, he was holding something under his arm.

"What have you got there, Hunter?" she asked.

"Silence, Woman," he said grinning. "I'm trying to do this properly. Miss Amber Morand Bradshaw, owner of Irene's Dairy, mother of Minna Grace, companion to Camelot Bradshaw and the most beautiful woman I've ever known, will you do me the honor of marrying me?" He went down on one knee awkwardly, still holding the parcel.

Cam came over and bumped into Hunter, practically knocking him over.

"Come here, you crazy mutt," Amber said pulling the dog away. For once he actually minded. "Now, as I understand it, there is supposed to be a ring involved in most proposals. That package looks too big to be a ring," she said, casting him an oblique glance. She was on the cusp of laughter.

"It is my understanding that the proposee must give the proposer her answer before an engagement is finalized with a gift. And I'm still waiting," he said, kneeling.

"Yes, you crazy idiot, of course I will marry you," Amber said with a huge grin. Her eyes sparkled as she pulled him to his feet.

"As an artist, I thought perhaps a painting would be more appropriate than a ring," Hunter said and pulled the wrapped package from behind his back.

Remembering Ina untying the string from the package that contained the icon, Amber felt the earth almost hesitate in its spin. Time stopped for a moment. Her heart pounded and her palms were sweaty. Pulling the paper away, Amber saw Hunter's painting.

It was of two cottonwood trees in early spring. The little white parachute seeds of the trees were being released making a white veil around the trees. The sky was very blue. Looking closely among the tree roots, Amber saw two tiny faces, perfect images of Frank and Ina. Further up the tree trunk, hidden in a knot in the wood, was a miniature of Aunt Irene's face. Among the crown of leaves she saw her mother's face, Claire's, her father's and Mr. Freedman's. In the topmost branches Hunter had painted three faces, his, hers and Minna's. Each face was outlined by a ribbon of miniature botanically exact cottonwood leaves. In the wide sky above the crown of leaves were two small empty squares. Amber couldn't stop her smile.

"And what, may I ask, are the empty frames for?" she asked.

"Those, my love, are for our future children," Hunter said, as he took his future wife in his arms.

AT CHRISTMAS, HUNTER CUT DOWN an enormous pine tree and lugged it into the house. Minna was entranced by the tiny white lights they installed on the tree. Amber had to scold Cam, trying not to laugh, for pulling the old blown glass ornaments off the tree, crunching them in his mouth and spitting out little pieces of glass. Luckily, the nutcase didn't swallow any of them, but not wanting to take any chances, she moved them higher on the tree. Amber had told Minna the tree was off limits. The baby would toddle up to the tree, shaking her head "no." Sometimes she shook her head so hard, she plopped down inadvertently on her little bottom.

Gusts of snowflakes swirled outside the old farmhouse making them feel as if they lived in a snow globe. Carols rang from the old player piano. On Christmas morning, it was the dog who helped Minna open her presents, tearing away the paper with his teeth.

Their wedding was to take place at the end of the week. Amber had struggled with the decision of whether she should wear Aunt Irene's wedding gown for the ceremony, or whether it should always be kept as a memento to her life. She took a long walk down the country road, trying to decide. The air had an icy edge and powdery snow swirled in a sweep of blue sky as she listened, hoping to hear Aunt Irene's voice once more. In the end, when she lifted the beautiful antique dress out of the chest and absorbed the scent of the lavender-infused tissue paper, it felt like the right thing to do.

THE MORNING OF HER WEDDING DAY, Joanna was helping her get ready in her bedroom at the farm.

"I believe you have forgotten something," she said.

"What?"

"It's the old wedding rhyme. You need something old—the dress is old. Something new—your hair piece. Something borrowed and something blue," Joanna twinkled and handed her a blue satin garter. "It was from my wedding to Will," she said.

"It's going to be your turn next to be a bride, Joanna," Amber said as she slipped the garter on her leg. She and Amber's father had announced their engagement a few days before.

"I'm so happy to be officially becoming part of your family, Amber. I'm committed to your dad and we love each other deeply. And, of course, I'm getting to be a step-grandmother," she said looking at the baby. Minna was sitting in her seat, dressed in a little white gown and booties and blessedly sound asleep.

"The only thing I regret today, Joanna, besides not having my mother, Aunt Irene and Claire here, is that I haven't taken the time to find Minna's father. I wish I had more to go on than just his last name. I'm not sure if I ever told you his full name. It's J. J. Stryker."

"Oh my God, that's my son!" Joanna said, sudden tears filling her eyes. "I was married as a young woman to Donald Stryker. He died of cancer only a year after the baby was born. Johnny's back in town now, living with some good friends. He quit the band and has enrolled in community college. He was completely devastated when he learned about Claire passing away, but he's definitely back and almost his old self again."

"My guess is that Claire was going to meet your son when she left the hospital after seeing our father. She must have told him she wanted them to be a couple again. When she told him about the pregnancy originally, he said he wasn't ready to be a father."

"I'll make sure he is now. It's past time my son grows up," Joanna said, smiling. "I just realized something. His band was playing at a club in Michigan around the time we lost your sister. That's what the Michigan map was about. Claire was going to hear him play."

"Hunter and I would very much like to adopt Minna, but of course J.J. will need to be consulted and give his permission. Whatever he decides, your son will always be welcome in our lifed and in Minna's. So, Miss Joanna, this means you're not a step-grandmother after all," Amber said. "You're the real deal."

Her father knocked on the bedroom door. He pulled a black velvet case from under his tuxedo-clad arm. It contained her mother's pearl necklace and earrings. He set the boxes of flowers, pink roses for the attendants, white roses, stephanotis and baby's breath for the bride on her dresser.

"Your bridesmaids are arriving," he said.

Amber looked out the window toward the cottonwood trees and saw Cassidy's car pull up. She got out of the car and waved. Cassidy was going to be her Maid of Honor and Megan would be her Matron of Honor.

Emma pulled in a few minutes later. She was going to be a bridesmaid. She had picked up Lizzie, the perfect baby-sitter, who was going to be a junior bridesmaid. Right behind Cassidy's car, Ryan's pick-up pulled in. Megan got out of the truck and headed toward the house with her dress draped over her arm. Ryan lifted little Connery out of the car and took him over to the hammock. He laid the little boy wearing his hooded snowsuit and boots down in the snowy hammock and pushed it slowly as the child's eyes closed in sleep.

As AMBER AND HER FATHER STOOD at the back of the old church when the music began to play, he bent his head and asked, "Are you ready, Sweetheart?"

"I've waited all my life for this moment," she said and they smiled at each other. "The only regret I have is that mom and Claire aren't here. At the head table for the reception, there is an empty chair for my sister with a placecard with her name on it. I had Hunter draw a little hummingbird on the card and a pair of angel wings," she felt tears sting her eyes.

"The night Claire came to the hospital, I apologized to your sister for succumbing to alcoholism and neglecting you both after your mother died. I told her you still felt guilty for the day you forgot to get her from school. She laughed and said she had long since forgiven us both. I hope knowing how she felt will help you, Amber," he said. "My failings were far worse than yours."

"All of that is over and done with, Dad. Living here, falling in love, and becoming Minna's mom have set me free. And if you still feel guilty about those old days, you need to forgive yourself, too."

Waiting at the back of the sanctuary with her arm on her father's, Amber saw Hunter standing by the altar. He had asked Ryan to be his best man and they were standing side by side. Joanna was seated in the first pew, holding Minna in her arms. Mr. Freedman was sitting with her. The organist played "Joy to the World" as Hunter slipped the ring on her finger. When the minister said "You may kiss the bride," the entire congregation applauded.

Walking down the aisle to back of the church after the ceremony, Amber saw nearly all the people she loved best in the world. Every one of the local farm families were there. Only three were missing. She blew three kisses in the air, one for her mother, one for her sister and the last for Aunt Irene.

As she and Hunter reached the back of the church, the final entry from Ina's journal came to Amber so clearly it was as if her great great grandmother had spoken them aloud.

I couldn't forgive my husband until I knew the answer to one last question. Trembling inside, I asked Frank if my little spotted dog had been sacrificed to pay for our journey.

"Ina, my wife, did you think I took her to the knacker man?" he asked. His face turned white and shocked. "I would never have done that. Remember how much the neighbor boy loved your dog? I gave your dog to him. She couldn't come with us."

I felt ashamed and looked away. He lifted my chin with a finger.

"All this time, have you not known how much I love you?" Frank asked, a confused frown on his face. "I always have, Ina. The first day I saw you, I fell in love with you. I give you my word. This long journey was undertaken only because I wanted us to be together—to live and to watch baby Irene grow up."

That night I took my husband into our white spool bed, the bed he made for us. I have told him that I want another child.

Standing in the receiving line, Amber touched Hunter's arm and he bent to listen. "Do you remember the empty frames in your proposal painting?" He nodded. "I want to put some little faces in that frame soon."

"As do I," Hunter said and gave her a smile of such sweetness it brought joy to Amber's heart.

AUTHOR'S NOTE

I N WRITING *THE COTTONWOODS* I'VE SOUGHT to recapture a lifestyle that has mostly vanished and pay a modest tribute to those wonderful people and that sacred space—the family farm. It's a story based on my own ancestors.

On nights when I have trouble sleeping, I summon my seven-year-old persona with my shining brown braids, dark eyes and bare feet. It is evening and my childhood self enters the old farmhouse through the summer kitchen door. It slams behind me and I see my grandmother's face as she bends forward over the stove. She's holding a lighted match to start a fire under the wrought-iron burner to heat the kettle.

"Don't forget to wash your feet," Gram says as I walk toward the bathroom and sit on the edge of the tub. "Use the cold water. No use wasting hot water on a little girl's dusty feet. Your little sister is already in bed."

I hardly register the oft-repeated refrain but it comforts me. Everything is always the same at the farm, no wild arguments, no drunken stumblings, no hiding to escape—the nomenclature of my life at home. With clean feet, I walk upstairs and open the door to my bedroom. The window is open and I hear the rustle of the cottonwoods. I strip off my short dress, toss it over the footboard and pull back the covers. My little sister smiles sleepily at me. The scent of fresh-cut grass and summer sunshine rises from the sheets my grandmother hangs on the clothesline in warm summer wind. I close my eyes and a wave of bliss washes across me.

When does a story of a family truly begin? My mother's side of the family began with my great grandfather, a smiling young ne'er do well from Switzerland named Frank Remund who arrived in the U.S. in 1890. Frank Morand's optimistic and determined character in the story is based on my great grandfather's personality. Unlike Frank Morand in the book, however, Frank Remund brought no treasures with him to this country. Nonetheless, without much to offer, he managed to court and marry my great grandmother, Ina. She was a stern woman with a prim mouth who taught children in one-room schools in the Dakotas. In those days, it was the frontier.

After the wedding, they settled down in a small town in Minnesota and despite Frank's minimal formal education, he somehow managed to become Superintendent of Schools. Although they were comfortably off, owned their own home and had a baby daughter (my grandmother, Lillian) Frank Remund had a dream—a dream of a dairy farm. His dream would radically change his wife's fate and the direction of the family. There would be others.

Over his wife's objections, Frank bought our family farm in Wisconsin and informed his wife they were moving. Ina Remund was a strong woman and from what I know of her, I believe she would have initially refused to go. In time she must have acquiesced, but her likely bitterness about the loss of her comfortable life gave me the inspiration for the character of Ina Morand. I don't know who planted the cottonwood trees that became the sentinel guardians of the farm, but in my mind it was Ina.

Eventually Ina and Frank had two more children, their sons Paul and Charles, my great uncles. When I was a child, they owned two dairy farms on the same gravel road, side by side. The scene in *Cottonwoods* where Frank's leg is amputated by an alcoholic doctor on the old tin-topped table is factual. Amazingly, that indomitable man ran a dairy farm and raised three children with only one leg. My cousin still owns that table.

As Frank and Ina's children grew up, and my grandmother Lillian became a teen-ager, she met and fell in love with George Erickson. He was another boy with a dream—a dream like Hunter's—one in which he became a successful artist. It was a plan his father actively discouraged. He insisted that George go to business school. George refused and instead went to the prestigious Philadelphia Fine Arts Academy on his own dime and continued to court Lillian whose parents also opposed the relationship. They argued that George was unlikely to be successful enough to support her. When they died the farms would be willed to Lillian's brothers. Like Aunt Irene in the story, she was expected to marry.

Against all odds, George realized his destiny. He married my grandmother and became a famous and financially successful American illustrator (artist name Eugene Iverd) who painted covers for all the great magazines of the day. A single one of his paintings sold at the time for the same amount public school teachers made in an entire year. Today they are worth five and six figures.

After George died, his brother Carl went to visit Mr. Norman Rockwell. When Carl mentioned that his brother was Eugene Iverd, Rockwell took him back to a storage room. He opened a file cabinet containing every magazine for which Iverd painted a cover. "I thought of him as my greatest rival," Mr. Rockwell said. When Amber orders art for the farmhouse, the painting Cassidy purchases (The Two Master's) was painted by my grandfather, Eugene Iverd. The original painting is still in the family.

Ultimately my grandmother and her brothers passed away, leaving only my great Aunt Irene living alone and running the farm until she finally entered a nursing home. In life, Aunt Irene was not a spinster as she appears in the book. Her maiden name was Lundgren and she was married to my uncle Paul. I was in my mid-twenties when Aunt Irene decided the time had come to leave the farm. I was divorced with two small children by then and about to marry a man I loved beyond reason. One day I got a call from my aunt who asked if I could possibly go to the farm for the summer, fix up the old house and comfort Aunt Irene in her last days. It was June, the month I had always left for the farm as a kid, and an irresistible simmer of delight rose in me. But I was working, in graduate school, about to be married and deeply in love. So in the end, I gave my dream away for the greater good, remarried, raised my children and helped raise my husband's.

When Aunt Irene passed away, the farm was willed to a cousin who sold it to the Lundgren family who still live down the road. Today that family keeps their calves on our old farm and twice a day one of the long-legged Lundgren boys walks down that dusty road to feed them, just as Hunter does in the story.

The Native American Freedmans in the story also existed. They lived across the road from my Uncle Charles' farm and my great grandfather Frank was fascinated by their culture and their ability to feed themselves from the land. He spent many hours talking with the father and his son.

Now only silvered grasses bend like sea-waves in the wind where my grandmother's farmhouse once stood. The house was burned to the ground decades ago, an exercise for fire fighters in training. Feeling the searing heat of those flames, I still get a lump in my throat. But, the big red barn still stands—empty except for a few calves, and a tattered hammock still swings between the ancient cottonwood trees, moving as if touched by an invisible child.

LYN FARQUHAR (PENNAME LYN FARRELL) holds a master's degree in English and a Ph.D. degree in Education from Michigan State University. During her academic career, Lyn served in multiple administrative roles with the College of Human Medicine, retiring as a full Professor.

When Lyn retired from Michigan State, she returned to her first love of writing and self-published a YA Trilogy. Subsequently she and her daughter, Lisa Fitzsimmons, wrote a 7-book mystery series, *The Mae December Mysteries*, published by Camel Press under the penname, Lia Farrell. Her marketing efforts for *The Mae December Mysteries*, as well as much work by Camel on a subsidiary rights deal with Harlequin, have resulted in sales of 22,000+ (to date) for the series. She has recently started a new series, *Rosedale Investigations*. The first is titled, *The Blind Switch* and was released in January, 2021.